Duel of
Hearts

Duel of Hearts

Diane Farr

A SIGNET BOOK

SIGNET
Published by New American Library, a division of
Penguin Putnam Inc., 375 Hudson Street,
New York, New York 10014, U.S.A.
Penguin Books Ltd, 80 Strand,
London WC2R 0RL, England
Penguin Books Australia Ltd, Ringwood,
Victoria, Australia
Penguin Books Canada Ltd, 10 Alcorn Avenue,
Toronto, Ontario, Canada M4V 3B2
Penguin Books (N.Z.) Ltd, 182–190 Wairau Road,
Auckland 10, New Zealand

Penguin Books Ltd, Registered Offices:
Harmondsworth, Middlesex, England

First published by Signet, an imprint of New American Library,
a division of Penguin Putnam Inc.

ISBN: 0-7394-2922-1

Printed in the United States of America

PUBLISHER'S NOTE
This is a work of fiction. Names, characters, places, and incidents either are the product of the author's imagination or are used fictitiously, and any resemblance to actual persons, living or dead, business establishments, events, or locales is entirely coincidental.

To NORMA JEAN GOLLING
whom I can never thank enough

1

Delilah Chadwick was rarely at a loss for words. This, however, was too much. She stared at the sheet of elegant, hot-pressed paper, reading, over and over, the single paragraph it contained. No matter how many times she read it, its contents did not change. The words did not magically rearrange themselves. She read them one more time, just to make sure.

The letter still said what it said.

She turned the sheet over. The reverse side contained only her direction: *Miss Chadwick, Chadwick Hall, Squires Road/Trowbridge End, Wilts.*, written in precise and tidy cursive. Nothing more.

Lilah took a deep breath and found her tongue. "Is this a joke?" she demanded. It was a purely rhetorical question, of course. The sender of the message was many miles distant. She extended her arm dramatically, dangling the offending missive from her outstretched fingers as if it were covered in filth. "Where is the rest of it?"

Her father's secretary regarded her mildly over the rims of his spectacles. "There is no 'rest of it.' "

"One page?" Her voice rose an octave. "One *paragraph*? Impossible!"

Mr. Applegate, a long-suffering young man, recognized the rising note in Lilah's voice and begged her to be calm. She ignored this suggestion and rounded on him, eyes flashing. "Did you know of this, Jonathan?"

Mr. Applegate removed his spectacles. "No." Honesty compelled him to modify this statement. He cleared his throat, his eyes no longer meeting hers. "Not exactly."

This tiny adjustment to his denial robbed Lilah, once again, of speech. She dropped into a chair, staring at him as if he had just sprouted horns. Mr. Applegate's long acquaintance with Miss Chadwick led him to suppose that her inability to speak would be of short duration, so he hurried to fill the brief silence.

"I was not expecting to receive this message, nor anything like it. But I did know that your father entertained some thought of remarrying one day."

"*What?*" Her voice nearly cracked with outrage. Jonathan winced.

"It was all very vague," he said hastily. "Just a hope, you know, that he expressed to me once or twice. He had no one in mind, of that I'm certain. No real plans. I am nearly as astonished as you are, to learn that he has located a suitable female—and that she is inclined to accept him. It must have happened very quickly." He smiled encouragingly. "But I'm sure Sir Horace has chosen carefully, and that Miss—what is it? Mayhew—I'm sure Miss Mayhew will prove a worthy successor to the late Lady Chadwick."

Lilah's bosom rose and fell with indignation. "Are you *acquainted* with this woman?"

"Well, no. Naturally not."

"Then you cannot be sure of anything." She flew out of her chair and began flitting around the room, putting Jonathan irresistibly in mind of an agitated hummingbird. Delilah Chadwick was a petite little thing, but she invariably filled a room with her presence. He had often wondered why this was. Most men would have called her pretty, but her combination of brown hair, fair skin, and green eyes, though pleasing, was hardly unique. There was nothing extraordinary about her straight nose and determined chin. In fact, there was nothing remarkable in any single feature of her face or form—yet Delilah Chadwick was definitely greater than the sum of her parts. She drew the eye as irresistibly as one of those jewel-colored birds from the tropics.

"There must be some mistake," she exclaimed at last, lighting momentarily near the window.

"Papa and I have no secrets. We consult each other on everything. He would have told me, were he contemplating such a—such a *crazy* step! But he said nothing to me, nothing whatsoever."

Jonathan quirked an eyebrow at her, but decided it would be wise to keep his thoughts to himself. It did not surprise him that Sir Horace had failed to confide these particular plans to Delilah. Sir Horace Chadwick was a pleasant, easygoing chap, an excellent sort to have as one's employer, but there was no denying that he lacked backbone when dealing with his daughter. Well, who could blame him? Lilah was a handful. Jonathan could easily imagine how she would have carried on, had her father told her he was searching for a bride. She would have enacted a scene similar to the one she was performing for Jonathan's benefit—and Sir Horace disliked scenes.

Lilah resembled her mother, and Lilah's mother had been French. To Jonathan's mind, that explained everything. But the same qualities that had captivated Sir Horace in the mother made the daughter impossible for him to control. Lilah and Sir Horace adored each other, but the smooth running of the household and Lilah's sunny nature were dependent upon Sir Horace offering no opposition to his daughter's will. Jonathan knew it, Sir Horace knew it, and the entire household knew it. Lilah alone was unaware of the degree to which her whims were catered to. A pity, really. Lilah wasn't a bad sort. If she had any inkling of the way everyone tip-toed around her—

"Jonathan!"

He blinked. Lilah, still standing by the window, was turning huge, accusing eyes upon him. "You aren't listening. How long have we been friends?"

Her abrupt changes of subject always knocked him off balance. "How—how long?" he stammered, nonplussed. "Well, let's see—"

"Years! Years and years."

This struck Jonathan as an exaggeration. "Four years," he said firmly. "I've been in your father's employ four years."

Her impatient little shrug told him that, technically, four years *was* years and years, but that she wasn't inclined to belabor the point.

"There, then!" she said, on a note of triumph. "You're practically a member of the family. You know perfectly well that something peculiar is going on. Papa always, *always* includes me in his plans. And something like this—something that obviously affects me! Why, this news—*if* it is true, which is yet to be determined—would upset our entire household. It would change everything. He surely would have told me, he would have *consulted* me, before foisting a stepmother on me. As for marrying a stranger—no! It is utterly unlike him. You haven't met her. I haven't met her. Who *is* this woman?"

Since he had no ready answer for this question, he offered none. He watched in sympathetic silence as Lilah darted restlessly from window to table to chair to window. Her expressive brows, which normally flew in a dramatic upward slant, were knitted in a frown of concentration. "I'll tell you what it is," she announced, halting once more by the window. Genuine worry clouded her features. "My unfortunate father has fallen into the clutches of a harpy."

Jonathan was startled. "What makes you think so?"

"There can be no other explanation. Nothing else makes sense." She shivered dramatically. "Some mercenary harridan is taking advantage of Papa's good nature. You know how he is— too gentle by half. He's been *bullied* into this match. I can feel it."

Jonathan knew better than to argue with one of Lilah's "feelings." He coughed. "Now, Lilah," he said soothingly, "your father is not in his dotage. It's unlikely he would contract an engagement against his will; such things happen very rarely. Before you fly up into the boughs—"

Too late. She was all fired up now, her green eyes blazing with determination. "I'm going to

6

London," she announced. "This"—she flicked the letter contemptuously—"this Mayhew woman, or whatever she calls herself, must not be allowed to drag my poor father into a marriage he neither wants nor needs."

Jonathan rose from his seat behind the desk, alarmed. "Now, Lilah, pray consider! You are jumping to conclusions. We have no reason to believe—"

"We have every reason to believe." Lilah, preparing for action, was briskly stuffing the letter into her skirt pocket. "Why else would Papa's message be so brief? No details whatsoever! As if he were ashamed, or frightened, or—or sending me a secret message between the lines, begging for my intervention."

"A secret message? No, now, really—"

"At any rate, I shall go and meet the creature. And then"—her eyes flashed—"we shall see."

As she headed briskly for the door, Jonathan took three quick strides and intercepted her. "Lilah, think!" he begged, taking her by the shoulders. "If you meddle in this matter, it is I who will be blamed. Sir Horace will say, and rightly, that I ought to have stopped you."

Her eyes softened with humor. "Dear Jonathan," she said, affection warming her voice, "Papa would never be so unjust as to blame you for my actions. Has *he* ever been able to stop me from meddling?" She reached up to pat his cheek.

"Papa has no one to blame but himself," she said firmly, "for sending me such a maddeningly brief communication on such an important matter. And I will make certain he knows it."

She was gone then, in a flash of snapping silk, to set the household by the ears. Mr. Applegate sighed and returned to his desk, ruefully rubbing his patted cheek. With Sir Horace in London, he was the closest thing left to an authority figure in the house, but he had no power to quell Lilah's impulses. He had no real hope that Lilah's old governess, Miss Pickens—kept on as a sort of companion, so that Sir Horace could travel from time to time—would call a halt to her shenanigans, either. If Lilah said she was leaving for London, leave for London she would.

He wondered idly what she would do when it dawned on her that her father had taken the berline. There was no suitable traveling coach in the carriage house, but he did not suppose for a moment that such a trifling impediment would stop her.

He was right. Less than three hours after receiving Sir Horace's epistle, Lilah and Miss Pickens, together with two trunks, three valises, and a towering stack of bandboxes, were being shoehorned into the barouche. Jonathan sauntered out onto the portico to view the excitement. A parade of harassed-looking servants carried things to and fro while Lilah, on her feet and balanced like a sailor in the open carriage, issued a series of rapid-fire instructions to the housekeeper and the head groom. Miss Pickens, wearing the dazed look of a woman who would indulge in strong hysterics if given the slightest encouragement, cowered feebly in the corner of the carriage, clutching her vinaigrette in one hand and her parasol in the other. The parasol quivered and swayed as the carriage rocked beneath the onslaught of packing. One of the bandboxes rested atop Miss Pickens's knees, partially obstructing her view. The trunks had been piled around her feet, hemming her in as if to prevent escape. Lilah was the only person in sight who looked as if she were enjoying herself. Jonathan could not repress a chuckle.

Hearing his low laugh, Lilah glanced up and favored him with a saucy smile and a wave. Jonathan strolled forward. "I wondered which carriage you would take," he remarked. "What will you do if it rains?"

"Silly! I am not traveling all the way to London in the barouche. Grayson is driving us only as far as Bytheway. We will hire a proper traveling coach there."

"Had you sent word to the Swan, old Hopkins would have issued you the best he has and saved you the trip."

"Pooh! Trust the landlord of that greasy inn to choose my coach? No, thank you! Besides, sending a servant there and back would have wasted too much time."

Mr. Applegate gave up. He confined the rest of his advice to a mild admonition to Miss Pickens, as the barouche lurched into motion, to take good care of Miss Chadwick. Miss Pickens's reply, muffled against the bandbox, was inaudible. Lilah gave him a brilliant smile and another jaunty wave as they moved off. He ducked back into the house, hoping, rather nervously, that that wasn't a kiss she had thrown. It had looked suspiciously like a kiss. What an alarming thought.

Lilah settled contentedly against the high-backed squabs as the barouche bowled down the drive. Nothing gave one such a feeling of satisfaction, she reflected, as dealing masterfully with a crisis. Papa's situation was all very dreadful and mysterious, of course, but Lilah felt more alive than she had in weeks.

Miss Pickens was saying something. Her eyes were all that could be seen over the top of that upended bandbox, but they were fastened on Lilah with a distinct look of reproach. Lilah reached across and pulled the bandbox flat so she could see the whole of Miss Pickens's face. "What are you saying, Picky dear?"

"I am saying," uttered Miss Pickens, "that I saw you throw a kiss to Jonathan Applegate as we drove off."

Lilah looked mischievous. "Well? What if I did?"

Miss Pickens's thin bosom quivered with indignation and alarm. "Oh, Lilah, no! How *can* you? I wish, I *do* wish you would heed me, if only once in a while! You must be more careful, my dear. You really, really must. Fortunately Mr. Applegate knows you quite well, and will make allowance for your natural high spirits. At least, we may hope that he does! But you could easily give another man, a man who did not know you well, the wrong impression. Anyone might think you were *flirting* with him."

Lilah laughed. "Poor Picky! I am a sad trial to you, I know. But I *was* flirting with him."

Miss Pickens threw up her hands in horror. "No, no! You mustn't! Really, Lilah, you mustn't! Your father's *secretary*? Merciful heavens, child, you'll be the death of me! Mr. Applegate is a level-headed young man, and I daresay we may trust him not to get carried away, at least not by any notion of looking seriously at one so far above him, but—"

Lilah made a little moue of disgust. "Level-headed. Is that what you call it? I call it wooden-headed. I've given him any number of hints, and he ignores them all."

Miss Pickens shuddered. "This is what comes of burying yourself in the country," she declared mournfully. "Why, oh why, do you dislike London so? If only you would go with your father, at least every so often. At least for the Season! I do wish you would give the metropolis another chance, my love. Had you a wider social circle, you would not think for a moment of—of casting out lures to Mr. Applegate. Of all men!"

Lilah tilted her head thoughtfully. "You think not? He comes of good stock, you know. A most distinguished Hampshire family. It's not Jonathan's fault that he was born a younger son and must make his own way in the world."

"But he's penniless, my love!" uttered Miss Pickens in a horrified whisper. "No prospects at all. Not that you need to care for that so very much, situated as you are, and of course one is not supposed to mention it, but never mind. Every prudent woman considers such things, whether she mentions them or no. And on top of that—well, here's another thing we are told that females should not think of, but we do! Mr. Applegate is not particularly handsome, is he?"

Lilah tossed her head defiantly. "I think he's adorable. Those sweet little spectacles—and the way his hair always looks as if he doesn't own a looking glass—and that befuddled look he gets—"

"Good heavens! You find that attractive?"

"Well, I suppose not every female would," admitted Lilah. "But I think Jonathan is a dear. Dearness is a rare and wonderful attribute in a man." Her eyes twinkled. "I know you think me a flibbertigibbit, incapable of rational thought, but I assure you I have given this a great deal of thought. I believe that if I am ever to marry, I must find a mild-mannered man, a man who is gentler and more biddable than I. He must be my opposite in temperament. My parents were temperamental opposites, and such a match worked very well for them. Did it not?"

Miss Pickens opened her mouth to say something, then shut it again without answering. Lilah decided to press her. "Well? Did it not?"

"It worked well for your mother," said Miss Pickens darkly.

Lilah beamed. "Yes, that's what I mean. I need to find someone like Papa."

Miss Pickens looked as if she would like to amplify her previous statement, but Lilah's mind had already jumped to another topic. "As for this Mayhew woman," she announced, "she may think she has found an easy mark in poor Papa, but when I arrive upon the scene she will soon learn her mistake. What can she be like, I wonder? Eugenia Mayhew! She sounds haggish. The sort of crone who would try her best to keep her stepdaughter firmly under her thumb. Well! She won't succeed." Lilah's chin jutted mulishly. "And if she so much as *tries* to come between Papa and me—"

"Now, then, Lilah," interposed Miss Pickens

nervously, "you've no evidence to suggest she will do any such thing. You are letting your imagination run away with you, my love. Miss Mayhew may be perfectly amiable."

Lilah looked skeptical. "Hum! Every step-mother I've ever encountered, or heard tell of, was a tyrant. Yours was, wasn't she?"

"Oh, my, yes. A dreadful woman. That is— no, you are jumping to conclusions again!" Miss Pickens clasped and unclasped her hands in agitation. "There are exceptions to every rule, you know. And even if there were not, there is no reason to suppose you will be as unlucky as I. Indeed, it would hardly be possible. Your position will be quite, quite different from what mine was. Why, I was a mere child when my father remarried, and we were—we were not wealthy. But all this is beside the point." She sat bolt upright and took a deep breath. "Pray remember, my dear Lilah, that you and I have a duty to your father. Whatever our opinion of second marriages in general, or stepmothers in general, we *must* give your father's bride the benefit of the doubt."

These fell words struck new dismay into Lilah's heart. "My father's bride! Do you really think it will come to that? It sounds so—so" —she bit her lip—"so un-Papalike!"

2

The White Swan at Bytheway was the only inn for miles in any direction. This was the secret of its success, if success it could be called. Its proprietor, Mr. Hopkins, was not accumulating wealth at the same rate as other innkeepers along the turnpike. On the other hand, he was not sinking into poverty at the rapid clip his spectacularly lax management deserved.

When crossing Mr. Hopkins's threshold, Lilah lifted her skirts a little higher than usual. The Swan had an aura of neglect that made one look carefully before one stepped. She halted in the low-ceilinged foyer and, as her eyes adjusted to the dimness, glanced about her with distaste. Mr. Hopkins's attempts at cleanliness and order fell woefully short. The floor felt sticky underfoot, the walls and ceiling were black with smoke, and daylight struggled to penetrate the film of grime that coated the windows.

Miss Pickens tiptoed up and clutched Lilah's

arm. "My dear Lilah, this is a nasty place," she whispered. "Are you quite, quite certain—"

"Yes, I am," said Lilah shortly. "Although I wish we had some alternative. Look at the cobwebs on that chandelier. Disgusting!"

As if called by this remark, Hopkins himself waddled out from the taproom. His eyes brightened as he recognized the daughter of the most important landholder in the neighborhood, and he came forward at once, wiping his fat hands on the dish towel tied at his waist—futilely, Lilah thought, since the rag was far from clean.

"Miss Chadwick, is it not? Yes, yes, yes, I would know you anywhere! An honor, a privilege to see you, miss, I'm sure. How may I serve you today? And Miss—ah—"

"Pickens."

"Yes, yes, Miss Pickens, how d'ye do? What can I do for you ladies?"

Lilah gave him a bright, businesslike smile. "I require your best traveling coach, Mr. Hopkins, as speedily as you can provide it."

If she was expecting his obsequious manner to translate into prompt action, she was disappointed. The landlord's face fell ludicrously. "Oh, dear. What an unfortunate coincidence. I'm afraid I've only one left. Yes, indeed, only the one, and it be far from the best. Business being what it is, you understand. And—"

"Well, never mind," said Lilah, her heart sink-

16

ing. "Whatever its condition, I'll take it." An unpleasant vision of Miss Pickens and herself
having to scrub the interior before boarding
flashed through her mind, but she sternly banished it. This was an emergency. She would do
what she must.

The landlord licked his lips nervously. "Well,
that's just it. I'm afraid you are too late. As I
say, I've only the one coach left. And I promised
it, not ten minutes ago, to Lord Drakesley." He
flapped his towel in the direction of the
taproom.

Lilah's brows snapped together. "Who?"

"Lord Drakesley." Mr. Hopkins drew himself
up with an air of importance. "An *earl*, no less,"
he confided. "Peer of the realm."

Lilah's foot began to tap with annoyance. "I
know what an earl is."

Thus deflated, Mr. Hopkins shot her a glance
filled with resentment. "Yes. Well. At any rate,
his lordship's curricle lost a wheel, and he hasn't
time to wait while it is repaired. He—"

"What! He has a curricle with him, and you
gave him your last remaining coach?"

Mr. Hopkins swelled like an insulted toad.
"Certainly I did," he huffed. "He wanted one. I
had one. He offered me a handsome price. And
why not? Curricle's not driveable until the
wheel is fixed. Gent's in a hurry—got plenty of
rhino—peer of the blinking realm! Meaning no

17

offense, ladies, I'm sure," he added, as Miss Pickens clucked at his deteriorating language. "At any rate, you're too late. It's all arranged. Promised and paid for. His lordship'll be off as soon as—"

"He is still here?" Lilah's eyes brightened.

"Aye, he's in the taproom. But—"

Lilah did not wait to hear the end of his sentence. She swept past Mr. Hopkins and into the taproom. Ivy covered most of the windows, so the taproom was even more dimly lit than the entry hall. She hesitated on the threshold.

The room had only one occupant, an extremely large and unkempt man who sat with his back to her, draining a tankard. Lilah thought he looked more like a highwayman than an earl. There was nothing the least bit elegant about him. He appeared to be dressed all in leather, and he was exceedingly dusty. She could easily imagine him pulling a pistol on her and demanding, "Yer money or yer life." Still, she did not care to show disrespect to a man of his rank—assuming that this odd specimen belonged to the aristocracy. She infused a note of polite deference into her voice as she addressed him.

"Lord Drakesley?"

He did not immediately respond, but continued swallowing. He must be slaking a fearsome thirst. Perhaps he had not heard her. She took a step closer and tried again, a little louder.

"Lord Drakesley? May I have speech with you?"

He wiped his mouth with the back of his hand and swiveled halfway round on the bench. His expression was anything but welcoming. Her first impression was of thick brows drawn down over fiercely gleaming eyes. He looked like a hawk disturbed while feeding.

"Who in blue blazes gave you my name?" he growled.

She drew back, startled by his brusqueness, then stiffened her spine. It was absurd to let him frighten her. "The landlord, of course," she said coolly. "Why? Is it a secret?"

The man's scowl became downright menacing. He rose slowly off the low bench, the gradual straightening of his body somehow more intimidating than a hasty movement would have been. "From the likes of you, it is."

Lilah's eyes widened in astonishment. "The *likes* of—what on earth do you mean?"

He did not deign to answer her. The derisive expression on his face struck Lilah as insulting. Her brows snapped together in a frown. Did he not perceive that she was a gentlewoman? A fine attitude, from a man so thickly powdered with dust that it was impossible to tell the color

19

of his hair! She felt her temper rise. "Perhaps you misunderstand," she said crisply. "I am not some farmer's daughter. I am—"

"I don't care who you are," he interrupted rudely. "And whether your father is a duke or a ditchdigger, he should have taught you not to bother strangers. Particularly men. More particularly, lone men. And *most* particularly, lone men in public inns."

Lilah's jaw dropped. "How dare you? No one speaks to me in such a tone—let alone a *stranger!* Who gave you permission to take me to task?"

"You did. You began this conversation, not I. Let it be a lesson to you." He tossed a coin down on the table to pay for his drink and gave her a brief, dismissive nod. "Good day."

He would have strolled past her, but she caught at his arm. "Wait! If you please," she added, catching the look on his face. "I see that I have offended you. Pray believe that I would never have approached you were the circumstances not extraordinary. But really, my lord, I *must* speak with you."

He towered over her. She had to tilt her chin to look him in the eye. He was younger than she had first thought—probably less than thirty. It was his massiveness, his solidity, and his arrogant air that made him appear older. And, of course, the scowl that was twisting his features at present. The scowl added years to his face.

20

"Now, look here," he said evenly, as if hanging on to his patience by his fingernails. "I'm a busy man. You are the fourth numbskull today who has wasted my time, wanting something from me. It's not that I dislike being manhandled by a pretty woman"—Lilah hastily let go of his sleeve—"but, frankly, I have nothing to say to you. And whatever it is you want to say to me, I'm betting I don't want to hear it."

He was right. How annoying.

Lilah glared at him. "You can't possibly know that."

A gleam of irony lit his features. "I grow more certain of it every moment."

Hostility was getting her nowhere. With an effort, Lilah pasted a pleasant expression on her face and tried a gentle laugh. "Now, Lord Drakesley, I know you don't mean to be disobliging," she said archly. "I should not have addressed you without an introduction, and especially not while you were swallowing. There! I apologize."

"Good of you," he said mockingly. "Now add to your goodness by stepping aside."

"I will," she said, giving him her most winning smile. "But first, I must request your assistance in a trifling matter." She saw the refusal in his eyes and quickly added, "As a *gentleman,* I'm sure I may rely on you."

He looked suspicious. "Rely on me for what?"

21

Lilah pressed her palms together and tried to look apologetic. "I am very sorry to inconvenience you. But apparently Hopkins has only one coach available today, and you have hired it. I need it."

"What a pity."

"Yes. But I understand you have a curricle, and need only wait for a wheel to be repaired." She smiled encouragingly. "I daresay a wheel repair won't take so terribly long, and then you may be off."

One of his brows arched, in amusement or disbelief—she wasn't sure which. "Oh, I'll be off sooner than that. Hadn't you heard? I've hired the landlord's coach. Good day."

"But surely you won't insist on—surely you won't take it for yourself?" Lilah was flabbergasted. "Don't you understand? *I* need it."

She had instinctively caught at his arm again. He gave her an exasperated look. "So do I. Kindly release my sleeve."

Was he dense? She tightened her grip, planting her feet in the way of a mule. "There is only one coach," she reiterated, trying not to lose patience with him. "You must not take it. I want it."

"Nevertheless, you cannot have it. I am taking it. Immediately."

"But my need is greater than yours!"

"No, it isn't. And don't confide your troubles

22

to me," he added. "I haven't the remotest interest in why you need the coach."

"Then I will only tell you that—that my errand is urgent," she stammered, not knowing how to combat his blighting indifference. "And it is! *Terribly* urgent!" She heard her voice rising and struggled to lower her pitch to a more reasonable-sounding level. "My lord, where, oh where, is your chivalry?" she chided him. "You cannot, you will not, be so churlish as to take the last coach."

"I will be exactly that churlish," he assured her, not in the least discomposed by her attempt to shame him. "Let go of me."

"But I *need* it!" cried Lilah.

"Yes, you have said so. Over and over. But the fact remains that I hired it, and you didn't." He reached across his broad chest with his free hand and plucked her desperate fingers off his coat. "Better luck next time. Good-bye."

Lilah was outraged. The ruffian, or earl, or whatever he was, actually turned his back and strolled out the door to the yard, having brushed her off as if she were no more important than a fly buzzing round him. She marched after him, head high and cheeks aflame with indignation. The yard was muddy from last night's rain, forcing her to halt on the stone steps outside the taproom door.

"You are the rudest person I have ever met,"

she shouted at his retreating back. Curious faces appeared in the windows of the inn, but Lilah ignored them. To her surprise—and gathering wrath—the rudesby actually chuckled.

"What a pampered life you must lead," he remarked. "Not accustomed to having your will crossed, eh?" He turned to look at her, letting his gaze travel insultingly over her form. "Yes. You even look spoiled."

Fury choked her. She placed her fists on her hips and glared at him. "And obviously *you* never go out of your way to oblige anyone."

"I do have that reputation," he agreed.

"Detestable man!" she exclaimed. "I see what it is. You *enjoy* being disagreeable."

"Frequently, yes, I do." Was that a grin flickering at the edges of his mouth? "Some occasions are more entertaining than others, of course."

The lad-of-all-work employed by Hopkins appeared round the corner of the inn, leading two horses. Lord Drakesley turned his attention to the battered traveling coach leaning on its poles near the White Swan's doorway. He peered into one of the windows and pulled back, grimacing. "This thing stinks."

"Serves you right," muttered Lilah.

She had not expected Lord Drakesley to overhear her childish remark. The man apparently had the ears of a bat. He shot her a derisive look, then indicated the Chadwick barouche that stood, piled with luggage, on the other side of the yard. "At any rate, you will not be forced to walk to your destination. You obviously have a barouche at your disposal."

"Don't be ridiculous," snapped Lilah. "I cannot dawdle along in an open barouche all the way to London."

"You need only 'dawdle along' to the next posting inn."

"In a pleasure carriage? It would take hours! And besides, what would become of me if they also had no vehicle to hire? No, no, I *must* take Hopkins's coach."

Lord Drakesley's exasperated scowl returned. "I am taking it, you naggy little wigeon! I've already paid for it." He surveyed the shabby berline digustedly. "Overpaid for it."

"I will reimburse you," she said quickly, deciding her best course was to overlook his unflattering characterization of her. "I will—I will pay you extra. To compensate you for your trouble."

"No." He glanced at her, and something in her face caused him to relent a little. "I'm sorry," he said grudgingly. "But you'll be more comfortable in your barouche than in this smelly old bone-rattler. And probably safer."

"Its aroma, pleasant or unpleasant, is immaterial to me," said Lilah stiffly. "And I do not care if it rattles my bones. I cannot stop to consider such trifles; I must be off without further delay. I will pay you whatever you ask."

Irritation darkened his features again. "You'll catch cold at this game," he informed her. "Money means nothing to me."

Lilah tossed her head. "A noble sentiment!" she scoffed. "Take care your pride does not beggar you."

"It won't. I'm rich as Croesus."

He said these words offhandedly, seeming to neither boast nor joke. Indeed, he turned with perfect impassivity to watch the horses being hitched up, as if he had completely lost interest in Lilah and her plight. She folded her arms and looked down her nose at him. "If you're as rich as all that," she opined, "you should buy a new coach and let me hire the smelly one."

The sarcasm in her suggestion did not go over Lord Drakesley's head. He looked at her again, a glimmer of humor detectable in the depths of his hawklike eyes. "I said money means nothing to me. Time, on the other hand, is the very stuff of life. And I don't intend to kick my heels in this repulsive backwater an instant longer than necessary."

He tossed a coin carelessly to the boy, who had completed the hitching of the horses, and bent to inspect the wheels. "Ugly, but sound enough," he remarked. He glanced over his shoulder at Lilah. "By the by, if you'd like to borrow my curricle, I'm told it will be ready no later than Wednesday."

"Thank you," said Lilah icily. "It may have escaped your notice, but I am a lady. I require a closed carriage. And it will not be convenient for me to wait until Wednesday, as I think I may have mentioned."

"I had that impression," he agreed, straightening. "Oh, well." He then leaned lazily against the coach, an attitude that struck Lilah as maddeningly possessive. She felt her bosom swell with indignation.

To her left, the main doorway of the inn disgorged Hopkins, who halted in the dooryard, bowing and scraping and clearing his throat. Miss Pickens spilled out behind him, her anxious face telegraphing that the bulk of Lilah's conversation with Lord Drakesley had been overheard.

"Ahem! Lord Drakesley. If I might be so bold, milord," began Hopkins, turning a dull red.

The earl's forbidding scowl descended. "What now?" he barked, rounding on the landlord.

It was not an encouraging response. Hopkins bowed lower, pursing his mouth nervously. "Ah—p'raps your lordship might not know—these ladies are very respectable females. Most distinguished persons, milord, and highly regarded in the neighborhood. I mislike to offend them in any way. Begging your pardon, I'm sure, but you must know I've got to live here, and can't afford to cause ill will—"

"What the deuce are you saying?"

Hopkins's voice took on a whining note. "I'm only saying, milord, and meaning no offense, that a compromise would be preferable to this brangling, if a compromise might be found—"

"I hope you are not talking about the coach." Lord Drakesley folded his arms across his powerful chest. The stance was not only intimidating, it made him look enormous. "I've heard just about enough regarding your stinking coach."

"Well, as to that, milord, the vicar had it last, and his wife is powerful fond of onions—"

"Do not prate to me of your wretched vicar and his utterly uninteresting wife."

Hopkins blanched. "No-no, milord," he stammered. "Certainly not. But I was, in fact, speaking of the coach. It appears that the ladies are in urgent need of transportation—"

"No."

"But, milord—"

"No."

"You have not yet heard what I mean to say!" finished Hopkins in a rush.

"If it has anything to do with my giving up this vehicle—"

"No, no, upon my honor! But I have just found out, milord, that the ladies are traveling to London."

"Of what possible interest is that to me?"

"Why—why, milord, that is your destination, is it not? Yes, I'm quite sure you told me 'twas London—"

"What if I did?"

Hopkins appeared nonplussed. Miss Pickens peered round his shoulder and favored Lord Drakesley with an ingratiating smile. "We share a destination, my lord," she piped brightly. "Might we not share a coach as well?"

Relief and dismay warred within Lilah's breast. Dismay won. "Oh, Picky, no!" she blurted. All eyes turned to Lilah. She cudgeled her brain for a reason for her outburst and immediately thought of one. "Pray recall that it is a closed carriage," she protested, casting her eyes modestly down. "Lord Drakesley must let us take the coach, for I cannot share it with a gentleman. It would be the height of impropriety."

"I see nothing improper in it," said Miss Pickens reasonably. "You cannot go alone with him, of course, but I will be with you. No one could object to so harmless an arrangement."

"I could," said Lord Drakesley.

Miss Pickens, apparently interpreting this assertion as a jest, tittered politely. She then stepped forth and addressed Lilah with the confidence and affection of long acquaintance. "Lilah, dear, you will not like to appear unreasonable," she said coaxingly. "We do not mind sharing a little space with his lordship. Indeed, we must be grateful, you and I. Only think how we are incommoding him! Were it not for our arrival, he might have gone on alone quite comfortably."

"I may yet," said Lord Drakesley conversationally. "For I have no intention of sharing the coach with you ladies." Miss Pickens turned shocked, reproachful eyes upon him. He coughed. "Well, frankly, ma'am, I have no objection to taking you up," he explained. "But as for that troublesome chit"—he jerked a thumb to indicate Lilah—"I'd rather be caged with a wasp."

Mr. Hopkins stepped hastily forward. "Now, now, there's no need to pull caps over this," he begged. "I'm sure we can arrange something satisfactory, with just a little cooperation—just a smidgen of goodwill, if I might be so bold to suggest it! Ladies, Lord Drakesley's groom is stopping here and will drive his lordship's curricle to London once it is repaired. Much of your baggage might be left here, for transport in the curricle. If you three travelers can agree on what items must go with you and which may be left behind for a few days—"

"All my luggage is absolutely vital," said Lilah quickly. "There will be no room for Lord Drakesley or any of his gear in my coach."

Something that sounded like a low growl came from Lord Drakesley's throat. Miss Pickens and Mr. Hopkins rushed to pour oil on the troubled waters.

"Oh, but for my own luggage, I am sure I need only one bandbox," Miss Pickens averred. "And you know, Lilah dear, we will have no immediate need for *any* of the trunks—"

"My lord, I'm sure Miss Chadwick has not thought it through. I'm sure she will be reasonable," babbled Hopkins. "And if Miss Pickens is willing to dispense with most of her own items for the time being—"

"I see no reason why Miss Pickens should be inconvenienced," Lilah interrupted, her voice cool with disdain.

"And I see no reason why *I* should be inconvenienced," announced Lord Drakesley. "This conversation is at an end. Good day."

He moved to climb into the coach. In a moment, he would be gone. For half a moment, Lilah could not believe her eyes. Had she *lost*? Incredible! She was such a formidable opponent in any battle of wills, it was rare for her to meet resistance, let alone defeat.

Frantic, she ran forward and clutched at his coat. "Do not go!" she cried. "My lord, I beg of you—see reason! You are inconveniencing two ladies, something I am persuaded your good breeding will not allow. If you take that coach, we will be stranded."

He paused on the step, looking back at her in patent exasperation. "The coach is mine, brat. Unless you would care to change your tune about sharing it with me?" He bared his teeth in what was clearly meant to be a smile. "I might be persuaded to take you up, were I confident that you would not delay me further."

His tone was so jeering, Lilah knew he expected her to spurn his offer. He was, all too obviously, waiting only for that before climbing into the coach. Her chin jutted stubbornly. A *brat*, was she? Ha! She would not give him the satisfaction of seeing her behave like the spoiled child he thought her. Besides, instant capitulation was her last hope. She pinned a sweet smile on her lips.

"Oh, my lord, I would not dream of delaying you. Come along, Miss Pickens! His lordship has decided to share the coach with us after all, and, upon reflection, I see no point in declining his offer."

Lord Drakesley appeared startled. Then his brows contracted in one of his ferocious scowls. "This is sudden! I thought you insisted on taking the coach yourself?"

She shrugged lightly. "I would prefer it, of

course. But if Mr. Hopkins has let the coach to you, why, I suppose I have no recourse."

His scowl darkened. "Hang it all! I don't *want* to share the coach with you."

Her smile brightened. "Then it was particularly kind of you to offer," she said sweetly. "Thank you."

She was highly gratified to see that her apparent surrender had wiped the smugness from his expression. It was a Pyrrhic victory, but the sight of the earl's discomfiture, and his obvious annoyance, made it almost worthwhile. The outcome was not to her liking—but it was a consolation to see that it was even less to his liking. She half expected him to withdraw his offer immediately, but he did not. He muttered a rather shocking oath that Lilah pretended not to hear, then stalked back into the inn, announcing savagely that if he *must* wait for the ladies' baggage to be transferred to his coach, at least he would refresh himself meanwhile. Lilah breathed a little easier when he had gone.

Well. She had committed herself. She and Lord Drakesley would be sharing a coach. This was not what she had intended, and the journey would doubtless be an unpleasant one, but she consoled herself with the thought that at least she was en route to London in a proper traveling coach. And the insufferable Lord Drakesley had been forced, after all, to accommodate her.

3

As Lord Drakesley had foreseen, a brief delay ensued while the ladies' baggage was piled atop the rickety coach. As soon as their reluctant escort had disappeared into the Swan, Lilah scrambled into the coach's cabin. She pulled Miss Pickens after her, beckoning hurriedly. "For heaven's sake, make haste!" she urged. "I would not put it past the man to take the forward-facing seat and force us to ride backward. He may be an earl, but he is no gentleman."

Miss Pickens obligingly clambered in. "Well, earls are a different breed, my dear. We must make allowances for his rank. I daresay he receives so much deference as a matter of course, he has come to expect it from everyone he meets."

"He won't get it from me." Lilah's chin jutted mulishly. "You should have seen him a while ago—flashing his title and swaggering about,

34

distributing largesse to the lackeys and generally behaving like the Grand Turk! Disgusting, I thought it."

But Miss Pickens's face had assumed an extraordinary expression. "Mercy on us! What is that reek?" she exclaimed as she settled onto the narrow bench beside her charge.

Lilah sniffed the air, then coughed. She struggled to remove the leather curtain covering the window on her side of the compartment. "Onions," she said in a strangled tone. "I think." Having succeeded, she leaned into the opening and fanned briskly with one hand, trying to pull fresh air into the confines of the coach. "The great thing is, Lord Drakesley's odor won't matter a whit. Did you see how filthy he was? I wanted to tell him that powdered hair is no longer the fashion, but I didn't think he would see the joke."

"Now, Lilah! He's been traveling in a curricle, you know. It's natural for a man to collect a little dust that way."

"Kindly stop defending him," said Lilah crossly. "It puts me out."

"Nevertheless, you are blaming Lord Drakesley for a situation that is entirely Hopkins's fault. He must know he runs the only posting house for ten miles or more. I cannot imagine why the wretched man doesn't secure a few more vehicles."

"If he maintains them as poorly as this, I daresay the rest have all fallen to pieces."

When Lilah saw Lord Drakesley emerging from the inn she promptly sat back against the squabs, assuming an elaborately dignified posture. She would not give him the satisfaction of seeing her sulk, but, on the other hand, she needn't fawn on him the way Miss Pickens seemed prepared to do. Out of the corner of her eye, she saw the earl's enormous body striding swiftly across the yard. The coach rocked violently as he pulled open the door and clambered in.

"Well, well. This is cozy," he said dryly. "Mind if I put my feet in your lap?"

Startled, Lilah looked at him—and was relieved to see that he was joking. The space was, indeed, cramped for a man of his bulk. For the first time, she felt a twinge of sympathy for his reluctance to share it. This would be a tedious journey for him, with his long legs folded into the narrow confines of the aisle and his head nearly touching the ceiling. The jouncing of the carriage would doubtless knock his skull against the roof from time to time. Alone in the coach, he might have stretched out and made himself more comfortable.

He had obviously availed himself of a washbasin. She had to admit, it had done him some good. The film of road grit that had leeched all the color from his person and his clothing had been, for the most part, removed. The leather duster and thick muffler that had made him look like a highwayman had also been discarded, revealing a well-cut suit of ordinary clothing. He was dressed in perfectly respectable blue and buff. His hair, damp combed, appeared dark brown. He had evidently changed into clean linen. Why, he looked halfway human. Even his eyebrows looked more civilized. It was impossible to think of him as attractive, but at least he no longer looked as if he made a living by lurking about with a pistol in his pocket.

He seemed to notice her scrutiny. An ironic gleam appeared in his deep-set eyes. "I clean up well, don't I?" he drawled.

If he hoped to embarrass her, he would be disappointed. Lilah's chin lifted. "Moderately well, my lord," she said coolly.

The coach started forward with a lurch, throwing her briefly against his knee. She ignored the embarrassing contact and pressed her feet tightly together, squeezing herself into the corner as far from him as she could. This, unfortunately, wasn't very far. Beside her, Miss Pickens was hanging on to a strap provided to steady travelers during the rocking of the coach. The strap on Lilah's side of the vehicle, she noted belatedly, was broken.

The coach swung round the turn onto the

highway and Lilah was pitched again, willy-nilly, almost into Lord Drakesley's lap. She regained her balance with an effort, trying not to blush, and fixed her gaze determinedly out the window. It seemed that Lord Drakesley's eyes never left her face, and she was fairly sure he was enjoying her discomfiture. Odious man! She tried to appear unconcerned.

"We are now, officially, traveling companions," he commented. "I think introductions are in order."

Lilah shot him a cold look. "We will not be thrown together for longer than a day or two. I see nothing amiss with calling each other 'my lord' and 'ma'am.'"

"Or, to differentiate between you ladies," he suggested, "how about 'my lord,' 'ma'am,' and 'your highness'?"

Lilah choked. "I do *not* expect royal treatment!"

"Good, because you're unlikely to receive it," said Lord Drakesley affably. "Let's dispense with the animosity, shall we? It grows tiresome. My name is Adam Harleston. I'm the ninth Earl of Drakesley. I've had the title since the age of ten months, so everyone has called me Drake for as long as I can remember."

She eyed him doubtfully. "Are we to call you Drake as well?"

"Yes. Why not?"

"It sounds disrespectful."

His deep-set eyes gleamed. "How touching. Where was this concern for my dignity ten minutes ago?"

Lilah tossed her head. "I am not concerned about your beastly dignity," she said frostily. "I am concerned about how *we* will look, if Miss Pickens and I address you so informally."

"Oh. So your concern is for yourself. Now *that* makes sense. You had me worried there, for a moment; I thought I might have misjudged you."

Lilah drew herself up to her full, if diminutive, height and opened her mouth to say something pretty blistering. She was forestalled by Miss Pickens, who leaped hastily into the breach. "Very obliging of you, my lord, I am sure—most obliging!" she babbled. "I'm sure we will be glad to call you anything you like. Whatever you prefer. Lilah, dear, pray—! His lordship is being very kind, most condescending, to let us use a name his intimates use. Why, we only met him this morning, and here he is, treating us quite like old friends. Very good of you, my lord, very good of you. We will be proud to call you—ah—Drake." She gulped involuntarily, as if calling an earl by his nickname caused her physical pain. "Drake," she repeated gamely, and managed a rather wan smile. "You say it is taken from your title?"

He bowed. "Naturally. Now tell me, if you can, why the fastidious creature to your immediate right hesitates to call me Drake but publicly calls you Piggy."

Miss Pickens blinked and Lilah gasped. "I do not call her Piggy!"

"I distinctly heard you call her Piggy. Shockingly disrespectful, I thought."

Lilah bit her lip, struggling not to laugh. "*Picky.* You may have heard me call her Picky. Short for Pickens." She turned to her companion, contrite. "I'm sorry, Picky dear. I should be more careful."

Miss Pickens looked mortified. "I own, I do not care for the nickname," she confessed. "But it never occurred to me that a stranger might hear it as Piggy."

"I shall call you Miss Pickens," promised Drake. "Whatever the princess does."

Lilah's urge to laugh vanished. "I am not a princess," she said stiffly. "My father is a baronet. My name, if you must know it, is Miss Chadwick."

The oddest expression descended onto Drake's features. It was the first time she had seen him nonplussed. He stared, his brows knitting. A muscle jumped in his cheek. "What did you say your name was?"

"Chadwick," said Lilah, surprised. "Delilah Chadwick."

She could have sworn he turned pale. "Never tell me you are related to Sir Horace Chadwick!"

Lilah and Miss Pickens looked at each other, then back at Drake. "Why? Are you acquainted with my father?" asked Lilah, puzzled.

"Good God! Then—d'you mean your *father* is Sir Horace Chadwick?" He raked a hand distractedly through his still-damp hair. It immediately sprang up into an unruly thatch of cowlicks.

"Ye-es," said Lilah cautiously. "What's the matter?"

Drake suddenly looked as if he would like very much to jump out of the coach. "I should have guessed as much," he ejaculated bitterly. "The way my luck has been running, I might have known this would happen. Confound it! Of all people to encounter on the road—of all people to be forced to travel with—his *daughter*! Good God!"

"Have you run mad?" demanded Lilah, incredulous. "My father hasn't an enemy in the world."

"He hasn't met me yet," said Drake darkly. His lip curled as he looked at Lilah. "I should stop the coach and put you out on the road right now. I should drive off and leave you here, alone with Miss Pickens and all your blasted luggage. I daresay your father would leave London at once and ride to your rescue."

"Of course he would," said Lilah promptly. "And you would be clapped into Bedlam, which is obviously where you belong."

"I begin to think I would be happier there," growled Drake. "Blast it! What a chapter of accidents."

Miss Pickens leaned timidly forward. "My lord, you are distraught," she said soothingly. "What has occurred to vex you so? Sir Horace is a virtuous, kindly man, I give you my word. I have lived in his household these dozen years or more, and know him well. He is no man's enemy."

The rickety coach suddenly hit a bump and all three of its occupants flew straight up and knocked their heads on the ceiling. This did nothing to improve Drake's temper. He leaned out the window and shouted, "Wake up, you cowhanded whipster! You'll land us in the ditch!"

"Beg pardon, milord," came the faint reply. The driver sounded aggrieved. "You did say you wanted all possible speed."

"Aye, but let's arrive with no bones broken!"

"Very good, milord."

Drake pulled his head back in and glared at the ladies. "You were saying?" he inquired with savage politeness. "Ah, yes! Extolling the virtues of Sir Horace Chadwick. Well, save your breath. Is he, or is he not, a man of middle age?"

Lilah was still rubbing her head. "Since he is my father, you must know he is," she said crossly. "What's wrong with middle age?"

"Fifty years or more in his dish, I daresay," said Drake in a voice of loathing.

"Forty-five, if it's any business of yours. Which it isn't!" said Lilah with spirit. "And what has that to say to anything? It's absurd to take a man in dislike because he is forty-five! You'll reach that age yourself one day—if no one murders you first."

Drake scowled. "When I am forty-five," he announced, "I shall not spend my declining years seducing innocents who are young enough to be my daughter."

Lilah nearly jumped in surprise. "I should hope not!" Then a crazy idea occurred to her. Her eyes narrowed. She leaned toward Drake, her voice becoming dangerously silky. "Do not—do *not*—tell me that that incredibly offensive remark had anything to do with my father."

Miss Pickens made a faint squawking sound. The two combatants, intent on each other, ignored her.

Drake leaned forward until his face was scant inches from Lilah's. "It has everything to do with your precious father," he said through his teeth. "In fact, there is no remark I could make about Sir Horace Chadwick that would be offensive enough to describe his conduct."

43

Lilah's eyes felt as if they would pop from her head with astonishment and wrath. "You must be demented!" she gasped. "My father is a respectable, upright man, not a—a *lecher!*"

His lip curled in a sneer. "Call it what you will. I have it on excellent authority that Chadwick has spent the past seven weeks persecuting a certain young lady—a lady of birth but no prospects. Since she is an orphan, I daresay he thought she had no one to protect her, no one to defend her from his unwelcome advances. He is about to learn his mistake."

Lilah, relieved to discover that Drake had simply been misinformed, uttered a trill of scornful laughter. "Well! You could scarcely be farther off the mark. I have just received word that my father is about to contract a marriage. Now, how could he find time to court my future stepmother if he were busy seducing a young girl?"

Drake looked startled, but only for a moment. His scowl became fiercer than ever. "Marriage!" he exclaimed, straightening as much of his spine as the low compartment would allow. "So that's the way of it. He has used his title and his fortune to turn Eugenia's head. Well, I have a piece of Spanish news for Sir Horace Chadwick! I have a better title and a bigger fortune, and I'm jolly well going to marry her myself."

Lilah felt the color draining from her face.

"Eugenia?" she said faintly. "Eugenia Mayhew?"

Drake looked sharply at her. "That's the name. My second cousin, once removed. I've meant to marry her since I was fifteen years old."

"But—but—no, we cannot be speaking of the same person! How old is your Miss Mayhew?"

"Six-and-twenty. What's the matter?"

Lilah pressed her palms to her cheeks. "Merciful heavens." The scenario she had dreaded, of being placed under the thumb of a powerful crone was being replaced by a new, even worse, nightmare: the vision of finding herself subordinate to a child bride.

She turned to Miss Pickens, blinking in bewilderment. "Picky, did you hear? Miss Mayhew is quite *young*. Can that be possible?"

Miss Pickens flushed uncomfortably and tugged at her gloves, a nervous gesture so habitual to her that every pair she owned had been stretched out of shape. "Yes, my love, I heard. Well. Not what you expected, I daresay. But she will be a most amiable lady, I'm sure, if Lord Drakesley vouches for her—"

Lilah could scarcely comprehend what Miss Pickens was saying. Her brain was awhirl, adjusting to this new set of circumstances. "Oh!" she interrupted, tears stinging her eyes. "My unfortunate papa! He must have taken leave of his senses. He's a modest man, a reserved man. Why would he make such a figure of himself? The dreadful creature has ensnared him somehow, luring him with her wicked wiles."

"Eugenia has no wiles, wicked or otherwise," said Drake hotly. "She is a gentle, dignified lady—utterly without pretense and completely free from odd humors. She is, in fact, a paragon of every feminine virtue." He looked pointedly at Lilah. "Unlike some females I could name! I've known Eugenia since she was twelve years old, and she's never once argued with or contradicted me."

Lilah gave a disdainful sniff. "If she fails to argue with *you*, she's either a simpleton or a prig. Why would any man wish to marry such a bore? Especially my father. Why, he might marry whomever he pleased." Drake's bark of disbelieving laughter caused Lilah's cheeks to heat. Her voice rose in anger. "My father, I'll have you know, is a prince among men! Gentle, chivalrous, and thoughtful, always considerate of others. He would never dream of bullying or browbeating a woman." She jabbed her finger accusingly at Drake. "And *those* are the qualities a lady truly admires in a man, whatever some of you men may think."

"He sounds a perfect milksop," snorted Drake. "That's not the kind of chap to appeal to

Eugenia—or any other woman with an ounce
of spirit."

"Much *you* know about it!" cried Lilah, furious. "You have never even met my papa."

"And you have never met my Eugenia. You
may take it from me, she is the last woman in
the world to cast out lures to an old man."

"Papa isn't old!"

Miss Pickens covered her ears with her hands.
"Oh, stop! Pray, stop it!" she pleaded breathlessly. "I cannot bear to hear another word."

Drake and Lilah were concentrating so completely on their battle that Miss Pickens had
been utterly forgotten. Caught, Lilah felt
ashamed of herself. She quickly hugged Miss
Pickens's thin shoulders and begged her pardon,
blushing. "I don't know what came over me,"
she confessed. "Shouting like a fishwife. Your
poor head! Truly, Picky dear, I am sorry." She
caught a glimpse of Drake out of the corner of
her eye and her expression darkened. "Although, you must admit, the provocation was
extreme."

Miss Pickens mumbled and sniffed into Lilah's shoulder, then sat up, straightening her
bonnet and fumbling for her handkerchief. "I'm
sorry to be such a wet-goose." She gulped. "My
lord, I don't know what you will think of me.
It's just that I—I never could bear to be around
any kind of argument or strife."

"Good for you," said Drake unexpectedly. "There's no excuse for us, Miss Chadwick. Let us beg Miss Pickens's pardon at once."

"I have already done so," said Lilah stiffly.

"Then so do I."

He gave the distinct impression that his apology was conditional, and that he offered it only because she offered hers first. Lilah struggled to quell her indignation. Miss Pickens's lacerated nerves were more important—at the moment— than putting Lord Drakesley in his place.

Whatever his faults, he did not seem to nurse a grudge. Lilah's feathers were still thoroughly ruffled, but Drake appeared admirably calm, even sympathetic, as he addressed Miss Pickens. "It reflects well on you, madam, that you are sensitive to the sound of quarreling. Don't be embarrassed. Your interruption was an excellent thing; I applaud it. In the heat of the encounter, Miss Chadwick and I lost sight of the most important point."

Lilah looked askance at him. "And what, in your opinion, is the most important point?"

"That you and I are allies." He almost smiled at her. "It is absurd for us to bicker when we are, in fact, in agreement. Your father's marriage to Miss Mayhew must be stopped."

Lilah immediately felt guilty. "Oh, dear," she said faintly. "You go too fast, my lord. I had not thought that far ahead. Not to actually *oppose* the marriage—at least, not irrevocably. I had thought to meet Miss Mayhew before making up my mind. I wanted to see how the land lay, as it were—"

"Well, you see how the land lies," said Drake reasonably. "You were picturing an older woman for your father. You doubtless hoped he had chosen a motherly soul who might, if all went well, take a fancy to you. Such a woman might actually have been acceptable to you. In some ways, she might have made your life easier."

"Yes," Lilah admitted. "Although I would never dream of encouraging Papa to marry simply to make my life easier."

"Be that as it may, you will instead be saddled with a stepmother barely older than yourself. This is an entirely different kettle of fish."

Lilah's forehead puckered with puzzlement. "But this is exactly why I think there must be some mistake!" she exclaimed. "I can understand, upon reflection, why Papa might wish to remarry. I have often thought that he missed the companionship of someone his own age. But to marry a woman so much younger than himself—no, I cannot understand that. Unless—" She bit her lip.

"Unless?" Drake prompted. Laughter lurked in his voice.

Lilah twisted her hands together in her lap.

She turned anxiously to Miss Pickens. "Picky, do you think it might be *my* fault? It occurs to me that I may have let a few ill-considered remarks drop—complaining about the servants and so forth. Do you think I led him to believe I feel overburdened by my responsibilities since Mama died? Do I complain too often of boredom or loneliness? Perhaps he thinks I would welcome the companionship of a girl near my own age."

Miss Pickens did not reply. For some reason, she even looked a little embarrassed. But Lilah brightened, warming to the idea. "Why, I daresay one frank conversation with Papa will scotch the whole scheme. I will tell him that I *enjoy* tending to the household's needs, and that you provide the only companionship I require. He need not marry on my account. If he wishes to find a truly suitable lady, someone to give him mature companionship, he may take his time and do so. A widowed lady, perhaps, with years of experience in managing a large household. A bride in her twenties would be as out of her depth as I am. More, in fact, since she would be completely unfamiliar with Chadwick Hall. What can Miss Mayhew do that I cannot?"

Miss Pickens fluttered and murmured, and Drake uttered a bark of jeering laughter. "She can give your father an heir," he said rudely. "A young wife is uniquely able to do that."

Seeing her charge stunned into silence, Miss Pickens hurried into speech, blushing and blessing herself. "My dear Lilah, I fear that Lord Drakesley is quite, quite correct—all very natural, of course, but so distressing! I own, it was the first thing that occurred to me. A common reason to remarry, you know, for a man with only one child, and that child a girl. A pity that poor Sir Horace could never quite like his uncle's oldest boy. What was his name, my love? Reggie, I think. Or was it Richie? At any rate, I always thought him a trifle wild, and now that he's grown up he's scarcely better, and Sir Horace never approved of—well! They do say boys will be boys, but, really, they only seem to say that about a certain *type* of boy, and one hardly likes to think of a boys-will-be-boys type of boy, which Reggie certainly is—or, I should say, *was*—inheriting an estate, let alone a property one personally cares for. Wickedness rewarded! Nothing could be more distasteful."

Beneath the flow of Miss Pickens's gentle chatter, Lilah had had time to recover her poise. "There is nothing wrong with Reggie," she declared crossly. "Once he has sewn his wild oats he will doubtless settle down and make a good master."

Miss Pickens patted Lilah's knee sympathetically. "I hope you are right, my dear. Although, if he does—or *when* he does—what will become

51

of you? Well! We mustn't think about that. No sense in borrowing trouble. And, of course, if your father should marry Miss Mayhew and produce an heir, your position will be equally precarious. So, as far as you and I are concerned, it's really six of one and half a dozen of another, isn't it?''

Lilah stared blindly at Miss Pickens's kind, worried face, feeling as if her blood were turning to ice water. Perhaps it was the jolting of the carriage and the lingering smell of onions that was making her feel so sick. She swallowed hard. "What nonsense you are talking," she said, a bit unsteadily. "I will always be first in Papa's heart."

Good heavens. Was that *pity* she saw flickering in Miss Pickens's eyes? Intolerable! Lilah braced herself against the swaying of the coach and tried to appear calm. She had had a shock, but she would recover. The notion of one's father marrying to produce an heir was, naturally, repugnant—but understandable. At least it meant that Papa had not, as she had first feared, become enamored of a scheming hussy. He was contracting a marriage of convenience. He had neither lost his wits nor been trapped by some Machiavellian female. This was not, could not be, a love match. He was marrying because he needed an heir. Perfectly sensible. Utterly practical.

For a moment, she felt slightly better—which told her, more clearly than any argument would have, how much of her initial reaction had been simple jealousy. She had feared, on some primal, unconscious level, that Miss Mayhew would supplant her in her father's affections. It would be terrible indeed to find oneself relegated to second place, after so many years of being the center of Papa's universe. What a relief, to realize that he was contracting a loveless marriage.

Except that Miss Pickens had just uttered a terrible truth. Miss Mayhew was the least of Lilah's worries. Papa would, if he could, sire a son. Any man might, eventually, become disenchanted with his new wife. But a son? A son would take precedence over the wife *and* the daughter. Immediately. Permanently.

Her fears stirred again, stronger than before. Alarm rushed through her like a shot of brandy, making her feel hot and sick. Drake was right. She must, if she could, put a stop to the marriage. Perhaps it was ignoble of her—well, it almost certainly was—but she had no choice. Females had so little power in the world. She had to hold on to whatever portion she had, however she could.

She became aware that a silence had fallen while she wrestled with her demons. Drake's eyes were on her, watchful and shrewd. He seemed to guess the direction of her thoughts, for a wry smile twisted his mouth. "An unpleasant prospect, isn't it?" he remarked. "I'd offer you my sympathy, but I'd rather offer my help. What do you say, Miss Chadwick? Shall we put our heads together?"

The suggestion was appealing. Too appealing, when a tiny voice within her whispered that it was probably wrong. Anger and confusion rushed through Lilah. "Wild horses could not persuade me to team up with you," she snapped.

Drake rolled his eyes piously toward the ceiling. "May I remind you, Miss Chadwick, that it is dangerous to speak without thinking."

Despite his apparent solemnity, she could see he was laughing at her. Lilah flushed with mortification. He was right. Her unruly emotions had led her to blurt out something uncivil. Now *she* looked like the rudesby! Why did this dreadful man rattle her so? It cost her something, but she managed to incline her head and mutter, "I beg your pardon. I did speak without thinking."

His self-satisfied grin made her wish she could retract her apology. "Thank you," he said smoothly. "Now I hope you will think for a moment. We must convince Sir Horace and Miss Mayhew, singly or together, to break their engagement. It's a tall order, but it seems that you and I share—ah—forceful personalities. Working alone, either of us might prevail. But together, Miss Chadwick—together, we almost certainly will."

Miss Pickens fluttered in protest. "Oh, my. Dear sir, do you think it wise? Really, I don't think I can condone any actual *interference*. It would be most improper. Unseemly! We must not insert ourselves into such a delicate matter— and one that is really none of our business."

Drake bowed courteously toward Miss Pickens. "I was not suggesting, ma'am, that you become involved in this." His eyes gleamed as they met Lilah's. "Miss Chadwick, what say you?" he asked softly. "Shall you and I join forces?"

Looking into the deep-set amber eyes across from her, Lilah felt a strange spark of exhilaration. It was unsettling, but undeniable. This terrible man, of whom she thoroughly disapproved, brought something out in her—something primitive. Something the civilized part of her mistrusted and disliked. Just being around him somehow turned her into a shrew, and now . . . now he was deliberately appealing to the darkest part of her nature, the part of herself that she admired least.

And she was responding.

She could feel the tug, as if her internal moorings were straining against a sudden, strong tide. Would they snap? She didn't know. They had never been tested before.

Her mouth had gone strangely dry. She had to swallow before she could speak. "I promise nothing. I will . . . I will think on it," she said unsteadily. She did not want to give him even that much, but it seemed the best way to avoid further argument. She needed a little space in which to think.

Preferably, a space that did not contain Lord Drakesley. His presence seemed to addle her wits.

4

No one noticed when the rain began. So long as its pattering was covered by the creak and rumble of travel, the interior passengers were unaware of how wet the weather had become. What they did notice, through the leather flaps covering their two small windows, was the gathering darkness. The light coming through the chinks had gradually grayed and gone dim.

"How gloomy it is," Lilah exclaimed at last. "It can't be that late, can it?" She reached to unfasten the curtain beside her and peer out.

"Wait!" warned Drake, but too late. She had pulled the flap loose. Water instantly poured in and sluiced down the side of the compartment to the bench where she sat. With a startled exclamation, Lilah leaped from her seat and across the aisle, landing in the only available spot—the place beside Drake.

Her move had been purely instinctive. Anyone in her position would have done the same. And when Drake reached past her with his long arms to refasten the curtain, he had no choice but to lean against her while his fingers wrestled with the catch. After all, she was in the way. There was nothing improper in his touch. There was no meaning attached to their forced intimacy.

So why did Lilah feel as if someone had unexpectedly punched all the air out of her?

Once, when she was about ten years old, she had fallen out of a tree. She would never forget the frightening sensation. The world had spun and the breath left her lungs with a whoosh, leaving her stunned on the ground, helpless and dizzy. With Drake's body crushed against hers, Lilah stopped breathing and, for a confused moment, could not remember how to begin again. The sensation was similar to that long-ago fall from the tree—she felt as shocked, as helpless. And nearly as breathless.

But, no, this was different. She had never experienced anything quite like this. Crazy thoughts jostled in her brain. Every nerve jangled. She was acutely aware of the weight of him. The heat of him. She felt his body press hers from shoulder to thigh, branding her.

A monstrous idea reared its head. Was she *attracted* to him? Impossible! She couldn't be. But then, if not, what was the matter with her? Oh, this was terrible.

It was also the most thrilling feeling she had ever experienced.

Could she keep it to herself? Merciful heavens—she mustn't let him see how strongly his touch had affected her! How embarrassing. Why, she didn't even *like* the man. What would he think of her, if he knew he had bowled her over simply by fastening that silly curtain? He'd think she was demented. Or worse! Wanton. Contemptible. Oh, he *did* bring out the devil in her. What to do? What to do?

The catch on the curtain was apparently giving him a great deal of trouble. He was pressed against her for what seemed an eternity, while his fingers worked the wet leather. At last he sat back and Lilah could breathe again.

"Thank you," she managed to utter. She stole a peep up at him. That was a mistake. Their eyes met—and locked. In the closeness of the carriage, mashed onto a bench too small to hold the both of them, his nearness was inescapable.

Invisible sparks seemed to fly between them. Lilah saw at once, with mingled fear and relief, that the sparks flew both ways. The connection between them was instantaneous, and so strong she felt as if she could almost read his mind. Could he read hers? Attraction flashed and pulsed between them, as irresistible as it was inexplicable. Drake seemed to like it no better than she did. His expression grew fierce. She felt herself paling. Yet, for a long and fascinated moment, neither could look away.

Drake broke the contact first, turning his head as if with an effort. "You are welcome," he said hoarsely. "But don't do it again. I don't know what idiocy possessed you—"

"How was I to know the window would leak?" flashed Lilah. It was a relief to vent her emotions in anger. Anger was simple. Anger was understandable.

"Common sense," he snapped, immediately rising to her bait. "Which you seem to lack."

Miss Pickens shuddered and intervened, breaking up what might have been a refreshing little skirmish. "Lilah," she pleaded timidly, "pray let me change places with you. Your seat cushion is wet through."

Lilah felt a stab of irrational disappointment at having her quarrel interrupted, but her better self prevailed. She took a breath, mentally shook herself, and faced Miss Pickens.

"That won't be necessary," she said with gentle firmness. "It is like you to offer, Picky, but I shan't allow you to sacrifice yourself on my account. Pray remain where you are. Lord Drakesley and I are perfectly comfortable."

"Speak for yourself," Drake muttered. Lilah longed to jab him with her elbow, but repressed the unladylike impulse.

Miss Pickens looked distressed. "Oh, my dear child, it isn't seemly for you to ride facing backward while I keep the forward-facing seat. And I have it all to myself, too! You cannot ask me to take the best seat while my betters are inconvenienced. I would be ashamed."

"I'll take it," offered Drake.

Lilah, exasperated, glowered at him. "For your information, riding backward makes Miss Pickens ill."

"Oh. In that case, she can stay where she is. In fact, I insist on it." Devils danced in his eyes as he looked down at Lilah. "But I see no reason why you shouldn't be forced to sit in the puddle. I daresay it would teach you a valuable lesson."

"Thank you," said Lilah with awful politeness. "But I have no need of *lessons,* valuable or otherwise."

"On that, we have a difference of opinion," remarked Drake. "Oh, well." He shifted slightly on the too-small seat, stretching his legs, as best he could, across the narrow aisle between the benches. Lilah tried not to notice the muscles bunching in his thighs. "At least this hellish journey can't last much longer. The mud will probably force us to halt at the next inn."

"Oh, no." This daunting thought shook Lilah out of her odd preoccupation with Drake's body. She blinked at him in dismay. "Do you

61

really think so? We haven't covered nearly enough ground today. I *must* reach London no later than tomorrow."

Drake's mouth hardened into a thin line. "And so must I. Time is of the essence. We may have to drive past nightfall tomorrow, but we'll reach London. Whatever the weather. The great thing is, we'll be able to change coaches if we stop. I don't intend to go a mile farther than I must in this rattletrap."

Lilah brightened. "I hadn't thought of that. Why, we might even hire *separate* coaches."

Drake immediately reached up to rap on the ceiling. "An excellent idea. I shall instruct the driver to halt at the next inn, mud or no mud."

Unfortunately, they were traveling through a sparsely inhabited area of rolling pastures and irregular stands of woods. Drake checked their progress periodically through the flaps on Miss Pickens's side of the coach, but the only buildings discernible through the rain were far from the road and seemed to be farmhouses.

The rickety coach was forced to travel more and more slowly as conditions worsened. Every so often, it seemed to float sideways as it skidded in the mud, and still no roadside inn or habitation appeared. Miss Pickens began to look quite sick with dread.

Lilah leaned across Drake's lap and took her old governess's hand in a sustaining clasp. She

reminded her that they were not, after all, nego-
tiating a mountain pass. "We shan't skate over
the edge of a cliff," said Lilah bracingly. "Tipping into a ditch is the worst that can happen."
Miss Pickens, her anxiety not noticeably eased,
only moaned in reply.

By now, the rain had become a downpour,
drumming with increasing intensity on the roof.
The coach tilted and slipped forward for a moment. Lilah thought it prudent to let go of Miss
Pickens's hand and sit back; it would only add
to Picky's distress if she pulled her from her
seat. But as she slid back into place, she was
startled to feel Drake's arm go around her. Lilah
froze as a frisson of dark excitement flashed
through her veins, jangling her nerves. She
stared up at Drake, her eyes wide with alarm.

His face seemed very close to hers. Too close.
She was acutely aware of his arm behind her
back like a band of steel, his enormous hand
gripping her. With his arm thus out of the way,
her body was molding itself to his, willy-nilly.
It was a strange sensation . . . but there was
something wonderful about it, something both
compelling and comforting. His eyes held hers,
but she could not read his expression.

"Let me hold you," he said. His voice seemed
carefully devoid of inflection. "The strap on
your side of the carriage is broken."

Lilah frowned at him. "I don't need—" she

began, but the coach gave another sudden lurch and she forgot what she was going to say. Miss Pickens uttered a miserable little cry and clung to her strap, nearly losing her seat. But Drake's arm tightened around Lilah, holding her close. Keeping her safe. She found that she had instinctively grabbed at his coat and was now clinging to him in a way that struck her, once the danger was past, as quite shocking. Why, they were actually *embracing*. Really, if Miss Pickens hadn't been preoccupied with her own misery, Lilah was sure she would have delivered a thundering scold.

Lilah quickly disentangled herself and assumed a more dignified posture. "Thank you," she said stiffly. It was best to pretend he was offering her a service, nothing more. She tried to ignore the blush heating her cheeks and prayed that he would have the decency to do the same.

He did. "You are welcome," he said gravely, as polite and distant as if he were merely holding a door for her. She was grateful for this unexpected display of good manners—until it occurred to her that his motives for feigning disinterest were highly questionable. He had certainly not removed his arm. If anything, he held her more intimately than before.

Miss Pickens suddenly seemed to notice the peculiar scene confronting her. She eyed Lilah and Drake askance. "My lord, you must not allow Miss Chadwick to encroach upon your space," she said severely.

Drake's face was a mask of politeness. "I am comfortable enough, Miss Pickens," he assured her. "I only hope you do not think I am taking liberties."

Miss Pickens, still hanging on to her strap for dear life, turned pink beneath her pallor. "Oh, no, my lord, I would never suggest such a thing. I am sure you would never do anything so vulgar. But—"

"Thank you," Drake interrupted smoothly. "I am concerned for Miss Chadwick's safety. With no support on her side of the coach, she might easily be thrown from her seat."

Miss Pickens appeared relieved. "Oh! Naturally. I had not thought—that is, I had not noticed the state of—well. Never mind. How observant you are! So solicitous! Your concern does you honor, my lord."

"I am happy to be of service," he replied politely. Lilah, still suspicious, sneaked a glance at Drake's face. He looked down at her again, and she thought she saw a flash of enjoyment behind his bland smile.

"Exactly how long do you intend to keep your arm around me?" she inquired.

He must have heard the tart edge in her voice, for his smile widened. "For as long as you are in danger, Miss Chadwick." The smile widened further, and his voice lowered. Shielded by the noise of the rain he was able to tell her, in a voice only she could hear, "I promise you, I don't mind it a bit."

Lilah was too flustered by this to think of a good reply. Fortunately for her peace of mind, their forward progress, though slow, was genuinely treacherous. This robbed her of the necessity to bleat out a maidenly protest. She could, instead, be grateful for the strong arm encircling her, since it really did prevent her from being thrown about. The fact that it was Drake's arm was, she reminded herself, immaterial.

The moment finally arrived, however, when the driver, with a shout of relief, turned the weary horses into the yard of a roadside inn. For the last time, Lilah felt herself thrown against Drake's body by the turn.

"Thank goodness," she said brightly, and pulled out of his embrace. It seemed to Lilah that he kept his arm around her a fraction of a second longer than absolutely necessary, but he did release her at last. She busied herself in pulling up the hood of her traveling cloak and fastening it tightly at her throat, while the driver whistled up an ostler and pulled the coach as near the door of the inn as he could.

The rain was still pounding down. The din made conversation difficult and outside activity impossible to hear, so it was no wonder that Miss Pickens recoiled when the door beside her was yanked open. An unrecognizable figure who may or may not have been their driver, thoroughly drenched, with water streaming from the brim of his low-pulled hat, gestured impatiently for Miss Pickens to step out so he could usher her into the doorway visible a few yards behind him. Clucking faintly, Miss Pickens stepped out.

The man's arm was extended for her, and she surely clutched it, but nevertheless her feet slid out from under her. Miss Pickens shrieked. The man caught her before she went down, but her shoes were obviously ruined and the hem of her gown was now six inches deep in mud. One of the inn's servants sprang forward to assist, and Lilah watched in dismay as Miss Pickens, huddled miserably between the two men, was half dragged into the inn.

Lilah hung back, eyeing the distance from the coach to the inn with misgiving. "Perhaps we should wait a bit," she suggested nervously. "It can't rain this hard forever."

Drake snorted. "Don't be a pudding-heart. Water won't melt you."

"I'm not a pudding-heart," declared Lilah, stung. "But this is my favorite traveling cloak, and it's new. I don't want it ruined."

Drake said something under his breath. The

roar of the rain drowned out every word except "female." Lilah guessed at the rest. Her chin jutted stubbornly.

"It has nothing to do with being female," she informed him. "I am simply being practical. Although a man 'as rich as Croesus' might not understand such mundane matters."

"Oh, if you're going to throw that in my teeth—"

"I'm not throwing anything in your teeth! I'm merely—"

"What a contentious chit you are! Sit in the coach till doomsday; it's all one to me. I'm not going to sit here like a gapeseed and argue with you." The coach swayed as Drake grasped the narrow doorjamb and heaved himself off the seat. There he paused for a fraction of a second, squinting out at the rain. It was blowing in sheets across the yard.

"Damn," he said, without heat. Apparently resigned to his fate, he stepped through the doorway and onto the step, then splashed down onto the ground. Lilah watched forlornly as Drake disappeared into the pelting rain, leaving her alone in the abandoned vehicle.

Well, whatever Lord Drakesley may think, she did *not* intend to sit in the coach until doomsday. One of the inn's servants would return for her in a moment or two and help her make a quick dash for the door. She was wondering if she should try turning her cloak inside out, so that the worst of the damage would occur to the lining rather than the exterior, when the door on her side of the coach suddenly burst open. She turned with a frightened squeak, thinking it had blown open—and, indeed, with both doors open the rain immediately blew into the interior—but, to her astonishment, it was Drake who had opened it. He had evidently walked around to her side of the coach rather than into the inn. And before she could say a word, his long arms reached in and unceremoniously pulled her into the storm.

"There's no help for it," he said unemotionally. "Hang on." And he swung her neatly up into his arms. Her feet never touched the step, let alone the ground. Good heavens, he was strong. Lilah instinctively flung one arm up around his neck and hung on.

He held her in his arms like a baby and strode toward the inn. It was an outrageous stunt. What did he mean by it? Lilah decided to worry about that later. For now, she turned and pressed her forehead against Drake's wet coat, hiding her face from the rain. Being carried as if she weighed nothing was a novel sensation. She felt powerless—which had never been one of Lilah's favorite ways to feel—but with her body cradled in Drake's massive arms, there was something oddly pleasant about feeling out

69

of control. She wondered, dreamily, if drunkenness felt like this. If it did, she understood for the first time why people might find it addicting.

A small waterfall pattered down on her shoulders, signaling that Drake was stepping over the threshold of the inn. The roar of falling water immediately lessened. He took two more steps, then halted. Lilah opened her eyes, lifted her head, and looked into Drake's face.

They were in a small anteroom or foyer with walls of rough-hewn logs and plaster. They were alone. Further on, the foyer opened into a larger room where firelight and voices signaled the presence of Miss Pickens, gently complaining, but the foyer itself was deserted. Behind Drake, the door stood open to the yard. She heard a distant shout from what must have been the stables, and the splash of running feet as a boy came to take the horses' heads.

The contrast between the utter stillness immediately surrounding them and the noise and activity on either side, made it seem that Lilah and Drake were stranded together on a private island. They had halted, by accident or design, in a space between two worlds. The open door behind them led back to the tempest. The open door ahead led to the coziness of the firelit inn. But in the foyer, they belonged to neither the storm nor the refuge. They stood wrapped in an intimate solitude, lit only by the flicker of a single torch smoking and dancing in the wet wind. He did not set her on her feet. She did not struggle. He held her, and she allowed herself to be held. Time spun out like candy floss, sparkling and sweet and fragile as gossamer. They stared, studying each other with a startled, almost wary, amazement.

Lilah remembered that earlier she had thought Drake was not handsome. She must have been daft. He had the bones of an aristocrat, with strong features, a high-bridged nose and square jaw. The deep-set, hawklike eyes were compelling. Beautiful, too, like the eyes of a predator. They were a hazel that appeared almost golden when the firelight struck them.

She watched the wavering light glance across the planes of his face, mesmerized. It was impossible to tell what he was thinking. He must be a man who habitually hid his thoughts from others; his expression was masklike in its neutrality. But his eyes blazed with a stark emotion she could not name. She recognized it, whatever it was, because she felt it too. With their eyes locked in wordless, intuitive communication, Lilah felt something flare and burn in the core of her being, heating her from the inside out.

She wanted something. She wanted . . . she

wanted . . . Why, this was strange. She didn't know what she wanted. But she felt every nerve in her body stretch taut with longing.

Suddenly, their private island was rudely invaded. A flash of light and exclamation of concern heralded the entrance of Miss Pickens with a lamp and the landlady with towels.

"Lord Drakesley, you are dripping on the floor. My poor Lilah! Are you wet through?" uttered Miss Pickens, holding the lamp anxiously aloft.

Drake seemed to tear his eyes from Lilah's with an effort, directing an annoyed frown at the intruders. The landlady, undeterred by his scowl, beamed a welcome. "Come you in, my lord. And you, my lady. *Tsk!* Nasty weather for a journey, isn't it?" She handed one of the towels to Drake and stood respectfully back, waiting for Drake and Lilah to step away before attacking the pool of rainwater they had left on her floor.

Embarrassment seemed to seize both Drake and Lilah at the same time. He moved to set her on her feet, and she quickly slid down his body and stood beside him.

"Thank you," she said, shaken. She turned her attention to the two women hovering helpfully nearby. "I am only wet in patches, but I'm afraid Drake is soaked to the skin," she told Miss Pickens.

This unfortunate remark caused a vivid image to seize Lilah like a fit: Drake peeling off his wet clothing. Paralyzed by her own imagination, she gulped and fell silent.

Miss Pickens fixed Lilah with a startled, disbelieving gaze. Since she was still occupied in fighting off unbidden fantasies, it took Lilah a moment to comprehend her old governess's sudden disapproval. Then, with a shock, she realized that she was still clinging to Drake, and he to her. Mortified, she moved quickly away and busied herself in shaking out her cloak and untying the strings of her hood.

Meanwhile, the landlady had taken a brisk swipe at the floor and was ushering Drake into the room beyond the foyer. Her voice, cheerfully prattling, floated back to Miss Pickens and Lilah. "Well, it's going to be a wet night and no mistake, but we'll see to it you're kept warm and dry, my lord."

Lilah was about to follow, but Miss Pickens pulled warningly on her arm, stopping her. "My dear Lilah, what will the landlady think?" she whispered, seeming much agitated. "Two single ladies, traveling with a bachelor! It must look very odd. She seems a most respectable person; I am afraid she will refuse to house us."

"Well, for heaven's sake!" said Lilah, exasperated. "You should have thought of that before. It was you, after all, who insisted that we share a coach with Drake. Did you think we would reach London in a day?"

Miss Pickens looked unhappy. Before she could speak, however, the evils of their situation were forcibly brought home to Lilah; the land-lady, in the adjoining room, had a penetrating voice. And she was saying to Drake, "I hope Lady Drakesley did not suffer any injury? Your companion was telling us, a moment ago, how bad the road was."

"Oh, dear," said Lilah faintly.

"Just so," murmured Miss Pickens, agreeing. "We must put a stop to this before it be-comes awkward."

"It is already more than awkward," objected Miss Pickens, but Lilah swept her determinedly aside and entered the room. The landlady was behind a counter, thumbing the pages of an enormous ledger. Drake leaned on the counter, still dripping.

"It's not often we house guests of your rank, but I think you'll find the beds comfortable and the linens well aired," the landlady declared. "No need to bring your own sheets to *my* inn, if I do say so myself. We're nearly full tonight, but the best bedchamber was vacated only this morning so I'll be pleased to put you and Lady Drakesley in it. I've a smaller room down the hall for—"

"For me," said Drake smoothly. "I'm a single

74

gentleman. You may give the larger room to my cousin, Miss Chadwick, and her companion."

The landlady looked up from her ledger, appearing surprised. Her gaze traveled doubtfully from Drake to Lilah. She was all-too-obviously replaying her memory of Drake carrying Lilah across the threshold, and struggling unsuccessfully to place that picture in an innocent context.

Lilah flashed her most confident smile and nodded at the landlady. "That will do," she said brightly. "Miss Pickens and I will gladly share a room."

The landlady pursed her lips for a moment, and her manner noticeably cooled, but she assigned the rooms Drake requested without demur. As she was being shown to her room it occurred to Lilah that Drake had not stretched the truth by much when he called her "cousin." If Papa married Eugenia Mayhew, she and Drake would, in fact, be connected through the marriage. Cousin Drake! The notion was not only alarming, it was somehow distasteful.

They really *must* scotch that marriage.

5

The landlady had not exaggerated. The beds at her inn were comfortable, clean, and dry. Nevertheless, sleep eluded Lilah for a long while. Too much had happened this day. Long after Miss Pickens was gently snoring beside her, Lilah lay awake, unsure which was to blame for her restlessness: the storm that was rattling the windows or the storm that was rattling her composure.

Her thoughts raced chaotically as she listened to the rain and wind. Worry about her father plagued her, but the bulk of her agitation seemed to be centered on the irritating Earl of Drakesley. He occupied her thoughts to an annoying degree, and refused to be banished from them. When she finally fell asleep, her dreams were feverish and highly colored. And they featured Drake. She awoke feeling keyed up, cross, and far from rested.

Morning had dawned unexpectedly sunny.

Miss Pickens apparently saw nothing suspicious in the care Lilah took with her toilette, and actually voiced approval when she donned her best muslin. "How pretty you look, my dear!" she said. "I am so thankful that Sir Horace had dresses made up for you in London. It seemed an extravagance at the time, for who knew that we would find ourselves in such exalted company? But now that we are forced to travel with an earl, I own it is a comfort to feel that we need not be ashamed of our appearance. I daresay you look as elegant as any lady of rank."

"As elegant as Lord Drakesley, at any rate," Lilah replied, pulling a face. "Not that that's saying much."

"He's a most unpretentious man," said Miss Pickens, as if agreeing with her.

Lilah refused to be drawn into praising Lord Drakesley. "Unpretentious? Is that what you call it? I suspect he is just too arrogant to care what anyone may think of him." She leaned toward the small looking glass mounted atop the washstand, carefully fastening a delicate earring to dance against the background of her shining hair. "I think he may be queer in his attic," she said darkly. "Do you know, Picky, he actually *bragged* to me about his wealth? Told me he was rich as Croesus. I hardly knew where to look."

Miss Pickens looked shocked. "No. Really?

My dear Lilah, you must have misunderstood him. No man of breeding would mention such a thing."

"My point precisely. One hears that men of rank are frequently eccentric, but Lord Drakesley's behavior is beyond the pale. I've never met anyone so ill-bred." Lilah, satisfied with her appearance at last, straightened and picked up her gloves. "I shall be glad when our association with him is a thing of the past," she said airily, but she did not meet Miss Pickens's eyes as she said it. "In fact, I hope we will be able to hire a vehicle of our own today. We will let Drake have that smelly old coach all to himself. You and I can go by post chaise."

"Whatever you decide, my dear," said Miss Pickens, with a marked lack of enthusiasm. She trailed after Lilah as they descended the narrow stairs to the private parlor Lord Drakesley had reserved for their party.

Drake was there before them, and Lilah, to her surprise, felt a flutter of nerves when she saw him. She wasn't sure why this should be. He was doing nothing out of the ordinary. He was seated at a linen-covered table, prosaically consuming a mouthful of ham. But for some reason, the sight of him affected her in a most peculiar way. She halted inside the doorway, struggling to compose herself, while Drake rose to greet them, swallowing.

"G'morning," he said. Hardly an effusive greeting. Really, what *was* the matter with her?

"Good morning," she said. She was pleased to note that her voice sounded perfectly normal.

Miss Pickens peered brightly over Lilah's shoulder. "Good morning, Lord Drakesley," she piped. "Drake, I *should* say! Such a pretty morning. May we join you?"

"For breakfast, she means," added Lilah, smiling determinedly. "Miss Pickens and I will not trespass on your time beyond that."

One of Drake's eyebrows climbed. "Really? I'm not sure I follow you. But I'm never at my best until the third cup of coffee. Sit down, sit down, ladies. They serve a very tolerable breakfast here." He rang for the waiter and returned to his meal while the ladies took their places across from him. "I don't mean to hurry you, but how soon will you be ready to depart?"

"You won't hurry us," Lilah assured him brightly. She would *not* let him get the better of her. "We will be ready to leave by the time our arrangements are complete. We have not yet hired a post chaise, or had our baggage removed from your coach. But I daresay that sort of thing can be done in a twinkling."

Drake's brooding, hooded eyes regarded her, their expression hard to fathom. "If you are referring to that malodorous monstrosity we shared yesterday, your baggage has already been removed from it. And mine as well. Neither of us is taking that coach. We are traveling in comfort from this point forward."

The note of authority in his tone made Lilah's hackles rise. "I don't know what you mean by 'we,'" she said with an artificial-sounding laugh. "You may travel in comfort. That is entirely your own affair. But Miss Pickens and I will choose speed over comfort, and take a post chaise. I am not sure why you ordered my baggage to be moved without securing my permission—"

"Did you want it left on that reeking heap of firewood?"

"Of course not. But—"

"Then why the deuce are you ripping up at me? I did you a favor."

"I am not ripping up at you," said Lilah, sitting very straight in her chair. "But you should have consulted me before issuing orders on my behalf."

He leaned back in his chair, chewing in a ruminative way. The waiter entered, bearing coffee in one hand and tea in the other. He claimed the ladies' attention for a bit, but Lilah was unnervingly aware throughout her conversation with the waiter that Drake's eyes were on her. When the waiter left, Drake addressed her with his customary bluntness.

"What is bothering you, Miss Chadwick?"

"Nothing," she said crisply.

"You appear rattled."

"Well, I'm not." She dumped a dollop of cream into her coffee and stirred it vigorously, her teaspoon ringing sharply against the porcelain cup. "Kindly stop staring at me. And you may dispense with the personal remarks as well. They're rude."

Miss Pickens fluttered at her side, murmuring agitatedly. Lilah ignored her. She knew she was behaving badly, but could not seem to help it. Something about Lord Drakesley cast her into high fidgets.

Drake addressed himself to Miss Pickens, jerking a thumb at Lilah. "Is she always like this?" Sympathy sounded in his voice, as if he believed Miss Pickens was a saint to put up with it.

Miss Pickens, very pink indeed, hastened to reassure his lordship. "Oh, no, my lord—indeed, I know you are joking with us, but I feel I must tell you how kind, how universally kind Miss Chadwick generally is! Why, she is the best-natured girl imaginable. So sunny and cheerful! A smile for everyone. And clever—my word! I never met a child with a sharper mind. Truly, my lord, she is a joy to be around. Such a comfort to her papa . . ." It seemed to occur to her that she was entering dangerous territory, and her voice faded. She shot an anxious glance at Drake. "You must not judge Miss Chadwick harshly, Lord Drakesley. She has encountered much to overset her during the past twenty-four hours."

Lilah squirmed a little. "Thank you, Picky, that will do! Pray hand me the sugar tongs."

Drake skewered another slice of ham, still watching Lilah with a sardonic gleam. "I think you got up on the wrong side of the bed this morning, Miss Chadwick."

Lilah tried to keep the edge off of her voice. "Do you? I think you are deliberately provoking me." She gave him an overbright smile.

"You are easily provoked," he observed. "It seems to me that you lose your temper the instant you are forced to relinquish the reins."

Lilah dropped a sugar cube into her cup with great precision. "And it seems to *me*," she snapped, "that you seize the reins whenever you choose, without so much as a by-your-leave." She pointed the sugar tongs at him. "You, my lord, have a strong streak of the tyrant in you."

"Oh, no doubt," he said equably. "But so do you."

Lilah gasped. "*I?* I do not go behind your back and order your things to be moved! I do not demand to know when you will be ready to leave! I do not badger you to tell me what you are thinking! I—"

"Yes, yes, pray spare me a catalogue of all the

sins you have nobly refrained from committing!
You have also not ordered our baggage to be
combined and jointly loaded onto an alternate
coach." Drake paused long enough to fork a
morsel of ham into his mouth. "Which I have
done," he added, in case his meaning was
unclear.

Lilah stared at him, bereft of speech. He swallowed and touched the corner of his napkin to
his mouth. She could have sworn he was hiding
a grin. "Perhaps I should explain," he offered.

She found her tongue. "Yes! I think you
should."

"We spoke yesterday of going on from here
in separate conveyances. Now that I've had a
chance to think it over, I believe that's not a
good idea."

Lilah flushed with annoyance. "What you fail
to appreciate, however, is that *your* beliefs and
ideas are entirely beside the point! Who placed
you in charge of this expedition? By what authority do you—"

"Hear me out!" Drake growled. "If we hire
separate coaches after arriving together it will
raise eyebrows, and I think the landlady is already suspicious enough. Besides that, we have
unfinished business to discuss. We had better
have our ducks in a row before arriving in London. And there is a third consideration that just
occurred to me." He nodded toward Miss Pick-

ens. "You will make your companion ill if you jounce her about in a post chaise. They don't call them yellow bounders for nothing."

Lilah's lips compressed into a thin line while she struggled to master her anger and chagrin. She had not thought of that. Drat the man! He was right.

She turned to Miss Pickens. "Have you ever ridden in a post chaise, Picky?"

Her companion looked miserable. "Once," she admitted.

"And did it make you ill?"

Miss Pickens toyed nervously with her fork. "I own, it was not a pleasant experience. I took to my bed for two days afterward. But I am perfectly willing to go to London in a post chaise, Lilah, if you deem it best. Perhaps it will not make me so ill this time."

Lilah closed her eyes for a moment, then opened them with a sigh. "Picky, for heaven's sake. Why did you say nothing about this when I advanced the plan?"

Miss Pickens wriggled in her chair and tugged at her gloves, obviously distressed. "Oh, Lilah, pray don't scold me! It's not my place to complain. You must order things as you see fit. Indeed, I would have gone with you gladly. I know you are anxious to reach London as quickly as you can—"

"Not at the price of torturing you, dear friend.

This is absurd! What difference would an hour or two make? We are not flying to someone's deathbed."

Drake coughed. "Are we all in agreement? Let us take a well-sprung, comfortable coach. And travel together."

Lilah shot him a glance of acute exasperation. "Since you have already made those plans on our behalf, and transferred our belongings as well, we have no choice but to agree."

"You could order your baggage to be taken off the coach," he said.

Lilah was not deceived by the mildness of his tone. "I could," she agreed, "if I wished to make a spectacle of myself. You have placed me in a most awkward position. I cannot countermand your orders without creating a scene."

"I am surprised that that consideration carries weight with you. You had no objection to creating a scene yesterday."

Lilah's bosom swelled with indignation. "I didn't create that scene," she retorted. "You did."

A muscle jumped in his jaw. "I hope you intend to thank me for pointing out what should have been obvious to you—that Miss Pickens is susceptible to motion sickness. You should be grateful to me for stepping into the breach. Your skills in arranging a journey are lacking, Miss Chadwick."

Lilah glared. "I am not indifferent to Miss Pickens's comfort," she informed him icily. "Whatever you may believe! I had only thought to reach London in the shortest possible time. A post chaise, whatever else it may be, is speedy. *And,*" she added, her voice rising as her composure slipped a bit, "a post chaise holds only two persons! It would be worth a little bouncing, to dispense with your escort."

Drake's eyes narrowed. "Do you imagine I *want* to spend another interminable day in your company? My sole purpose in escorting you to London is to ensure that we present a united front to your father and my cousin. Need I remind you, my shrewish young friend, that if we fail to prevent their marriage, you and I will be forced to endure each other for years to come?"

Lilah gave an eloquent shudder. "No, you need not remind me. That very thought kept me awake most of the night."

"Then what the devil are we arguing about? Pass the salt."

The command was barked at Lilah, but Miss Pickens, who was sitting rather nearer the salt cellar than Lilah, passed it to him hastily. "Oh! Certainly, Lord Dr—certainly, *Drake*. Since you did ask us to call you that, and if we are to travel together, we must remain on a friendly footing, mustn't we? As to our mode of travel, Lilah, I'm sure his lordship knows best. He is

86

doubtless a far more experienced traveler than either you or I, and I daresay our best course is to rely on his judgment. I own, I am grateful that he thinks there is no particular advantage to our taking a post chaise. Now that there is no chance of our being forced to take one, I don't mind telling you I was dreading it! They are quite hideously uncomfortable. Pray be calm, my love, and allow me to hand you the butter."

Lilah felt a strong, if unladylike, impulse to throw a tantrum. She repressed it with difficulty and kept her eyes on her plate to hide the anger sparking in them. She did not trust herself to speak, so her contributions to the rest of the breakfast conversation were minimal. At the end of the meal she rose from the table, excusing herself so that she might finish packing the items in her room.

Lord Drakesley, leisurely salting his second helping of buttered eggs, barely glanced at her. "No need," he said. "I've already made arrangements for that as well."

"I don't understand. Arrangements for what?"

"I ordered servants to pack up our gear while we breakfasted."

Lilah struggled to keep her temper, but failed. She flung down her napkin like a gauntlet. "This is intolerable!" she announced, her voice shaking. "First you order my trunks moved from one coach to another without my permission, and then you send strangers to pack my things! I take leave to tell you, my lord, that your arrogance is insufferable!"

His angry scowl immediately descended. "And I take leave to tell *you*, Miss Chadwick, that you are behaving like a two-year-old. Remember, I agreed to take you along on the express condition that you not delay me."

Lilah placed her fists on her hips. "I would not have delayed you. You are still eating."

"Confound it, woman!" Drake pushed himself away from the table, looking as if he would like to strangle her. "Let's be off, then. I'd rather starve than listen to your carping."

Lilah felt a flash of triumph followed by a pang of guilt. What was there about this man that brought out the worst in her? She could not understand it. On the other hand, it would be absurd to apologize for her attitude. Her antagonism was probably good for him, she told herself firmly. It was obvious he seldom encountered any opposition to his autocratic ways.

Feigning indifference, she covertly watched him as he paid their shot, ordered up the carriage, and supervised the last-minute preparations for their departure. He did everything with a careless ease that both attracted and annoyed her. This was a man so accustomed to command that he took slavish obedience for granted. He expected it. Well! He had a thing or two to learn about Delilah Chadwick. She was no simpering lackey. He would receive her cooperation when he respected her as an equal, and not a moment sooner.

In less time than she would have thought possible, everything was ready and Drake was offering his arm to lead her to the coach. As she took it, she glanced up at him. They were standing in sunlight and he was hatless. Lilah's eyes widened. "Your hair is not brown," she blurted.

"Of course it is brown." He looked down at her, half amused, half exasperated. "What a personal remark, Miss Chadwick. I hope you are ashamed of yourself."

She felt herself blushing. "I don't mean to make personal remarks," she said. "It's just that it startled me."

"What startled you? No, never mind," he amended hastily. "I think I'd rather not know."

He held the door for her. She lifted her skirts daintily, but paused on the step. She studied him again, amusement bubbling through her. It was absurd to call his hair brown. Brown was ordinary. Drake's dark hair glinted beautifully in the sun, auburn and sorrel, cinnamon and honey, autumn leaves. Anything but ordinary.

"I had a chestnut mare once upon a time,"

she remarked. "You put me in mind of her. In more ways than one, I might add." She bit back a laugh. "*Couleur de diable!* You redheads are all alike." And she ducked into the coach before he could wreak vengeance.

She soon had to admit that the coach he had hired far surpassed yesterday's conveyance. It was spacious, comfortable, and so well-sprung that imperfections in the roadway could barely be felt. It was also drawn by a fast team handled by a skilled driver. Really, it was amazing what a difference rank and fortune made to the little things in life. Lilah was painfully aware that, left to her own devices, a mere Miss Chadwick would not be traveling with so much speed and comfort.

Still, by the time they reached London she was exhausted. They had been rocking along in silence for a while, and Miss Pickens was nodding, dozing, beside her. It was well past lamplighting time and the interior of the coach was dark, but now that they had reached the outskirts of town an occasional flash of light through the windows illuminated Drake's face opposite her. He seemed to be studying her, his eyes hooded and opaque.

She was intensely aware of him. The darker it grew and the less she could see, the more her other senses pricked awake, feeling the pull of attraction like invisible wires humming between them. The air seemed thick with electricity. Since she could neither ignore it nor acknowledge it, whatever strange bond existed between them was nothing but a nuisance. Lilah felt herself growing crankier by the minute.

Drake suddenly leaned forward, causing her breath to catch. For a crazy second she thought he would touch her—but he only spoke, his voice lowered in deference to Miss Pickens's slumber. "The address you had me give the driver. It is in Kensington?"

"Yes." Whispering to him in the darkness felt so . . . intimate. She shivered. "It was originally my grandmother's house," she went on. She feared she was babbling, but she feared the charged silence more. "My parents met and married in France, you see. And when Papa brought his bride home to England, her mother came along to see her daughter's new home. And then Mama was expecting me, so Grandmama stayed a bit longer, and after I was born the troubles started back in France and Grandpere was . . . arrested. So Grandmama bought a house in London and never saw Paris again. And this is the house she bought."

She thought she saw Drake's eyebrows lift. "So you are the granddaughter of a French *seigneur*. I should have guessed," he said dryly.

"At any rate, we will reach Kensington shortly. I think I should come in with you, if your father is at home this evening."

"You—you do?" Lilah wasn't sure why the thought of Drake crossing the threshold of her home made her heart beat faster. Drake. In Grandmama's home. Meeting her father. Drake, surrounded by furniture and rooms familiar to Lilah since childhood. Drake, invading Lilah's private world. A thrill of terrified excitement shot through her.

Drake seemed unaware that anything was amiss. "Yes," he said. "The element of surprise is essential to our attack. Your father will be surprised to see you, will he not? That gives you an advantage. Your advantage will be doubled if I arrive simultaneously, since he certainly will not expect to see me."

"Oh." Lilah cleared her throat. "Yes. I suppose that's true."

"Between the two of us, presenting a united front, I daresay this ill-advised engagement will not last another hour. We could be done with this entire business tonight."

The unspoken words *and never see each other again* hung in the air. Lilah took a deep breath. "You may be right," she said composedly, although there was a strange tightness in her throat. "Especially if you make it clear to Papa that you stand ready to offer for Miss Mayhew.

He may feel reluctant, you know, to cry off—if he has actually proposed marriage to her. But if we can convince him that the lady will suffer no disgrace, I think we can persuade him. You can easily make the case that Miss Mayhew will be better off as Lady Drakesley than Lady Chadwick."

It seemed to Lilah that the silence lasted a heartbeat longer than it should have. A slight frown creased her forehead. "You did say you wanted to marry Miss Mayhew. Didn't you?"

"Yes," he said shortly. "I did. I mean, I do."

"Well, then," said Lilah, relieved, "Papa need have no scruples. He can break the engagement without a backward glance." She managed a smile. "I think you are right. We will speak to my father immediately."

But when they reached her family's town house, they were met with the news that Sir Horace was not at home. In fact (the butler regretfully informed them), Sir Horace was not expected home for some several days yet. He had joined a party at Wexbridge Abbey and would return no sooner than Tuesday next.

Perhaps Drake was not destined to cross her threshold after all. At least not tonight. Lilah stood on the low steps of the town house, clutching her cloak round her, and tried to think what they should do. She was so tired. Beside her, servants ran to and fro, busily unloading her baggage from the coach. Miss Pickens bade a grateful farewell to Drake and ducked into the house, eager to reach any piece of furniture that wasn't moving. Her father's butler, Hodge, hovered respectfully and awaited Lilah's instructions. With an effort, she turned to address Drake.

"Do you still wish to come in, my lord? I could offer you some refreshment."

"No, thank you," he replied shortly. He was frowning in an abstracted way. "They will take excellent care of me at the Pulteney. I need a word with you, however."

He seized her elbow in a peremptory fashion and led her a few steps down the street, away from Hodge's listening ears. "This looks serious," he told her grimly. "Wexbridge Abbey is barely outside of London. There's no reason for your father to remove there unless it's to increase his intimacy with the Abbey's occupants."

Lilah was puzzled. "Why is that so serious?"

His jaw tightened. "Wexbridge Abbey belongs to my great-uncle. Eugenia is spending the Season there, under the aegis of my great-aunt."

"Oh. Oh, dear."

"If your father remains under that roof for several days, it's a safe bet that matters have progressed to a formal engagement. Or soon will."

"I see." Lilah's heart sank for a moment, but she rallied. "On the other hand, Hodge said it was a party, not a private visit. Perhaps my father is only one among a large group. That wouldn't be so very bad."

"Perhaps." He did not look hopeful. "At any rate, we should ride out tomorrow and see for ourselves. Will you come with me?"

"Certainly." She sternly repressed the flutter of excitement she felt at the idea of accompanying Drake to Wexbridge Abbey. What was the matter with her? This was business, not pleasure. "The sooner, the better, I suppose."

They agreed that Drake would call for her in the morning, but he arrived before she expected him. Lilah was still breakfasting. Hoping that his early arrival did not bode ill, she set down her cup with a clatter and hurried to the library to greet him.

It was odd, as she had anticipated, to see Drake standing in the familiar room. He seemed to fill it, his head nearly touching the low ceiling. He was standing near the fireplace but turned as she entered, nodding a curt good morning to her.

For half a heartbeat, Lilah could not find her voice. Her hand traveled involuntarily to her throat. She had not seen Drake dressed for London before. In fact, she realized, she had not seen him dressed for anything but arduous travel—and since his man had been left in By-theway with the broken curricle, she had not seen what the assistance of a valet could do for a man of Drake's stamp. She had fallen into the error of thinking that he must always have that careless, thrown-together look. Now she saw that a London valet easily counterbalanced whatever impatience, or lack of personal vanity, might bedevil his master.

Drake's morning coat of dark green superfine had obviously been molded to his form by the hands of an expert tailor. In the clear morning light streaming through the front windows, his hair was definitely a rich, dark chestnut, gleaming and beautifully arranged. His unusual coloring was wonderfully complemented by the green of his coat. Immaculate linen gleamed at his neck and wrists, and his buff-colored breeches clung fashionably to the muscles in his legs. There was nothing ornate or fussy about his appearance; there was a no-nonsense plainness in his lack of jewelry and the brisk tie of his cravat. He was still, in other words, Drake. But, she had to admit, the overall effect of town polish was . . . powerful.

"Good morning," she said, thankful that her voice did not crack. "You are early."

His gaze flicked over her appreciatively. She was wearing her favorite morning dress and was glad, now, that she had donned it. Unmarried girls were supposed to deck themselves in pastels, which rarely became her, but the deep rose of this particular frock made her skin glow pink and white. She would never be the beauty her mother had been—her face was too expressive, lacking the bland sweetness necessary to attract men—but in this dress she felt almost pretty.

"I have news," said Drake with his usual brusqueness. "My great-aunt Polly is hosting one of her masquerades this evening. I think we should abandon our plans to ride out to the Abbey this morning, and attend the masquerade instead."

Lilah was a little taken aback by this abrupt change of plan. "That's odd," she remarked. "Did your family know you were coming to London?"

He looked surprised. "No. I took off on the spur of the moment, just as you did. The party has nothing to do with me or my arrival. Aunt Polly gives these masquerade balls every year. She's famous for them."

"I see. But . . . how did the invitation reach you?"

"It didn't," he said patiently. "I heard about it from an acquaintance of mine who happened to be at the Pulteney."

Lilah blinked at him. "You *heard* about it. Is that all? Surely your great-aunt's ball is not open to the public. How can you and I attend it?"

He stared at her as if she were mad. "Why, we ride over there this evening and walk through the door, of course. It's perfect. Remember, we'll be in disguise. We can observe your father and Eugenia unawares. They won't even know we are there. Since they aren't expecting it, I daresay they wouldn't recognize us even if they looked directly at us."

She must have been staring at him with a very queer expression on her face, for he crossed to her impatiently. "It's perfect, I tell you. Talk about the element of surprise! Why, we can hardly fail. We'll get them both together—you handle your father, and I will tackle Eugenia."

Lilah pressed one hand to her forehead. "Drake. Are you suggesting we attend a private ball to which we have not been invited?"

"Now, don't turn missish," he warned. "We haven't time to indulge any idiotic scruples."

Lilah sank into a chair, unnerved, and listened in horrified fascination as Drake outlined the scheme. "This situation couldn't be better if we invented it ourselves," he told her, pacing vigorously to and fro in his enthusiasm. "I know it's irregular to show up uninvited, but Aunt Polly won't care a rap. She's not one of your high sticklers—in fact, she's probably the least stuffy woman in England. Perfectly respectable and all that, but she's never been one to stand on ceremony. Besides, I've run tame at Wexbridge Abbey all my life. I would have received an invitation, sure as check, if they'd known I could attend."

"Yes, but you *didn't* receive an invitation," objected Lilah. "And I wouldn't have received one in any event! Your family has never even met me."

Drake waved this off impatiently. "Aunt Polly's got your father stashed in one of her guest rooms, hasn't she? That's introduction enough. Will you be able to put a costume together on such short notice?"

Lilah gave a faint moan and covered her eyes with her hand. Drake dropped to a squat beside her chair and pulled the hand away. "Buck up, Miss Chadwick. It'll be fun." A rare grin flashed across his features, lit with boyish mischief.

Lilah eyed him doubtfully. "Fun," she repeated.

"Fun," he said firmly. He gave her a conspiratorial wink.

Lilah felt herself weakening. She bit her lip and looked away, afraid he would see, at such close quarters, the wicked sparkle beginning to rise in her. It *would* be fun. Did she dare? She was certainly tempted. Lilah had only been to one fancy dress ball in her life—a woefully tame affair. Everyone in her small circle had attended it, including the vicar. Something told her that the local vicar would not be present at a masquerade ball held in the height of the London Season . . . and hosted by the least stuffy woman in England.

She stiffened her spine and tried to look prim. "Very well," she said demurely. "Since it is, after all, your family's ball, I will bow to your superior knowledge of what they would find acceptable. If you see nothing amiss in our attending the masquerade, I suppose it would be silly for me to quibble."

"That's the dandy!" exclaimed Drake, rising to his feet. "I'll call for you at half past seven or thereabouts. We don't want to be the first to arrive, but it won't do to crash the gates too late, either. We'll do nothing to draw attention to ourselves."

Lilah choked back a laugh. "Nothing, except show up without an invitation. Heaven help us if they check them at the door."

"I'll tip the butler. Higgins knows me, too; if I lift my mask he'll let us in."

"But won't he think it strange?"

"Higgins? He'll think nothing of it. He's known me all my life." The brief grin lit Drake's features again. "You see," he explained, "people expect this sort of behavior from me."

"I see," said Lilah politely. "You have a reputation to uphold."

"Something like that."

"I'll try to bear it in mind. I did not know you had gone out of your way to *cultivate* rudeness. Silly of me! I should have realized that such spectacular boorishness is only achieved through years of careful practice."

6

*L*ilah pointed her toe. The tip of her shoe, a neat triangle of embroidered satin, peeped from beneath her skirts. The close-fitting, high-heeled slippers felt strange to her feet, since ladies nowadays rarely wore rigid footwear—but they did look perfect with the wide-hooped gown. Watching her reflection in the pier glass in her bedchamber, she fluttered her fan, turned this way and that, and finally swept into a curtsy. Excitement bubbled through her. She looked nothing like herself.

Miss Pickens, behind her, clapped her hands and beamed. "Lovely! You look like a queen. My dear Lilah, you were born too late. With your graceful carriage and tiny waist, you were made to wear stomachers and hoops."

"I cannot put my hands at my sides," Lilah complained, but the compliment pleased her all the same. "I wish these dratted hoops were an inch higher. I might rest my elbows on them."

Miss Pickens looked shocked. "Promise me

102

you will do nothing so gauche," she begged. "Snap your fan closed with your left hand— so—and rest the fingers of your right hand against the sticks. Oh, that is elegant!"

Lilah studied the effect of this pose in the mirror. It felt awkward, but looked graceful. The gown had tight sleeves that encased her arms from shoulder to elbow, then abruptly ended in a foaming fall of lace. With her hands held thus before her, the lace fell prettily against the flat front of her wide skirts.

"No wonder there was a revolution," Lilah remarked. "My grandmother's life must have been unbearable. It will be great sport to wear such an outfit for an evening, but what a punishment it would be to wear it every day! The costume alters everything—the way one moves and breathes and stands and sits. One must be conscious every moment of how one looks. Life at Versailles must have been horrid."

"Very true, my love. Although it wasn't the aristocracy that revolted, you know, but the peasants."

Lilah chuckled and turned sideways, peering once again at the mirror. She was fascinated by the peculiar shape her figure had taken, forced by the old-fashioned bodice to conform to the mode of a bygone era. Pressed by the wooden stomacher and tightly laced stays, her breasts were mashed absolutely flat, allowing the front of the gown to assume a smooth taper from neckline to waist. The style was oddly dainty and feminine—odd because there was nothing remotely womanly about the resulting cone of tight satin. On the other hand, she mused, the rigidity of the cone-shaped bodice contrasted dramatically with the soft flesh it forced to mound high above the neckline. Perhaps it was the impression of femininity bursting from its confines that made the gown so alluring. For alluring it definitely was.

Her grandmother's attic had yielded several trunks of carefully preserved court clothes from the previous century and an old, but still usable, box of hair powder. There were wigs, but Lilah had shuddered at the thought of donning one; they were heavy and nasty with old pomade. The powder would have to do. Miss Pickens helped her dress her hair high and off her face— although it was too short to achieve the loftiness of some of the wigs—and together, with much laughter and sneezing, they inexpertly powdered Lilah's hair. Now the weird whiteness of her hair somehow made the delicate bird's wing sweep of her brows appear startlingly dark, and in the absence of surrounding color her green eyes, framed by sooty lashes, glittered like jade-colored ice. When she put the gown back on and tied a tiny silk mask over her eyes, the transformation was complete. Lilah stared at the pier glass, pleased and astonished.

And a little frightened.

She was going to a masquerade. *Secretly* going, for she hadn't been invited. And she was going with Drake. Alone. This was probably the naughtiest thing Lilah had ever done. Her heart beat faster at the thought, and the mysterious girl in the mirror smiled a catlike smile. *Fun,* Drake had promised her. Yes. This was going to be great fun.

Drake called for her punctually that evening, and she fairly danced down the stairs to meet him, as giddy as a schoolgirl. He paused in the hall and looked up at her, his hawk eyes glinting with appreciation. "Very pretty," he said. "Been raiding your grandmother's attic?"

"*Précisément, m'sieur,*" Lilah replied saucily. She swept a dainty curtsy. "I am glad it meets with your approval."

"Who are you supposed to be?"

"Marie Antoinette."

He gave a derisive snort. "Too common. There will be a dozen Antoinettes. You are not the only lady with access to her grandmother's attic."

Lilah looked resentfully at Drake's costume, which, as far as she could see, was nonexistent. He appeared to be wearing ordinary evening dress. "I could come up with nothing else on such short notice. And look at you! You have not even bothered with a costume."

"One of the many advantages of being male," he told her, with the hint of a smile. "I have brought a domino. That will suffice." He showed her the black silk cape he carried over one arm.

She looked down her nose at him. "There will be more men in dominoes, I daresay, than ladies dressed as Marie Antoinette. So do not scold me for lack of originality."

"Was I scolding you? Heaven forbid." He took her hand and leaned toward her, whispering close to her ear. "Go farther back in time and be Madame de Pompadour," he suggested wickedly. "You look very like her in that gown."

Lilah glanced sideways at him, unsure whether he meant to compliment her or not. "Madame de Pompadour was not a respectable person," she told him primly.

"No," he agreed. His eyes traveled over Lilah's petite form. "But she was enchanting."

Lilah flushed with pleasure. "Was she?"

"She captivated a king."

Lilah tossed her head daringly and assumed her best French accent. "*Alors!* I would like very much to captivate a king. Do you think such a one will attend the masquerade of your aunt?"

"I'm fairly confident of it. There is usually at least one Louis Fourteen, and several Louis Sixteens for good measure."

She opened her eyes at him. "Louis Fourteen, Louis Sixteen—but no Louis Fifteen?"

"Alas, no. It's difficult to impersonate a king whose sole distinguishing feature was his excellent taste in women."

"Ah, my poor Louis. He was not enough flamboyant." She tapped her chin with her index finger as if thinking. "I must, of a certainty, be La Pompadour tonight."

Drake's shoulders shook. "Your father is likely to murder me for this," he remarked. "Let us hope he is too distracted by my theft of his bride to realize that I encouraged his daughter to impersonate a courtesan."

Lilah reverted promptly to her own accent. "*Encouraged* me?" she gasped, indignant. "Forced me, you should say! This entire plan is yours from start to finish."

"Lower your voice, for pity's sake." Drake caught up Lilah's cloak and tossed it to her. He then placed a firm hand at her waist and bundled her hastily out the front door. "And stop squawking," he commanded, stepping past the footman to open the door of the coach for her himself. "You'll bring Miss Pickens down on our heads before we get safely away."

Lilah did stop squawking, but her eyes widened as she took in the details of the small, but elegant, coach. She halted on the step, resisting the insistent hand pushing at the small of her back. "Are we riding in a closed carriage together?" Panic edged her voice.

"I will ride beside the coach, as escort."

"Oh. Th-thank you."

Feeling foolish, she allowed herself to be handed in and, with difficulty, sat. It took nearly a minute to arrange the folds of her skirt to her satisfaction, but she finally decided upon a posture that would result in a minimum of crushing to the voluminous costume. Out the side window, she saw Drake swing easily into the saddle of an enormous black gelding, and they were off.

He was right about Miss Pickens. It would have been disastrous to bring her into the picture. Lilah felt slightly guilty when she thought of how she had misled her faithful henchwoman. She hadn't lied to her exactly. But the reason why Miss Pickens had not objected to this adventure was that she was under the impression (an impression Lilah had not corrected) that Drake's great-aunt was expecting them. And she doubtless believed that the party was taking place on the other side of Hyde Park, not out in the country somewhere. Lilah had told Miss Pickens that she was going to see her father tonight and meet her father's intended bride. This was true, as far as it went—but Lilah suspected that Miss Pickens would never have let her out the door had she known that Drake and Lilah were planning an ambush. And certainly not if she had known that Drake was actually taking Lilah out of London.

She journeyed toward the ball in solitary state, like Cinderella in her gilded coach—wearing gorgeous and unfamiliar clothing, heading for an unknown destination, and without a clue as to what the evening would bring. Lilah wondered if Cinderella had felt this nervous. She probably had. Lilah, unlike Cinderella, was not flouting the authority of an all-powerful stepmother. She had no stepmother to defy—at least, not yet. Doubtless her would-be stepmother would disapprove of Lilah's actions tonight as thoroughly as Cinderella's stepmother had. She could only hope that she and Drake succeeded tonight, so Eugenia would never have the chance to lock Lilah in the attic to punish her.

Despite Drake's assurances to the contrary, Lilah could not help picturing Miss Mayhew as a thoroughly nasty and spiteful person. She was probably warty. And hook-nosed. Yes. She *must* have a hooked nose.

Pleasantly occupied in these silly fantasies, Lilah failed to notice when the lights of London were left behind. The sun had gone down some time ago, and the sky had deepened to a star-spangled purple. From time to time she caught a glimpse of Drake as he rode up beside the coach to say something to the driver, but for the most part he stayed out of sight. It seemed a long time before the coach slowed and turned into a long drive choked with carriages. Lilah could not stand the suspense; she placed her hands against the window frame and leaned out like a child, peeking ahead.

Trees arched above the drive, nearly meeting in a tangle of limbs overhead. The darkness beneath would have been complete had it not been for the glow of carriage lamps lining the drive and the splash of light from nearly every window of the house that lay a hundred yards or so from where her coach had stopped. It was a large house, larger than Chadwick Hall, but not palatial. Even at this distance she could hear the sound of rollicking music and the roar of many voices conversing at once. There seemed to be laughter lacing the roar, and a few feminine shrieks. It must be quite a party.

Lilah swallowed. Her throat suddenly felt dry. Exactly how wild would this gathering be? She had never attended any party, let alone a *fast* one, unchaperoned. Masquerades, she had always been told, were dangerous. Hidden safely behind their disguises, people behaved scandalously, doing and saying things they would never normally dare. What this shocking behavior entailed had never been very clear to her, but she had a feeling she was about to find out. Drake's horse suddenly loomed up beside her, startling her. He leaned down toward her from the saddle. "Shall we walk from here? The drive is graveled."

She nodded, afraid that if she spoke he would hear the nervousness in her voice. He swung lightly down off the horse and handed the bridle to his waiting groom, then reached for the handle of the coach door and helped her to alight.

"Put on your mask," he ordered. She obeyed, tying the strings with trembling fingers. Drake followed suit, donning his mask and domino, then extended his arm to her. With a deep breath, she took it. He paused for a moment, looking down at her. She looked up inquiringly, but his expression was impossible to read through his mask in the half-light.

"Courage, Miss Chadwick," he said lightly, and squeezed her hand for comfort. "If Higgins refuses to admit us, it will only be Lord Drakesley and an unidentified companion who have been turned away in disgrace—not you. And at least it was a pleasant evening for a drive."

She gave him a rather shaky smile. And together they walked to meet whatever lay ahead.

7

She was swimming in an ocean of noise. Dazzled by the riot of light and color all around her, Lilah halted in the foyer and waited for Drake to catch up with her. He was conferring with the butler and, she suspected, tipping the old man lavishly. She saw the butler's well-trained face slip momentarily into a broad smile before he bowed and waved Drake in.

So, Drake had been right. Whatever trials were in store for them this night, at least they had not been humiliated at his great-aunt's door.

As he stepped past the bowing butler, Drake flashed a conspiratorial smile at her. Lilah felt her breath catch. She had not looked at him fully until now, in the glow of dozens of candles and against this glittering backdrop. He was overwhelming. The black silk domino and mask reminded her of her initial impression: he looked more like a highwayman than an earl. The flowing cape shrouded his tall person from neck to

112

heel, making him seem a towering figure of menace—or romance. She wasn't sure which. But when he moved toward her and the swirling silk parted, revealing the understated elegance of his evening attire, her impression shifted again. He looked like both a highwayman *and* an earl. The combination should have been incongruous. In Drake, it was not.

Confusion and alarm chased each other through her thoughts. She felt much too drawn to him. It was dangerous. *He* was dangerous. He reached her side, overshadowing her, forcing her to look up to meet his eyes. She didn't like it. She disliked men who dominated, men who had that hateful air of command—an attitude Drake had in abundance. She disliked feeling powerless and weak. And he definitely made her feel weak. When her eyes met his, something at the core of her being, something vital, turned to mush. She couldn't think properly. She couldn't breathe properly. Her knees trembled.

And she didn't like it one bit, she told herself, fighting the sensation as his gloved hand touched her bare arm, guiding her across the foyer to the ballroom. No, she didn't like it at all.

The din emanating from the ballroom was actually supportable, once they were in the ballroom itself. The confines of the marbled foyer had amplified the racket, but the ballroom had a high, airy ceiling and french doors open to the spring evening. From his height, Drake still had to lean in to speak to her, but she had no difficulty distinguishing his voice from the cacophony around her.

"Congratulate me."

"For what, pray tell?"

"We arrived unscathed, we entered without hindrance, no one other than Higgins knows we are here, and Higgins is sworn to secrecy."

She looked up at him. He was glancing around the room with an expression she recognized, even through the mask, as keen anticipation. Drake was enjoying every moment of this ordeal.

"The setup is perfect," he said exultantly. "Why, it's almost as good as being invisible. We shall come upon Sir Horace and Eugenia unawares, and in disguise. They'll have no chance to brace themselves for confrontation. They will be too flustered to withstand our persuasion."

"Yes, it is a marvelous plan," she agreed, biting back a laugh. "But you have overlooked one important fact."

He glanced down at her, one eyebrow raised. Lilah tucked the corners of her mouth into a demure smile. "Everyone else is in disguise, too."

She had to suppress a giggle as she watched

Drake take a second look at the crowd swirling around his great-aunt's ballroom. His expression gradually changed from anticipation to chagrin. What she had said was true; the advantage of their being disguised was wiped out by the disadvantage of everyone else being disguised. It was all very well to speak of coming upon the couple unawares—but how would they know Sir Horace and Eugenia if they saw them?

An annoyed frown creased Drake's forehead. "We'll find them," he vowed. "We have one advantage, anyhow—we know they are here. Pretend to converse with me, but look about you. It will be easier for you to recognize your father than for me to recognize Eugenia."

"Why do you think so?"

"The ladies are thoroughly disguised. Many of the men are simply wearing dominoes, as I am. Sir Horace may be among them."

"You are right," she said approvingly. She may be allied with a lunatic, but at least he was an intelligent lunatic. "Papa is a modest man, so I would be surprised to see him wearing anything too outlandish." She scanned the crowd, her nose wrinkling with distaste. "At the very least, I hope he is not that idiot dressed as a pig."

Drake led her on a slow promenade round the circumference of the room. Their progress was frequently impeded by collisions with

115

laughing couples and knots of loudly conversing people. Lilah did not recognize a soul. It gave her a peculiar feeling to scrutinize the oddly dressed throng and realize that she was surrounded by the *haut ton*. Was that woman in the monkey mask a duchess? Did the overstuffed courtier in the devil costume hold the fate of hundreds of tenants in his hoof-clad hands? "I weep for England," she murmured, biting back a laugh.

Drake's hand was momentarily knocked from her wrist when a tipsy sheep caromed into her, spilling his glass of champagne down his woolly front. "Beg y'r pardon!" shouted the sheep. "Bad luck, what? A shocking crush. I say, I s'pose I'll shrink now, eh? Ha! Ha! Wet wool, you know! Shrink!"

Lilah was saved from falling into conversation with the sheep by Drake's firm hand reconnecting with hers. She bestowed an apologetic smile upon the jolly soul—who seemed to take no offense when Drake pulled her bodily away from him—and, clinging tightly to Drake's hand, squeezed between two laughing ladies to catch up with him.

"I can't see anything," she complained. "We'll never find them this way."

"You're too short," Drake said grumpily.

"Well, you needn't say it as if you *blame* me.

We can't all be giants like you. If I describe my father, can you look for him?"

"Not unless he has some distinguishing characteristic he couldn't possibly disguise. I don't suppose he's hugely fat, or one-legged, or anything like that?"

Lilah choked. "No. No such luck."

"What a pity." Drake was scanning the room again. Suddenly his eyes narrowed. "Ah. Come this way."

"Do you see Eugenia?"

"No, but I see a way to make you taller." He seized her hand and began pulling her toward the wall.

"Drake," said Lilah warningly, trying unsuccessfully to free her hand, "if you *dare* put me up on stilts—"

"No, no, nothing so alarming," he promised. Then, as they had reached the wall, he swung around and took her by the waist, chuckling wickedly. "Although I'd give a pony to see you on stilts. Especially in this costume."

She gasped. "Dreadful man! I'm wearing hoops."

"Precisely. Stilts would provide a most entertaining view."

Before she could formulate a reply sufficiently withering to put him in his place, someone suddenly knocked into her from behind. She stumbled forward into Drake's chest. His hands steadied her, but did not push her away. Lilah pulled back quickly; their brief contact had not only made her forget whatever she was about to say, it had thrilled her in a terrifying way. What, oh what, was the matter with her?

"Step up," he said. His voice sounded strangely hoarse. "On the plinth."

He jerked his head to indicate the decorative column standing waist high near the wall. It appeared designed to hold a statue or vase, but at the moment it stood empty. One of the revelers had doubtless knocked down and broken whatever decorative object it had originally held. Lilah eyed it with misgiving. "I cannot step up on that thing. It is too tall."

"I will lift you."

"No!" cried Lilah, panic sharpening her voice, but it was too late. His strong hands encircled her waist and she sailed up into the air. With an outraged splutter, she scrambled onto the plinth. It was the only place her dangling feet could find a purchase.

The column seemed much higher than it had looked from the ground, and too small for safety. Her feet were planted, but she was afraid to stand upright. "Are you mad?" she panted. She was bent nearly in two, clutching his shoulders as she tried to find her balance.

He did not immediately reply. To Lilah's intense mortification, his gaze appeared riveted to what her squirming had placed directly in his line of vision: her chest. The rigid bodice of the old-fashioned gown bared the top half of her breasts and mounded them high above the neckline. When she bent at the waist, they bulged nearly to her collarbone. For an instant, she was afraid they would pop out entirely and spill right into his face. Something in his expression indicated he would not object to that.

"Lift me down," she ordered, albeit unsteadily.

"Not on your life." His eyes gleamed as his gaze traveled slowly up her throat, lingering briefly on her lips before continuing up to meet her eyes. A shock of heat shot through her when their eyes met, as if electricity had leaped from his eyes to hers, searing along all her nerves.

"You are blushing," he said.

His voice was so soft it should have been inaudible, but somehow she heard every nuanced syllable. It was as if her ears were instinctively attuned to his particular pitch, and when he spoke she hummed and quivered like a piano tuner's fork.

"Of course I am blushing," she said with a fair assumption of hauteur. "You are embarrassing me."

119

"Why? You look beautiful up there. Like a Dresden figurine." His teeth flashed in a brief grin. "Just strike a pose and hold still."

"Strike a *pose*? You wretch, I cannot even stand."

"Yes, you can. You are perfectly safe. I will catch you if you fall."

"What a horrible man you are," she observed, resigned. "For pity's sake, at least give me your hand."

He complied, and she rose rather shakily to an upright posture. Raucous cheering immediately broke out among a group of interested spectators nearby, all of whom seemed to be men. Since she had not noticed the small crowd their behavior was attracting, Lilah was so startled she nearly fell. Drake's hand steadied her.

"Careful," he warned under his breath. "Steady on. Remember your role."

"What role?" she gasped, mortified. "Drake, let me down at once!"

"Excellent," he said approvingly. "Now hit me with your fan."

She promptly complied.

"Ouch," he muttered, rubbing the top of his head. "Very convincing." He looked over at the knot of hooting men and flashed a broad grin. "I told her I'd put her on a pedestal," he called to them, "and worship at her feet."

Laughter and applause greeted this sally. One

of the men shouted, "The lady had something better in mind, my friend!"

Lilah wanted to sink through the floor. Through the haze of humiliation she felt Drake's hand squeezing hers reassuringly. She looked down at him, almost sick with shame, and saw that he was trying to signal her with his eyes. "Pompadour," he mouthed.

She understood in a flash. It was not Delilah Chadwick who stood on the pedestal, vulgarly displayed for the entertainment of strangers. It was La Pompadour. Lilah had forgotten, for the moment, that she was in disguise. She doubted if Madame de Pompadour had ever done anything this undignified, but never mind. Whatever Lilah did this evening, her reputation—and La Pompadour's, for that matter—would survive, for neither lady was actually present. She immediately breathed easier.

Under the cover of rude male laughter, Lilah tossed her head and frowned prettily. *"Tiens!"* she exclaimed in her mother's clear, carrying voice. "Your homage does not please me, m'sieur. I shall find another worshiper."

The men immediately rushed the pedestal, vying, with much laughter and horseplay, for the honor of becoming her new acolyte. One of the crowd was her wine-stained sheep; she was glad, now, she had not spoken to him. Let him think she was French. Let them all think it.

Feeling much more secure, Lilah—or, rather, this unknown coquette she had become— dropped Drake's hand and balanced daintily on her perch. She smiled and pouted, gestured with her fan and clapped her hands, doling out encouragement to one gentleman and discouragement to another as the fancy struck her. At the same time, she spared some attention to study the room spread out before her.

It was amazing what a difference a few feet of height made. Even with a gaggle of fatwits distracting her and crowding around her knees, she could see everyone and everything in the ballroom from here. The orchestra was placed in a low balcony on the opposite side of the room, where she could see them sawing away like mad. Dancing couples swirled and bumped in the center of the room, their agility impeded by their costumes. She saw several men who might be her father, but could be certain of nothing. There was so much movement and so many masks, it was impossible to pick one man out of the throng.

Eventually she caught Drake's eye and gave him a tiny shake of her head. He had drifted back to the outside of her ring of new admirers, but at her signal he immediately shouldered his way through them to her side. "That's enough," he commanded. "None of you are worthy of my goddess."

"Nor are you," said Lilah pertly. The men all laughed, but parted good-naturedly to let Drake claim her. She supposed they thought him her acknowledged suitor. Perhaps some of them recognized the earl and didn't care to annoy a man of his rank. Or bulk. At any rate, the men all took their leave of her and wandered off in search of additional sport.

Drake held up his hand. She looked down her nose at him for a moment, refusing to take it. "You, sir, are unconscionable," she informed him. "What if those dreadful men had done me a mischief? They smelled very strongly of spirits."

"You seemed to be holding your own," he said dryly. "I take it you did not recognize your father?"

She shook her head. "It is impossible."

"We should get out into the center of the room. Come down and we'll dance."

She frowned. "Stop ordering me about. It makes me cross."

He chuckled. "Sorry. Force of habit. *Please* come down and we'll dance."

She cocked her head. "I didn't quite hear you."

"Ah. Please come down. May I have this dance?"

"Much better." She placed her hand in his and hopped.

He caught her. Suddenly the music seemed to swell; it filled her head with sweet swirls of melody, deafening her to all other sounds. Drake's impossibly strong arm held her at the waist, crushed against him, his face only inches below her own. Her feet dangled, useless; she was suspended in the air with nothing between her and an ignominious fall but Drake's solid muscles. She balanced there against his broad chest and stared into his upturned face. There was a peculiar roaring in her ears—or was it the orchestra? Dizzy, she gazed into Drake's eyes, framed by the slits of his black silk mask. Devils danced in their depths.

"Put me down," she said. Her voice sounded nothing like her own.

Laughter rumbled in his chest; she could feel it vibrate beneath her. "Stop ordering me about," he said, mimicking her. "It makes me cross."

She tried to look severe. "*Please* put me down."

He did, but with obvious reluctance. She slid all the way down his frame. When her feet touched the floor she stepped hastily away, shaking out her skirts. "Thank you," she said stiffly. She wished she had a bigger mask. The flimsy scrap of silk she had employed disguised her features, but did little to hide her blushes.

Drake did not comment on the pinkness of

124

her complexion. He merely offered his arm. "Shall we? Your French accent is very good, by the way."

"My mother was French."

"Ah, yes. How could I forget?" His eyes had returned to the crowd around them. "Eugenia's speech must strike your father as sadly flat compared to his first wife's pretty accent."

A pang shot through Lilah at the thought. "Let us hope so. My mother did have a lovely voice."

"You must take after her."

Lilah glanced up at her companion in surprise. Was Drake complimenting her? Before she could decide, he seemed to catch himself, appearing vexed that he had spoken without thinking. "But Eugenia's voice is pleasant enough in its way," he said gruffly. "And she has other virtues."

They had reached the edge of the dance floor. Drake did not, however, pull her into the melee. They stood, irresolute, watching the red-faced, whooping couples. The dance in progress was some sort of country dance that involved men and women galloping about in concentric rings, trying to locate their partners among the horde. The dancers' fields of vision were severely limited by their masks, most of them had been sipping champagne for several hours now, and many of them were wearing costumes with tails to be stepped on or protrusions that struck glancing blows to dancers in their immediate vicinity. The result was much hilarity and little actual dancing.

"I would need something stronger than champagne to enjoy this mess," remarked Drake. "Let's withdraw and think of another plan."

Lilah could only be thankful. They fought their way back through the crowd to a high-arched doorway. Drake halted in it and they took their stand against the lintel. Lilah protested that they could see very little of the ballroom from here, but Drake's superior knowledge of the house and his great-aunt's party arrangements prevailed; he informed her that this exit led to both the ladies' and the men's cloakrooms. Anyone needing to visit the necessaries would pass directly in front of them. Lilah congratulated him on an excellent stratagem, and he bowed an ironic acknowledgment.

It was pleasant to have a respite from studying the crowd, a difficult task for a petite female. Lilah turned her attention to studying Drake instead. He had placed her with her back against the lintel and was leaning one hand negligently on the smooth wooden surface behind her, thus giving the impression that they were deep in a private flirtation and averse to being disturbed. His eyes were not on her, however; his gaze flicked past her to whoever approached the doorway. A chuckle rose in her as she watched the set of his jaw and the light in his eyes. She strongly suspected that he was having the time of his life.

"Are you fond of hunting, Drake?"

He glanced down at her in surprise. "Rather." A slow smile lifted the corners of his mouth. "You're a perceptive chit."

Drake was not a man who smiled often. One could not help returning such a rarely glimpsed smile. She felt an answering smile waver across her face, and devoutly hoped she did not appear too fatuous. Something about his smile made Lilah conscious of how close his body was to hers, and her attraction to this exasperating man was making her feel remarkably foolish.

"I'm perceptive enough when provided with clues," she said lightly. "I wonder—" She stopped, biting her lip. Oh, dear. She mustn't pry.

But Drake cocked his head as if listening, appearing approachable for once. "What do you wonder, I wonder?"

Very well. She would plunge ahead. "I wonder why you wish to marry Miss Mayhew. And why she doesn't seem to know it."

Drake's approachable expression immediately vanished. He scowled at her. "Of all the deuced cheek—"

"It isn't cheek." She lifted her chin defiantly.

"I need to know. It seems very strange, to me, that a lady who—" *It seems strange that a lady who could have you would marry anyone else.* Lilah gulped, shocked by her wayward thoughts, but rallied. "Strange that a lady who could marry an earl would choose to marry a baronet instead."

Drake's scowl darkened. "And that baronet not in the first blush of youth, either."

"Yes." Lilah decided not to take offense. It was, after all, what she had meant. Sort of. "Is it possible that Miss Mayhew does not know your intentions?"

He appeared to be struggling with whether or not to answer her. He must have decided that the question concerned her after all, as the daughter of Miss Mayhew's supposed fiancé. He finally gave her a grudging nod. "All right. I'll tell you what I think." He cast about for a moment, seeking the right words. His mouth finally twisted in a rueful look; to Lilah's astonishment, he actually seemed embarrassed. "I think she's playing a game with me. And I think she's winning."

Lilah was fascinated. "But how can that be? A lady would not encourage another gentleman's suit as part of a *game.*"

A crack of cynical laughter escaped Drake. "What an innocent you must be! Women execute these sorts of maneuvers every day. I just didn't think Eugenia was the kind of woman who would try it. Somehow I misjudged her. The more fool I."

"Do you love her?" Lilah blurted. She was immediately ashamed of asking such a personal question, but Drake did not seem offended by it. He was scowling, but not necessarily at her.

"Of course I love her," he growled. "We've been friends since childhood. I've always meant to marry her one day. I never said anything, however, so she evidently grew tired of waiting and decided to teach me a lesson." He dropped his hand from behind Lilah and thrust it through his hair, unwilling laughter shaking his shoulders. "Eugenia's not stupid. She made a clever move. It worked, didn't it? When I heard about some middle-aged chuff pursuing my girl, I thought it was a pretty good joke. But when I learned that she was ready to accept him, I dropped everything and ran hotfoot to London to thrust a spoke in his wheel."

Lilah frowned. "But does my father know that Miss Mayhew really intends to wed you, rather than him?"

Drake shrugged. "Who knows? The result will be the same, so it doesn't matter."

Her eyes flashed with indignation. "Possibly it matters to *him*! If you are right about this, Miss Mayhew is playing my father for a fool. He will look ridiculous if she jilts him to wed you. He may even suffer heartache."

Drake stared down at her in exasperation. "What difference does it make? Isn't that exactly what we came here to accomplish?"

She looked daggers at him. "It seems to me to make a great deal of difference," she informed him. "It is one thing to relieve my father of a commitment made half-heartedly. It is entirely a different thing to steal from him a lady he has grown to care for."

"I thought you were convinced that he only offered for Eugenia to give you companionship, or some such nonsense? Or to secure an heir?"

"Yes, but what if I am *wrong*?" cried Lilah despairingly. "I was picturing two adults, discussing their future reasonably—and now you tell me Miss Mayhew may have been enticing my poor father while secretly intending to pique *your* interest. If she is playing some sort of undergame—"

Drake looked fierce. "I keep telling you, Eugenia's not capable of enticing anyone! She's no siren. Why, she doesn't even know how to flirt. She's been very strictly reared—by my own mother, I'll have you know! She lost her parents at an early age and was brought up at Drakesley. I know her like a sister. She's a lady from top to toe."

"A game-playing lady!" Lilah snapped. "A manipulator! Or so you just told me."

Drake looked harassed. "Well, that's the part

130

I don't understand," he said abruptly. "But we'll get to the bottom of it. I would have said Eugenia was the last woman on earth to set a trap for a man. Any man. Even me." He hesitated. "Especially me! I can't imagine her duping one man, let alone two, so perhaps your father is in on the plot."

Lilah struggled with this for a moment. "I hope so," she said at last. "But I must say, it sounds extraordinarily unlike him. You say you cannot imagine Eugenia setting such a trap. Well, I can't imagine Papa helping her to set it! He's a very upright man. Such a scheme would strike him as sly and dishonorable. I know it would."

"Perhaps she appealed to his chivalry."

"Perhaps." She looked doubtful. "But Miss Mayhew has only just met him. Why would she take him so deep in her confidence? Not to mention that part of the plan must entail her *jilting* him—making him the target of malicious gossip. Anyone would dislike that, but Papa would hate it even more than most."

They stared at each other as if seeking answers to the mystery in each other's eyes. All they found was shared perplexity.

A rueful look dawned on Drake's features. "I may have misjudged Eugenia, but I've got you pegged," he said at last, softly, but with conviction. "You're a straight arrow, just as I am. The

131

problem is, neither of us is any good at understanding other people's deviousness. There are those who are on the lookout for deception and expect it—and see it coming. You and I do not. It takes a game player to understand another game player. We're out of our depth, Miss Chadwick."

"I'm afraid you are right." Lilah sighed. "Much as one hates to admit being so . . . so *simple*. But I know exactly what you mean; there are people who would look at this situation and understand in a flash what was really happening. You and I are not among them."

They pondered this glumly.

The ferocious look slowly returned to Drake's features. "I'll say this for us," he announced, righteous indignation warming his voice. "Neither you nor I would construct an elaborate plot to *trick* other people into doing what we want."

"Certainly not," said Lilah roundly. But then she added, with laughter quivering in her voice, "We would employ more direct methods."

8

It was bound to happen, Lilah supposed. Drake had made no real effort to disguise himself, and he was in a house that belonged to his family. Three giggling, chattering girls returning from the cloakroom pounced on him with shrieks of delight.

"Ooh, la, a giant among us! Who can it possibly be?" Then, in a flirtatious singsong: "I think I kno-ow!"

"Lord Drakesley, is that you? It is! I know it is."

"Drake, you wretch! Where have you been hiding? I didn't even know you were in town."

"A forfeit, a forfeit!" Much laughter and clapping of hands. "You must dance with me."

"No, dance with *me*!"

"No, no, he must dance with each of us—or all of us at once! That will teach him not to ignore his friends."

It was all very well for Drake to look dismayed; it was quite his own fault that he had been recognized, and just what he deserved. Lilah, feeling seriously annoyed, pressed herself against the wall and tried to blend in with the wallpaper. But she needn't have bothered. The girls had eyes only for Drake.

They pulled him bodily away from the doorway and into the ballroom. He was so tall that she could watch his progress for a few seconds more, his chestnut head bobbing like a cork tossed on a sea of masks and plumes. Then he vanished from view and she was alone.

Alone. Lilah took a deep breath, pressing one hand against her tightly constricted rib cage. She felt oddly bereft, and a little frightened, abandoned by her one ally at this party of strangers. She reminded herself that Papa was present . . . somewhere . . . and sternly quelled the silly sense of danger that had come over her. Papa did not know she was here, but never mind. She was at an exclusive party, surrounded by elegant people, not criminals. Nothing bad could happen to her.

A silky male voice spoke out of the darkness behind her. "Marie Antoinette, I presume?"

She whirled, startled, and saw a tall figure leaning lazily against the doorjamb of an open door to her right. She could not see his face; the blaze of light from the ballroom did not reach into the shadows where he stood. But his form was outlined by light coming from the room behind him. He was lean yet powerful, graceful as a dancer. And he was wearing impeccable evening attire instead of a costume. This man hadn't even bothered with a domino, as Drake had.

Her sense of danger increased. There was arrogance and mockery in every line of the stranger's being. His lack of costume indicated that he didn't care who recognized him, no matter what he did. This did not reassure her. Another man might have indicated, through his lack of costume, that he never behaved scandalously—even at a masquerade. This one had the aura of a man who behaved scandalously whether he was at a masquerade or no.

He straightened languidly and strolled toward her. "Speechless, Your Majesty?" Laughter lurked in his mocking voice.

"You . . . you startled me." Then she remembered her role and thankfully assumed it. It was like throwing a cloak over nakedness; she immediately felt safer. "I am not Marie Antoinette," she scolded, using her best French accent. "I am Madame de Pompadour."

The man was close enough now that she could see his face. He was quite young; possibly one of the Corinthian set, who prided themselves on equal degrees of elegance and athletic achievement. One of his eyebrows flew up as the corner of his mouth turned down, a perfect expression of sardonic amusement. "I see. How could I mistake? *Mille pardons,* my pretty Pompadour. I shall blame my error on the dimness of the light."

She snapped her fan open with one hand and fluttered it, bestowing upon him a haughty nod. "*Eh bien.* I forgive you the slight, *monsieur.*"

Keen interest suddenly flickered in his dark eyes. "Heigh-ho, what's this? I thought I knew you," he remarked. "But I don't, do I?"

He reached out and, outrageously, tilted her chin up with one lean finger. His hands were bare, and his skin felt shockingly warm as he lightly caressed her chin. "A mystery," he murmured, raking her with his bold eyes. "I do love a mystery. Who are you?"

Lilah's heart hammered with fear, but she managed a regal frown. She did not remove his fingers; it would be undignified to struggle with him. "Who I am, *m'sieur,* is none of your affair," she told him coolly. "To you I shall be only La Pompadour."

He laughed. "Very well, *petite.* I could do worse than to spend a few idle moments with La Pompadour. Every man's dream, in fact."

Would he never take his hand away? She tossed her head to dislodge his fingers, frowning crossly at him. "You should recall, *m'sieur,* that my heart belongs to the King of France."

"Not to mention your lovely body." His gaze

traveled insolently over her form, a wicked grin of appreciation spreading across his features. "You're a lush little morsel. His Majesty is a lucky man."

Lilah was too shocked to think of a clever reply. She simply stared at him, nonplussed. His grin widened. "Have I been too frank?" he inquired with mock contrition. "I hope His Majesty does not clap me in the Bastille for my insolence."

"*Fi donc,* I hope he does!" declared Lilah fervently. "I think you are a rogue, *m'sieur.*"

"Do you?" He pretended to find the idea surprising. "You know, I think you may be right, *chéri.* I must be a rogue." His eyes gleamed recklessly. "Only a rogue would poach on a king's private property." And before she knew what he intended, the stranger pulled her roughly into his arms.

His mouth came down on hers. He tasted strongly of champagne. Too late, she realized that he was half drunk. It would be difficult to convince him that she was in earnest. She struggled, but his arms tightened around her like bands of steel.

The kiss was not pleasant; it was terrifying. She could not get away. All she could do was press her own lips as tightly together as she could, to make her mouth hard and unkissable. Through the haze of alcohol he seemed to recognize her tactic, but his only response was a thick chuckle. He stopped kissing her, but he did not let her go. His face lifted an inch or two from her own, and he grinned again. It struck her as a singularly wicked grin.

"Give me a chance, *chéri*. Don't you prefer me to your fat king?"

"Let me go! You're mad."

"What a fiery little thing you are." His dark eyes mocked her. "I'll strike a bargain with you. Let me taste a little of that fire, and I won't pull off your mask. Otherwise"—he shrugged—"I'm afraid that mask will have to go."

"No!" Furious, she twisted her head back and forth to evade his laughing kiss, but to no avail. He seemed to have far more experience than she; he easily captured her mouth. He was growling playfully, but this was no game to Lilah. She worked one hand free and beat his shoulder uselessly with her fist.

She was concentrating so hard on defeating the scoundrel that she was utterly unaware of her surroundings. It seemed that the stranger's concentration was equally complete, because both he and Lilah were startled when a large hand reached between them, grabbed a fistful of the man's coat, and threw him bodily off her.

The stranger went sprawling backward and Lilah fell to a sitting position on the marble floor. Unhurt, she scrambled instantly back to

138

her feet with a little cry of relief, but the stranger looked a bit dazed.

It was Drake who had rescued her. Somehow, she had known it would be Drake. She rushed forward and seized his arm in a frenzy of gratitude. "Thank you," she gasped. "Oh, thank you very much."

He barely spared a glance for her, but stood, fists clenched, glaring at the stranger. "Are you hurt?" he asked brusquely. He shot the question over his shoulder, but his concentration remained fixed on his opponent.

"No," Lilah assured him. "Just shaken a bit. Oh, pray do not cause any more disturbance!" She was suddenly aware, agonizingly, of the curious stares they were drawing from the adjacent ballroom.

Drake looked to be in a barely controlled rage. It was almost frightening. In fact, had that rage been directed at her, Lilah thought it *would* be frightening. Under the circumstances, however, she was deeply grateful that her champion was immense, strong, and formidable.

He spoke again, this time to the rake. His voice was utterly cold and even, and somehow more intimidating than a shout would have been. "Get up, Rival."

Lilah had never seen a man half sprawled on the floor look so graceful and collected. Amusement lit his features, and he rose with admirable aplomb. "My, my," he drawled, twitching his coat back into place. "So theatrical! Really, my dear Drake, I deplore your tactics. It *is* Drake, isn't it?" He peered, squinting slightly, at the masked avenger towering at Lilah's side. "Yes, of course it is. I recognize the chip on your shoulder." His mocking gaze traveled to Lilah. "The lady is English," he commented, dusting his sleeve. Then he shrugged, laughing a little. "Ah, well. It was an honest mistake."

Now that the danger was past, Lilah was trembling with anger. "You forced your attentions on an unwilling lady," she told him hotly. "Dastard!"

The young man looked pained. "Dastard? No, no, I assure you. I am nothing worse than a rakehell. I will even apologize, if you insist."

Drake spoke through gritted teeth. "I insist."

The self-confessed rakehell turned to Drake, laughter lighting his dark eyes. "You? Really, Drake, apologizing to you would set a dangerous precedent. I will apologize to the lady." He turned back to Lilah and executed a beautiful bow. "Dear ma'am, whoever you may be, I beg your pardon for my—er—dastardly behavior. Pray chalk it up to the effects of excellent champagne on an empty stomach."

She curtsied stiffly, but did not reply. The man's grin flashed again, white teeth bared in his dark face. "Still so cold? I shall remove my unwanted presence. I fancy I will not have far to seek, to find a more willing partner." And with a last nod to Drake, he strolled off, not a hair out of place.

Lilah, in a glow of gratitude, turned to thank Drake—but he placed one hand in the small of her back and propelled her roughly toward the open doorway, the one that had been filled a moment ago by the rakish stranger.

"Wait! What are you doing?" cried Lilah. To her astonishment—and outrage—the blaze of anger in Drake's eyes, once focused on the stranger, was now directed at her. She had thought a moment ago that his anger would be terrifying. Now that she experienced it, however, answering anger shot through her and stiffened her spine. "How dare you shove me about? Unhand me this instant!"

"Stow it!" he snapped.

He pushed her, despite her resistance, through the doorway and slammed it shut behind him. They were in a small library lit by a single branch of candles. The candles matched nothing in the room, so they appeared to have been brought in from elsewhere. It was obvious that the rake, on the prowl for a willing victim, had opened up a room that the hostess had not intended to use and set it up for a trysting place. Ghastly! Lilah processed all this information at a glance—but did not spare a shudder for the

fate that might have awaited her had the
stranger somehow lured her in here. She was
too overwrought at the moment to care. Instead
she rounded on her erstwhile champion, spit-
ting fire.

"What is the meaning of this? Are you angry
with *me*?"

"Very angry! What the devil were you
doing?"

"I? Nothing!" Lilah fairly spluttered with outrage. "Don't you *dare* pretend that that scene out
there was my fault!"

Drake was pale with fury. "It *was* your fault,
you little fool! Don't you know better than to
go off alone with the worst rake in England?"

"Oh! Oh, how unjust!" gasped Lilah. "I didn't
go anywhere with him! He *accosted* me! And
how could I know who he was? You went off,
God alone knows where, and left me by myself.
I don't know any of these people—"

"All the more reason to be careful! Good God,
woman, do you have no sense at all? You can't
let a fellow like that paw you." He ground his
teeth. "And in *public*! Are you daft?"

"Let him?" Lilah nearly shrieked. "Are *you*
daft? I couldn't prevent him!" Her eyes narrowed. "And that reminds me of another thing.
You called him 'rival.' I heard you say it. And
I daresay others did as well, since you drew
quite a crowd, tossing us both on the floor! Well,

let me make one thing perfectly clear: You have no right, no right *whatsoever*, to call any man 'rival,' because you are *not* my suitor! I don't know how you came up with that idea. It's the most breathtaking piece of presumption I ever heard!" She advanced on him, her teeth clenched in impotent rage, and drove her index finger into his chest. "If you have begun to think of yourself in that light, you may stop now. I would rather die a spinster than marry you!"

He grabbed her hands and held them away from his chest, which she had been furiously jabbing with one finger. "Marry you? Marry *you?*" He sounded like he was strangling. "My God! I would rather be boiled in oil! I am going to marry Eugenia. Where have you been during the past three days? Haven't you listened to a word I've said?"

"I've listened," she panted, struggling unsuccessfully to free her hands. "I listened, and I heard you call that horrible man a rival. Well, he's no rival of yours!"

Drake gave her a very queer look. "I called him 'rival,' you crazy little vixen, because Rival is his name."

"His—his *name?*" Lilah stared at Drake. He did not appear to be joking her, but she gave a scornful sniff in case he was. "Ha! A likely story! I never met anyone with a name like that." She had a terrible, sinking suspicion that

143

she had just made a royal fool of herself. Her chin jutted stubbornly. "There is no such name as Rival. It's absurd."

"It may be absurd, but that's his name. His title, anyway." A slow, jeering grin spread across Drake's face. "So you thought I was jealous! You thought I saw some chap kissing you, and went all hot under the collar."

Lilah burned with shame. She could not meet his eyes. That was exactly what she had thought. She had made a perfect idiot of herself. Tears of anger and humiliation pricked her eyelids, and she blinked, furiously wishing them away. She would not let him see her cry!

Besides, why should she cry? So he hadn't been jealous. What did that matter? It wasn't as if she *wanted* to make him jealous. It was appropriate to feel embarrassed, but there was no reason in the world to feel . . . disappointed. She must be more shaken by the incident than she had thought.

"I don't care what you feel," she said, trying to sound as scornful as she wished she felt. Her voice betrayed her, however, coming out small and quavery. "I thought you had come to rescue me. Apparently I was wrong. I don't know why you intervened, and I certainly don't understand why you are so angry, but"—she lifted her chin defiantly—"I don't care. After this night's work is over, I hope and trust that I will *never* see you again."

Drake's hands, large and warm, had moved from her hands to her shoulders, his grip almost painfully tight. "You don't understand?" His voice sounded odd, hoarse and strained. He gave a queer little laugh. "You guessed right the first time: I was jealous. God help me! I was jealous."

Her eyes flew to his, wide and startled. Drake's amber eyes burned with emotion—she saw anger, bewilderment and self-mockery there. And something else, something hot and compelling that made Lilah's heart seem to leap in her chest and begin pounding with . . . fear? No, it wasn't fear, it was something else, something momentous, it was—

But then his mouth closed over hers and she couldn't think anymore.

9

Drake's kiss was rougher than Rival's had been. He held her too tightly. He ravaged her mouth. It should have been worse, far worse, than her previous ordeal—but somehow it drove every thought of that previous ordeal right out of her head. In fact, it drove every rational thought out of her head. *She* went out of her head. Out of her mind.

His kiss was ruthless. Fierce. Almost brutal. She should have loathed it. Instead, she loved it. She should have fought him. Instead, she clung to him. She should have been terrified. Instead, an answering ferocity rose in her, and she kissed him back with a wildness that swiftly matched his own. It was inexplicable. Insane. But she not only endured his kiss, she welcomed it, and melted before his onslaught like butter before a flame.

She heard his soft, hoarse exclamations urging her on, and dimly realized that the moaned response she heard was coming from her own throat. Their touch was more than physical; so deep a thrill could not be explained by the contact of mere flesh. It was their minds that met and linked in a primitive communication far deeper than words. The shock of recognition was like discovering, unexpectedly, that your soul had an identical twin.

Lilah clung to Drake as if he were a long-lost part of her, the missing half of the most important, cherished part of her being, heart of her heart, unexpectedly discovered after lifelong separation . . . a part of her she had not known was missing, but once met, instinctively recognized. Their souls joined like two drops of water the instant they touched. Joy filled her. Madness seized her. She could not get close enough.

Frenzied fingers tore at each other's masks, removing them, discarding them. His face, oh, his face. More skin to touch, closer, closer. More mutters, more gasps. More feelings. She was drowning in emotions she could not name. She clutched at Drake, writhing, pressing wantonly against his body, glorying in the feel of him. There was a tearing sound and then the pop of a waistcoat button.

Drake's button hit the marble floor and flew, skittering, across the tile, striking the baseboard on the other side of the room with a *ping* like a bell. This sound, at last, penetrated the fog of heat that enveloped them.

They fell apart at once, gasping for breath. Lilah's chest was heaving as if she had just run a race. The strange, wild joy she had felt was rudely dispelled by the breaking of their contact. Her emotions seemed to dissolve and float away like fog in a wind.

She pressed one hand to her bosom, struggling to fill her lungs while restraining her breasts. They seemed ready to spill out of the low decolletage; what was the matter with her neckline? The fragile lace must have caught on his buttons and ripped. Confusion shot through her, quickly followed by embarrassment. And consternation. She hardly knew where to look.

"What," she uttered faintly, "was *that*?"

Drake looked as dazed as she felt. He cleared his throat and shook his head like a dog emerging from water. "Nothing," he croaked. "That was nothing."

Now Lilah felt even more confused. "Rubbish," she said. Her voice was a little stronger. "Whatever that was, it certainly was not *nothing*."

Drake's button had bounced off the baseboard and flown back toward them; it was lying on the floor nearby. Needing an excuse to avoid Drake's eyes, Lilah reached down to retrieve it. Unfortunately, Drake dove for it at the same moment. They collided awkwardly and, at his touch, she jumped back as if burned.

"Sorry," said Drake. His voice still sounded strained. "Sorry." He straightened, tucking the button into his waistcoat pocket. Lilah dared not look up, but she could feel his eyes on her.

"Miss Chadwick. Lilah." He cleared his throat again. "Please don't be alarmed. These things happen."

Now she lifted her chin and looked at him. Levelly. "Not to me," she said with dignity.

His cheeks flushed a dull red. "No, of course not. Sorry! I didn't mean to imply . . . well, I didn't mean to imply anything. About you." His collar appeared to have suddenly grown too tight. "I just meant that, once in a great while, you meet a certain person who . . . well, what I mean is, not you personally. And not me, actually, until now. But I've heard of this sort of thing. One hears of it happening, you know, to other people. People meet people, and . . ."

Lilah stared at him, mystified, as his voice trailed off. "Drake, what on earth are you talking about?"

Her brisk tone seemed to brace him. He faced her and tried again. "Chemistry," he said more firmly. "Animal magnetism. What happened between us wasn't your fault, and it wasn't my fault. It was just a freak of nature. Like chain lightning, or earthquakes, or the aurora borealis."

Light dawned. "I see," said Lilah slowly.

"Like . . . like a shooting star. It flashes across the sky, and then . . . then it's gone."

"That's right," he said, appearing relieved. "And afterward, everything is just as it was before."

Sharp disappointment was stabbing through her. She knew it was irrational to feel disappointed by his attitude. She took a deep breath and reminded herself, with great sternness, that Drake was saying exactly what she had hoped he would say. He was right.

And even if he wasn't right, it was better to pretend he was. After all, what were the alternatives? Either their kiss had been meaningless, or . . . it had been important. The implications of their kiss being *important* were too frightening to face. Why, it would change everything. It would ruin all her plans. The entire course of her life would alter. Was she ready for that? Of course not. She had thought everything through very carefully, and she was going to marry Jonathan Applegate. A quiet man. A predictable man. A man of mild habits and calm temperament. A man who was her *opposite*, not . . . not her soul mate.

To strengthen her resolve, she tried to conjure up the face of Jonathan Applegate. She failed. Drake's overwhelming presence had wiped Jonathan's image from her brain.

Oh, dear.

Meanwhile, Drake had begun pacing. In his agitation, he raked his hands through his hair. It seemed to be a habit of his. Even when dry, she noted distractedly, his hair immediately sprang up into cowlicks when he did that. It made her want to run her own fingers through the thick, gleaming waves of chestnut, muss them up, smooth them down, feel her fingers slide through—

Good God, what was she thinking? She must stop this lunacy! Her thoughts had taken on a life of their own, flying willy-nilly down paths not of her choosing. Paths better left unexplored.

Drake's brow knitted in a fierce frown of concentration beneath his disordered locks. "I wish to high heaven I had never met you!" he exclaimed. The rudeness of this remark seemed to strike him, and he paused, adding in a milder tone, "Meaning no offense."

"None taken." It was an automatic response, but she meant it. "I understand you perfectly," she added. "I wish the same! But since we *have* met, and this terrible thing has sprung up between us—magnetism, did you call it? We really must address it somehow."

He eyed her with misgiving. "Well, I don't know how," he said bluntly. "Normally this sort of encounter leads to marriage, but I fancy you don't care for that idea any more than I do."

"No, I don't," she said fervently. "Please

151

marry Eugenia, and let me marry my Jonathan. You and I would be miserable together."

"Aye, that we would." But then his features darkened. "Who the devil is Jonathan?"

Lilah pulled herself up to her full, if diminutive, height. "Jonathan is no concern of yours," she said stiffly. "Suffice it to say, I have no interest in associating with, let alone marrying, a hottempered man like you. I require a peaceable man, a gentle man—"

"A man you can bully." He gave a rude crack of laughter. "You're right; I am not that man! And you, I need hardly say, are not the woman for me. We would be at each other's throats more often than not."

She glared at him. "I resent your tone, Drake! Are you implying that I would henpeck my husband?"

"Of course you would. I never met a more controlling female."

"In other words, you never met a woman strong enough to stand up to you," cried Lilah, bristling. "Heavens, what a wretched life awaits your unfortunate Eugenia! I sincerely pity her."

"Save your pity for someone who wants it," ordered Drake, an angry flush reddening his neck. "Eugenia and I never fight about anything, I'll have you know! She is the perfect woman for me. We are always of one mind."

Lilah gave a scornful laugh. *"Your* mind, no

doubt! She probably defers to you out of habit, because she's learned how exhausting it is to oppose you."

"Which is doubtless the reason why people defer to you! Or hadn't you thought of that?"

"People don't *defer* to me! *I* am not an all-powerful earl! I know you think I am vain and spoiled—"

"No, just spoiled."

"—but I am not! It's simply that I have been blessed with a high degree of—of leadership ability, and more than my share of good ideas. If others let me have my way it is because they honestly *agree* with me, not because I ride roughshod over them!"

Drake appeared to be breathing through his teeth. "So you think I ride roughshod over people?" he snarled.

"Yes, I certainly do!"

"Well, I think the same of you, so one thing is abundantly clear: we must avoid marriage at all costs! Good God, we would brangle day and night!"

Lilah shivered. "Horrible! If we agree on nothing else, my lord, we agree on that."

"Good."

They both breathed a little easier. After taking a moment to collect herself, Lilah even managed to smile at Drake. "I am glad you do not feel obligated to propose marriage," she said archly, trying to lighten the moment. "It would upset my father very much if I spurned an offer from an earl."

His rare grin flitted briefly across his face. "And I am glad you do not insist upon such nonsense. Any other female would have treated me to a bout of maidenly hysterics. Thank you for sparing me that."

Her smile warmed with genuine amusement. "You're welcome. But I'm not such a poor creature."

"No. That you are not." Drake's voice had softened. Dangerously. "You're no man's notion of a poor creature."

Their eyes met across the narrow room. Met, and held. There was a wealth of appreciation in his eyes—and infinite attraction. Lilah felt like she was drowning. He was drawing closer, and she could not bring herself to move, or even to look away. Caught in the grip of feelings she feared but could not suppress, she stared help-lessly into his eyes and let him approach.

Please don't kiss me, she begged him silently. Her panic must have shown on her face—and her inability to resist him. He halted, inches from her, and something like pain moved in his eyes. He lifted one hand to trace the edge of her cheekbone. She shivered at his touch.

"You have the most amazing face," he said, as if to himself. "Strong, yet feminine. Vivid.

Your expressions flash and pour like water over pebbles. I could watch this face for hours." His thumb moved across her cheek and his voice grew unsteady again. "What a pity that we cannot tolerate each other."

"Yes," whispered Lilah, giving him a crooked smile. "But we are too alike. Fire cannot marry fire. And neither of us is likely to change."

His amber eyes darkened. "I cannot touch you without wanting you," he said hoarsely.

Lilah felt suddenly faint with longing. It wasn't fair for him to say such things. She closed her eyes so the sight of his regretful face would no longer tempt her, and managed to whisper: "Then you must not touch me."

"Right." He dropped his hand with obvious reluctance. Lilah opened her eyes and caught him staring at her neckline. "Your lace," he said, his voice carefully devoid of emotion, "is torn."

She glanced down. It certainly was. Her left breast was nearly completely exposed where the fragile stuff had fallen away. The lace was now secured at only one corner, near her left shoulder. Drake reached for the lace, his large fingers surprisingly gentle, and pulled it back across her tender flesh. The soft scrape of his fingers against the top of her breast tingled like electricity. Lilah caught her breath.

At first she thought Drake's fingers were shaking. Then she realized she was trembling.

And then she saw that both things were true. Both Drake and she were utterly focused on the sensation of his fingers touching her body. They were oblivious to everything else in the world; nothing existed but his flesh lightly caressing hers. Together, they became completely engrossed in prolonging the delicious moment—and in fighting what it made them feel.

Feeling drugged, Lilah slowly raised her eyes to Drake's face. They stared into each other's eyes. Their lips parted. Their breath quickened. She had never before felt such desire for a man. She had never dreamed what power mere attraction could wield. She had not known such complexity of emotion was possible. And then his fingers slid between her breasts as he tucked the lace back into place, and Lilah discovered, beyond doubt, that desire was the strongest force in nature.

Neither Drake nor Lilah heard the door open behind them. They failed to notice the swell of sound from the ballroom. They did not even observe the light flicker and sway as the candles caught the draft from the open door.

But they did hear the outraged voice of Sir Horace Chadwick as he thundered, "What in *blue blazes* are you two doing?"

10

Lilah sprang backward with a little scream of surprise. In the doorway stood four people. It was easy to tell who was whom, for none of them were masked. One was her father, clad in a Puritan costume and looking angrier than she had ever seen him. Standing beside him, her hand lightly resting on his arm, was a tall, black-haired young woman in a pink domino. Lilah realized at once that this must be Eugenia Mayhew. Her appearance came as something of a shock. Whatever Lilah had expected, it had not been this: a homely beanpole of a woman who, despite her spectacular lack of beauty, radiated a poise that was almost regal. If her true object was to attach Drake through feigning interest in another man, she greeted the sight of Drake's fingers tucked into Lilah's neckline with admirable serenity.

Another, older, couple stood behind her father and the beanpole. The older lady was a comfortable-looking woman in a shepherdess costume, who peered through her spectacles at Lilah with great interest. She looked from Lilah to Drake and back again, for all the world as if they were on display at a zoo. Beside this lady, Lilah saw with chagrin, was the genial, tipsy sheep she had encountered earlier.

"Dear me," said the shepherdess mildly. "It's Drake." She did not appear shocked in the least.

The sheep's face noticeably brightened. "Why, so it is. Drake, my boy! Didn't know you were here. How are you?"

Drake, however, failed to respond. He appeared rooted to the spot, too flummoxed to move a muscle. Looking at him, Lilah was struck by the overwhelming irony of their situation: this was the exact opposite of what they had hoped to achieve! The plan had been to surprise Sir Horace and Eugenia, not to have Sir Horace and Eugenia surprise *them*. Now their plans lay in ruins. Lilah wondered if it were possible to faint from mortification. She rather wished it were. It would be a tremendous relief to lose consciousness right about now.

But her father turned on his heel to address the sheep. "Are you acquainted with this fellow, Nat?" he asked sharply. "Kindly tell me who is mauling my daughter!"

The sheep looked distressed. "Tut, tut, Horace! No need to fire up. It's Drake, old thing.

Polly's nephew Adam. One of the Harlestons. Daresay he didn't mean to maul your daughter. The Harlestons are like that, you know; act first and think later. They never mean any harm."

"Nat, dear," interposed the shepherdess. He turned to her inquiringly. "It doesn't matter what he *meant* by it," she said with an air of infinite patience. "Drake's carelessness may be deplorable, but he knows the rules as well as anyone. I'm sure we may count on him to do the right thing."

Eugenia turned to Lilah's father with gentle courtesy. "Adam is the Earl of Drakesley," she explained in a low and musical voice. "You have heard me speak of him. We call him Drake."

Lilah began to feel that she had wandered into a madhouse. Everyone except her father seemed preternaturally calm. She pressed her hands to her temples, feeling dazed. "I do not understand. Papa, what brought you into this room? And why did you bring all these people with you?"

Sir Horace's choler had visibly diminished. He was obviously much mollified by the news that the rapscallion he'd caught manhandling Lilah was an earl. Besides, even under the most extreme provocation, displays of temper did not come easily to him. He placed one hand over

Miss Mayhew's where it lay on his arm, as if unconsciously drawing strength from her quiet presence at his side.

"I came in here, Lilah," he said sternly, "in search of you. I was never more astonished than when I glimpsed you in the ballroom tonight! Why, I could scarce believe my eyes. And then to see you making such a figure of yourself—perched up against the wall, of all things! Had you been a few years younger, I would have turned you over my knee! At any rate, I lost sight of you after you jumped down. Someone pointed out which way you had gone, and I gathered together the three persons I particularly wanted you to meet, and went to find you."

Lilah felt her jaw dropping. "But—but—how did you know it was me?"

Sir Horace looked exasperated. "I could not mistake. You are wearing a dress from your mother's trousseau! Although God alone knows where you found it." His expression softened as he looked more closely at it, and his voice became gruff. "A man doesn't generally notice a woman's gewgaws and such, but I would know that gown anywhere."

Lilah was silenced. Her mother's memory seemed to flood the room with her lively, laughing presence. Nostalgia, and something like homesickness, squeezed Lilah's eyes shut for a moment. Eugenia Mayhew could never fill her mother's dainty shoes. Never.

But Sir Horace was facing Drake now, puffing his cheeks with disapproval. "Well, my lord?" he asked him sternly. "What have you to say for yourself?"

The gray-haired shepherdess stepped calmly forward. "I think introductions may be in order," she said with an air of great good humor. "Drake, the gentleman addressing you is Sir Horace Chadwick of Chadwick Hall. Sir Horace, this scapegrace is indeed my nephew's son. He is Adam Harleston, the Earl of Drakesley."

Sir Horace sketched a brief, rather jerky, bow. "My lord," he said stiffly.

Drake cleared his throat. "Sir Horace," he replied, bowing with slightly more grace.

The shepherdess looked from one to the other. Lilah could have sworn she saw her eyes twinkle. "Well. Since the only persons present who might finish the introductions seem momentarily incapable, I suppose I must bend the rules a trifle." She bestowed a kind smile on Lilah. "My poor child, this is all quite dreadful for you, isn't it? But you must not let Drake's want of conduct embarrass you. His impetuosity is legendary. None of us will hold you accountable for his bad behavior. You are Delilah Chadwick, are you not? Of course you are. I am Drake's

161

aunt Polly, and I'm very pleased to meet you. The sheepish fellow is my husband, Drake's uncle Nat."

The sheep dug an affectionate elbow into his wife's ribs. "Sheepish! Ha, ha! Very good, my love."

Lilah, blushing furiously, dropped into a curtsy. "How do you do?" she murmured, scarcely knowing where to look. She knew that her unwitting host's name was Peabody, so it wasn't as if she needed more information—but it seemed very odd that Mrs. Peabody had introduced herself and her husband by their Christian names.

The mystery was solved by her next words. Mrs. Peabody folded her hands comfortably against her generous midriff and announced with great satisfaction, "I see no need to stand on ceremony, Delilah. You may call us Aunt Polly and Uncle Nat. Since you will doubtless marry Drake without delay, I consider you quite one of the family."

Drake and Lilah were immediately jolted from their daze. They spoke with one voice: "No!"

It was an anguished cry, blurted straight from the heart. Drake's fingers writhed in his hair once more. Lilah clasped her hands before her in an attitude of prayer and rushed into impassioned speech. "Please! You have completely misunderstood. I know it looked very bad, but

I promise you, Drake has not—not *compromised* me. And even if he had, I would not marry him."

"And I wouldn't offer!" exclaimed Drake. Four pairs of shocked eyes fastened on him with varying degrees of reproach and horror. He gave a strangled moan and opened his mouth to explain, but Lilah had dashed to his side in quick support.

"No, of course you would not," she said warmly. "It would be the height of absurdity. And a waste of time as well, since you already know I would refuse you." She spread her hands beseechingly, addressing Polly Peabody. "Dear ma'am, we mean you no disrespect—"

"Despite the fact that we crashed the gates tonight," added Drake.

"—but there is no romantic attachment whatsoever between Drake and me, and we cannot, *must* not, marry."

"In fact, we dislike each other," said Drake earnestly.

"Extremely," said Lilah, just as earnestly. "Why, we've known each other for only three days and have nearly come to blows on more than one occasion. Have we not, Drake?"

"Yes, indeed we have."

That disturbing twinkle had returned to Polly Peabody's eyes. "How odd," she remarked. "You seem to me to be in complete agreement."

Drake scowled. "What we agree on, Aunt, is our mutual antipathy. I'd as lief marry a wildcat as spend my days with Li—Miss Chadwick."

"And I'd as lief marry a grizzly bear," retorted Lilah, stung. "At least they hibernate from time to time."

"Besides," said Drake suddenly, as if he had just remembered something, "I want to marry Eugenia."

This simple statement caused a sensation. Nat Peabody made a choking sound and goggled at his nephew. Polly Peabody threw up her hands, exclaiming, "Oh, Drake, *no!*" Sir Horace demanded testily to know whether *he* had gone mad or everyone else had.

But Lilah was watching Miss Mayhew. It seemed to her that the lady was taken aback, but only for a moment. Then she smiled. Her smile, though amused, was filled with rueful affection—and struck Lilah as a little wistful, too. For a moment, Eugenia Mayhew was almost pretty.

"Dear Drake," said Miss Mayhew warmly, "how lovely. Thank you."

Her response would have been equally appropriate had Drake handed her a bunch of lilacs. Lilah could read nothing more into it than pleasure at receiving a compliment. Apparently neither could Drake, for he looked nonplussed.

"Hang it all!" he exclaimed. "I've done it

wrong. Forgive me, Jenny. I'm a poor hand at making pretty speeches, and I've never offered marriage before." He strode swiftly forward and dropped to his knees before Miss Mayhew, plucking her hand from Sir Horace's sleeve and holding it tightly in his. The sight gave Lilah a strange pang.

Her unfortunate father looked as if he might go off in an apoplexy. "Now, see here—" he began, in a tone of outrage. But Drake's firm voice interrupted him, addressing Miss Mayhew as if there were no one else present.

"Jenny. Eugenia. I know I've taken you for granted all these years."

Amusement crinkled the corners of Eugenia's eyes. "Yes, Drake. You have."

"I believed I could claim you at any time convenient to me. I thought you would wait, however long I took."

"Yes. It was rather rude of you, wasn't it?" Miss Mayhew mused, gazing at Drake with a faraway look. "And shortsighted as well, if you intended all along to marry me one day."

"If? There's no *if* about it," he said impatiently. "I always meant to marry you. You must have known I did."

Miss Mayhew looked even more thoughtful. "Did I? No, not quite—although I did suspect it. I would have brought the subject up at some point, but I hesitated to put myself forward.

After all, I might easily have been mistaken. Your attitude toward me was never loverlike. It was merely . . . possessive."

A note of chagrin crept into Drake's voice. "I'm sorry, Jenny," he said gruffly. "I'm a thick-skulled chap, and only drastic action gets my attention. I drove you to this, didn't I?"

Miss Mayhew cocked her head as if puzzled. "Drove me to what?"

"This cockamamy flirtation with Chadwick. I don't blame you. In fact, it was a clever little stratagem, as far as it went. It was a dangerous game, and it didn't fool me for a moment, but it was a spirited thing to do for all that. I deserved it, too. I won't hold it against you after we are married."

Sir Horace exploded. "I've heard enough!" he exclaimed, seizing Miss Mayhew's arm and attempting to drag her hand from Drake's by main force. "I am a patient man, sir, but this is too much! The lady is spoken for."

Drake sprang to his feet, towering menacingly over Sir Horace. "By you?" he asked, his lip curling. "I think not."

Lilah threw herself between the two men, clinging to her father. "Papa, pray do not be overset," she begged, her voice throbbing dramatically. "Do you not see? Think! Lord Drakesley's suit is *good* news."

Her father's arms went around her reflexively,

but he appeared exasperated. "Lilah, give over, for pity's sake," he said testily. "The last thing I need now is a bout of your theatrics!"

She blinked at him, hurt. "But, Papa, don't you understand? You need not marry Miss Mayhew after all. Drake is willing to marry her instead. In fact," she added, warming to her theme, "you will be doing Miss Mayhew a *favor* if you jilt her."

"That," murmured Eugenia, "is entirely a matter of opinion. Is anyone interested in hearing mine?"

All eyes turned to Eugenia. Mrs. Peabody chuckled. "It seems to me, my dear, that yours is the only opinion worth hearing."

A faint smile curved Miss Mayhew's lips. "I never dreamed I might, one day, be forced to choose between two offers of marriage," she remarked. "I thought such things only happened to wealthy women, or those with great beauty. This is a lesson to me, for I have always envied women who received proposals right and left. I see, now, that the reality is quite different. It is a melancholy task to choose one man over another."

Both Sir Horace and Drake tensed, seeming to steel themselves for the worst. Miss Mayhew reached out and placed one slender hand on Drake's. He clutched it, and Lilah's heart twisted within her at the sight. *All for the best, all for the best,* she repeated in her mind like a litany, bracing herself for the blow that would surely fall.

But when Miss Mayhew's homely face smiled at Drake, it was a kind smile, not an adoring one. With her hand still in his, she slowly shook her head. "Dear, darling Drake," she said softly. "You have been my closest friend for many years. But I could never marry you."

Drake appeared stunned. She pulled her hand from his and patted him gently. "I mean that, you know," she told him with gentle firmness. "I cannot now, and I never could. Had Sir Horace and I never met, I believe my answer to you must always have been the same."

Lilah's heart seemed to leap and pound in her chest. Relief that she would not have to give Drake up to another woman—at least not immediately—warred with shame at her dog-in-the-mangerish emotions. She was also conscious, absurdly, of a flash of anger at Eugenia Mayhew for daring to turn down Drake's offer. How could the ungrateful creature wound him so?

But Drake did not look wounded. He looked furious. He shook Eugenia's hand off his sleeve. "Why?" he demanded. "This is utter nonsense. Confound it, Eugenia, I thought you loved me!"

"I do love you," she said firmly. "As you love me. Do not pretend you are *in* love with me, Drake. You know perfectly well that you are not, and never have been."

Polly Peabody stepped forward. "Well! This has all been vastly entertaining," she said brightly. "But I suggest we return to the ballroom."

Drake rounded on her, head lowered like an angry bear. "Blast it, Aunt—*no!* What the devil can we do in the ballroom, among that crowd?"

His aunt Polly smiled benignly, in no way discomposed by Drake's surliness. "Dance," she replied. And shooed them all through the door.

11

"She didn't even hesitate," Drake growled for Lilah's ears alone. "You'd think she would do me the courtesy of thinking it over for a bit. Hell's bells, I've known the woman all my life!"

He was dancing with Lilah in a perfunctory way. Both of them were too preoccupied with the events that had just taken place to mind their steps. Their moment of high drama had unaccountably fizzled, and they had been made to feel faintly ridiculous. For the first time, they were united in hostility toward something other than each other.

Lilah, awash with indignant sympathy, patted Drake's arm to console him. "It is a shame," she told him warmly. "I sincerely feel for you."

"But I cannot believe this is her final decision. It makes no sense." In his agitation, Drake swung Lilah violently in a circle. "Why would she choose an old man over a young one? Why would she choose a stranger over a friend?"

"For that matter," said Lilah rather breathlessly, "why would she choose a baronet over an earl? Drake, for pity's sake, slow down."

"Sorry." He slowed his steps. "Dash it, Lilah, there's something peculiar about the business. She turned me down flat! I don't mean to sound like a coxcomb, but—"

"Oh, you don't!" Lilah assured him. "I perfectly agree with you. I love my father—he is a most estimable creature, and quite young and vigorous for his age—but he cannot compare to *you* by any measure known to man. Or, which is more to the point, woman."

Drake stared intently into Lilah's eyes, perplexity and bewilderment writ large across his face. "Then tell me. Why do you think she chose your father over me?"

Lilah thought for a moment. Inspiration struck. "Why, I imagine she was intimidated by the crowd of people in the room."

Drake halted in his tracks, nearly causing Lilah to stumble. "Do you think that was it?" he exclaimed. "By Jove. You may be right. By Jove, you *are* right! What else could she say, with Sir Horace standing there?"

"Nothing," said Lilah triumphantly. "She had to decline your offer. I daresay she has already promised to wed my father."

"She almost certainly has. Lilah, you've hit it! I'll get Eugenia alone and try again." He seemed to notice something odd in Lilah's expression. His eyebrows lifted slightly. "Well? What is it?"

Lilah gave a short laugh and looked away. "Nothing. I merely wondered—" She hesitated. "Well, to speak frankly, there is something else about the business that strikes me as peculiar." A glimmer of mischief lit her features. "Everyone seems wild to marry Eugenia Mayhew. I confess, I do not see the attraction."

His eyes gleamed. "Never underestimate the power of a biddable woman. No, do not look daggers at me! I realize Eugenia will never be a beauty. And she's not the most entertaining woman you'll ever meet. But she's . . . restful. And superbly competent. She'll be an excellent and thrifty housewife. A quiet life and a well-run home are worth a great deal to a man."

Lilah pursed her lips demurely. "And, of course, one need not watch a plain woman too closely, since it is unlikely that another man will steal her away."

Drake looked glum. "So I thought," he admitted. "But apparently I was wrong."

Lilah choked. "Is nothing safe?" she asked with mock sympathy. "Is there no woman plain enough to ignore with impunity? Tsk! You might as well marry a pretty girl."

She looked up at him, her eyes full of laughter. But he was staring down at her with a

172

strange intensity that caused her laughter to fade. "I wonder if you are right," he said slowly.

Lilah suddenly felt a vigorous tap on her shoulder. Since she was entirely focused on Drake, she nearly jumped out of her skin. "There you are!" said the cheerful voice of Polly Peabody. "I wanted you to know, my dear, that I've sent round to Kensington for your things. They should arrive within the hour."

Lilah quickly dropped her hand from Drake's shoulder and turned to face her hostess. "I beg your pardon?"

Mrs. Peabody smiled patiently. "Since your father is stopping here at the Abbey, we have decided it would be wholly ineligible for you to remain in Kensington. Whatever the custom may be in the countryside, dear child, in London I assure you that single females do not reside alone."

Lilah blinked. "But—do you mean I am invited to stay *here*?"

She beamed. "Certainly. You cannot refuse, you know. Your papa and I have arranged everything. Your companion—what is her name, dear?"

"Pickens," said Lilah faintly. She was feeling a bit overwhelmed.

"Miss Pickens will be brought round in the morning. And as for you, Drake"—Mrs. Peabody bent a severe look on her nephew, peering over the top of her spectacles—"I hope you know better than to argue with me. I'm ready to box your ears as it is."

Drake looked mildly surprised. "I wouldn't dream of arguing with you, Aunt. You may house Miss Chadwick with my goodwill."

"So I should hope. But I'm housing you, too." She raised a warning finger. "Not another word! I won't be made a subject of gossip. My own nephew, staying at the Pulteney!" She gave a disapproving sniff. "Anyone might think we'd had a falling out. Well, we haven't, and I won't have it spread all over town that we have."

She gave a brisk nod and bustled away, leaving Drake and Lilah with their mouths agape. They turned back to each other, eyeing one another with misgiving. It was Lilah who broke the silence.

"I hope you won't take this amiss, Drake, but I am extremely reluctant to stay in the same house with you."

"I don't blame you. There's a very odd dynamic at work between us." He took a deep breath and expelled it, looking thoughtful. "On the other hand, both of us staying here will have certain advantages. Provided we take care never to be alone together."

"Oh, we must avoid that at all costs," said Lilah fervently.

It wasn't that she didn't trust Drake—although it was just as well if he thought that. She did not trust herself. Merely standing beside him as she was now, or dancing with him, gave her far too much pleasure. It wasn't normal.

"Very well," said Drake abruptly. "We'll make that a rule. We meet only when others are present. Agreed?"

"Agreed."

"Good. Because as long as nothing untoward happens between us, Aunt Polly's invitation is a godsend. If you and I went tamely back to London, we would never break up this ridiculous engagement scheme. Matters seem to have reached a critical point. In fact, I wouldn't put it past Eugenia to simply avoid us altogether until the knot was tied."

Lilah was much struck by this insight. "I believe you are right," she exclaimed. "I am not acquainted with Miss Mayhew, but that is definitely what Papa would do. He goes to great lengths to avoid what he calls 'unpleasantness.' If he thought we were going to argue with him day and night, he would do almost anything to keep away from us."

"Eugenia is the same way," said Drake grimly. "Craven, I call it! But if Sir Horace shares the trait, that cinches it. They will duck us if they can. If we are staying in the same house, at least they'll have fewer opportunities to give us the slip."

Lilah frowned. "But even if they are unable to avoid us, they will pooh-pooh whatever we say," she pointed out. "Only look how they treated us just now! As if we were simply putting on a show for their amusement." Resentment churned within her. "Papa seemed to think I was being *childish*."

Drake gave a brief nod. "Theatrical, he called it." He sounded both disgusted and sympathetic. "We were both made to look like fools. But we'll get the last laugh, Lilah, never you fear."

Lilah awoke late on Sunday morning and staggered grumpily down to breakfast. Her things had arrived at Wexbridge Abbey long before the end of the party, and when she was notified of this she had immediately retired— since the more time she spent in Drake's company, the more jangled her nerves became. However, going upstairs to bed had accomplished little. It had taken nearly an hour to wash the powder out of her hair, and the festivities below had gone noisily on until dawn. She had sat up, listening to the cacophony and waiting for her hair to dry . . . and brooding. She felt far from rested.

At least her appearance was fresh and neat. Mrs. Peabody had honored her by sending her own maid to help dress her hair this morning. The woman was definitely an artist; Lilah had actually smiled when she saw the result of the maid's labors. But her smile soon faded. She was in no mood this morning to be pleased.

She expected a solitary breakfast at this hour, but, to her surprise, Polly Peabody was in the breakfast room, consuming a substantial repast and chatting with Miss Pickens. Miss Pickens still wore her traveling cloak and was sipping gingerly on a cup of black tea—her custom when recovering from a journey of any length. Her thin face brightened when Lilah entered the room.

"Lilah, my love, good morning! Is this not delightful? So kind of Mrs. Peabody to invite us! She has been telling me a little of the Abbey's history and, I must say, I am looking forward to wandering the grounds—which she has told me I may do at my leisure. I am truly grateful. Such an opportunity does not often come my way. Only fancy, Lilah—Queen Elizabeth herself is said to have stopped here for a week's hawking, in the early days of her reign. Can you not picture it?"

Some of Lilah's crossness evaporated in the face of Miss Pickens's obvious enthusiasm. She smiled affectionately at her loyal companion. "I am glad for you," she said simply.

Polly Peabody, her mouth full of ham, waved Lilah languidly into a nearby seat before swallowing. "Miss Pickens seems to know a frightful amount of history," she remarked. "I am quite terrified of her."

Miss Pickens beamed. "I'm afraid I am a dreadful bore on the subject," she said. "I seldom have an audience for my favorite hobby-horse."

Lilah laughed, wrinkling her nose. "By that, she means that I showed little interest in sixteenth-century politics," she explained to her hostess. "Or any other period of history, for that matter. I was a sad disappointment to her back in the days when she struggled to educate me. You have offered her a rare treat."

"Well, that's lucky," said Mrs. Peabody, her eyes twinkling. "It's seldom that a genuine treat costs so little. I'm delighted to be able to provide it."

Lilah glanced surreptitiously around the room, wondering what was expected of her. No servants were anywhere in sight. Places had been laid for four persons besides the three now seated at the table, but dirty dishes and discarded napkins bore witness to the fact that two of the four missing people had already breakfasted and departed.

Mrs. Peabody saw Lilah's indecision and, with the same informality she showed in waving

178

Lilah to a seat, gestured toward the sideboard. "The coffee and tea are piping hot, and I can vouch for the eggs and ham as well," she said cheerfully. "You may need to stir the chocolate. Shall I ring for fresh toast?"

Lilah was taken aback for a moment. Apparently, she was supposed to wait on herself. What a novel idea.

"No, thank you. Not on my behalf," she replied politely, and carried her plate to the sideboard to explore the contents of various covered dishes. Strange. But as she lifted the covers and examined what lay beneath, choosing what to take and what to leave, she discovered that she rather liked filling her own plate. Mrs. Peabody's informal ways, although eccentric, had a charm of their own.

By the time she returned with her plate to the table, Miss Pickens and her hostess had moved on to another subject—one that enthralled Lilah even less than history did. She frowned in irritation as Miss Pickens lavished praise on the absent Lord Drakesley.

"And to think of him helping two strangers!" she gushed. "I never met with such extraordinary consideration. And in a man of his rank, too! He put me forcibly in mind of the Good Samaritan."

"The extremely reluctant Samaritan," said Lilah tartly, dropping into her chair with an indignant flounce. "You know you are talking nonsense, Picky. Why, he threatened at one point to put us out on the road simply because my name is Chadwick! The only extraordinary thing I saw in Lord Drakesley's conduct was his arrogance. Now *that*, I will own, is something out of the common way." She shook out her napkin with an angry snap, then paused. It hit her, all of a sudden, that she was maligning her hostess's nephew. She felt the color rush into her face, and her gaze flew guiltily to Polly Peabody.

Mrs. Peabody looked merely thoughtful. "It's true that Drake can be high-handed," she said agreeably. "He means well—most of the time— but I have often told him that his temper will be the death of him."

Lilah bit her lip, scarlet with shame. "I am so sorry," she said in a strangled voice. "I should not have said such things of your nephew. I am afraid I am . . . not myself this morning."

Mrs. Peabody smiled very kindly. "Never mind, my dear. You had a difficult evening last night, did you not?" She turned to Miss Pickens and confided, as if it were the most natural thing in the world: "Drake kissed her, you know."

Lilah gasped. The color burning in her cheeks seemed to drain in a heartbeat. And to think that, two minutes ago, she had thought Polly Peabody's eccentric informality *charming*!

Miss Pickens, frozen with her teacup halfway to her mouth, looked as if she had been turned to stone. Her goggling expression might have struck Lilah as comical, had she not been too horrified to appreciate it.

Mrs. Peabody appeared oblivious to Lilah's and Miss Pickens's reaction to her simple statement. She continued speaking, placidly spooning sugar into her tea. "We did not actually see them kiss, but what we did see was more than sufficient to tell us what had taken place. I wonder why Drake turned round and offered marriage to Eugenia, after demonstrating so conclusively his attraction to someone else? It strikes me as most peculiar. But perhaps I am old-fashioned." She glanced at the door and her face brightened. "Here is Nat at last."

Mr. Peabody rolled in, puffing and beaming, and nodded genially at the ladies. "Good morning, good morning, everyone. Good morning, my pet." He bent and planted a loud kiss on his wife's cheek, then straightened, rubbing his hands together with delight as he looked from Lilah to Miss Pickens. "Ah! This is cozy. How d'ye do? Nathaniel Peabody. Don't believe we've met."

Miss Pickens half rose in confusion, murmuring a few disjointed phrases. Mr. Peabody shook her hand heartily and sat down, taking the presence of a complete stranger at his breakfast table entirely in stride. He stole a bit of scone off his wife's plate and asked, as he popped it in his mouth, "I say, where's Horace?"

His wife frowned scoldingly at him over the tops of her spectacles. "Behave yourself, Nat, for pity's sake. What will our guests think? Horace and Eugenia have gone to church."

"Ah, yes." He swallowed contentedly. "Sunday. I should have thought they'd give it a miss, after dancing all night—but I suppose they want to be there when the banns are read. Not bad, these scones." He winked at Lilah. "Scottish cook this morning. French chap resting up after last night. Have you tasted the porridge?"

Lilah stared at him. She had the oddest sensation that time had stopped, leaving her suspended forever in the breakfast room at Wexbridge Abbey. "No," she said, her voice sounding high and faint. "No, I have not. Excuse me, but did you say . . . banns? Banns being read?"

"That's right." He cocked an eyebrow at her. "What! Didn't you know? Horace told me he'd written you. Had a notion that's why you showed up here last night."

Lilah pressed a hand to her forehead. "Yes, but Papa's letter said nothing of *banns.* I had the impression that . . ." Her voice trailed off.

She had had the impression that Papa's marriage to Eugenia Mayhew was nothing more than a vague possibility, something being talked of, not prepared for. There was a vast gulf between a marriage proposal and the actual reading of banns. Banns were serious. Banns meant that the marriage might actually take place within a few weeks! How could matters have progressed so swiftly?

While Lilah struggled with her emotions, Mr. and Mrs. Peabody continued the conversation. Nat turned to Polly for confirmation. "It's the second reading of the banns, is it not, my love? Yes, yes, I thought so. Being read in Wiltshire, I daresay, as well as here. And up in the Lake District somewhere as well, Drakesley's parish. Have to publish 'em everywhere the parties reside. Or so I believe."

"Yes, I think that's right," said Polly. "Unless the couple marries by special license, of course."

"No need for that; Horace and Eugenia are a sensible pair. Always thought there was something unseemly about rushing down the aisle, not bothering with banns. Silly stuff! Almost as bad as an elopement, if you ask me. Which no one did, of course." He chuckled good-naturedly. "At any rate, they're expensive things, special licenses."

Miss Pickens chimed in. "I had a cousin who married by special license. So extravagant! But she was ever the impatient sort."

Lilah sat silent, inwardly seething. Everyone

was acting as if Papa's betrothal to Miss Mayhew was nothing more than an interesting event! Could they not see how outrageous, how unsuitable, the match was? Could they not understand the anguish it was causing Lilah? A strong sense of injury began to swell her bosom. She felt . . . betrayed. Overlooked. Her feelings, her opinions, her concerns, her very *dignity*, were being ignored. If the Peabodys were correct, and this was the second Sunday the banns were being read, Papa had planned to marry Miss Mayhew without even *introducing* her to his only child! Was she worth nothing to Papa? Was she actually a cipher in her own home? Tears of anger and hurt pricked Lilah's eyelids.

When Miss Pickens began clucking contentedly about how much she looked forward to meeting the future Lady Chadwick, Lilah could stand it no more. She flew up out of her chair, quivering with emotion. "This is intolerable!" she cried, flinging down her napkin. "Does no one have any consideration for *my* feelings? Am I to be passed over? Will my father marry a total stranger without so much as a by-your-leave? I seem to have strayed into a nightmare."

Three pairs of eyes fixed on her with expressions ranging from mild surprise (Nat Peabody) to outright distress (Miss Pickens). Mrs. Peabody tsked sympathetically. "There, there, dearie, it's not as bad as that," she said in the tone one uses to soothe a screaming two-year-old. "We know Eugenia so well, and think so highly of her, we never stopped to think how the situation might strike you. Once you have had a chance to become acquainted with her—"

"I don't wish to become acquainted with her!" Lilah cried. She knew she sounded irrational as well as uncivil, but she was past caring. "I wish to return to Wiltshire with Papa and go on just as we always have!"

She had to stop herself from blurting out, *And I want my mother!* She pushed a fist into her mouth to keep from sobbing aloud, and fled the room.

But this was terrible. She was in a completely strange house. Her breath hitching, she ran into a disused salon across the hall from the breakfast room and slammed the door behind her. It was cold and dark, with no fire lit and the draperies pulled across the window embrasure. She didn't care. Cold and dark matched her mood beautifully. She vented her feelings by delivering a few savage kicks to a tufted ottoman, then sank onto the closest sofa, buried her face in an embroidered pillow, and wept like a child.

Exactly like a child. Good God, this was appalling. Shameful. What on earth was the matter with her? Why had all her emotions boiled up to the surface like this? She was carrying on like a madwoman. A *rude* madwoman, since she had begun her outburst at the Peabodys' breakfast table.

She sat up, struggling to scold herself back into control. What would Drake think if he saw her like this?

Now, there was another stupid thought. Why should she care what Drake thought of her? She didn't care. She didn't care. He was an ally at the moment, but not a permanent friend.

Somehow that thought made her even more miserable. It did, however, stiffen her spine. She dashed the tears from her cheeks with a resolute hand and took a deep breath. Enough. She would find Drake and tell him the latest bit of news. He may be the most irritating man on the face of the planet, but at least he was capable. If anyone could help her out of the present emergency, it was he.

She rose, shook out her skirts, and walked out of the room with her head high. She would keep a grip on her turbulent emotions, she promised herself. Even if, in order to accomplish this, she had to ignore two uncomfortable facts: that the very notion of going to find Drake had inexplicably lifted her spirits, and that no degree of urgency was sufficient to keep her from washing her face and tucking her hair back into place before she went.

Merely seeing Drake, of course, would neither strengthen nor comfort her. He had no magic power to make her feel better. It was absurd to feel more cheerful at the very thought of him. He might come up with an idea, but she knew perfectly well that he might not. This sense of pleasurable anticipation, this weird bubble of excitement, defied logic. It must be due to some disorder of her nerves.

12

Bribing a junior housemaid to tell her which of the bedchambers housed Lord Drakesley was the work of a moment. Lilah marched to the door and raised her hand to knock—then paused. The wondering eyes of the housemaid, fixed on her with a combination of awe and disapproval, reminded Lilah of the awkwardness of her situation. A young lady could hardly visit a single gentleman in his bedchamber. Pounding on his door and entreating him to come out would doubtless be beyond the line as well. She hesitated, then reluctantly let her hand fall.

"Thank you," she told the housemaid, with a nice air of hauteur. "That will be all."

The girl looked as if she would like to stay and see what Lilah did, but she obediently ducked a curtsy and scurried away. Alone in the dimly lit hall outside Drake's door, Lilah stood, irresolute. Was Drake asleep or awake? There was nothing to give her a clue. And the morning habits of gentlemen were, naturally, beyond her ken.

She leaned cautiously forward and pressed her ear against the door. Nothing. She listened at the keyhole. Nothing. After a swift glance up and down the hall to make sure she was unobserved, she took a deep breath and pressed her *eye* to the keyhole. She was almost relieved when this maneuver, too, elicited no information.

Lilah stood up, frowning. She tapped her foot against the carpet and thought. If Drake was still asleep, which seemed likely, she must wake him somehow. It was vital that she speak with him before Papa and Miss Mayhew returned from church. Knocking on his door was unacceptable, but there must be some other method, more subtle than knocking, she could employ.

She cleared her throat experimentally, then coughed. She coughed loudly and repeatedly, then produced a false sneeze that was almost a shout: "Ah-tishoo!" Hopeful, she listened for a response, her ears on the prick. Even a rustle or a creak might indicate that she had disturbed his slumbers, but she could discern nothing through the thick planks of oak.

"Drat," she muttered. Why couldn't the Peabodys live in a modern house with proper doors? These old abbeys were like fortresses.

She wandered down the hall to the next door, which was slightly ajar, and peeked in. Her eyes brightened. What luck! The room contained a harpsichord, probably moved to this disused room after the Peabodys acquired a newer, more fashionable, pianoforte. A trumpet might have been better for her purpose, but beggars could not be choosers. Besides, Lilah didn't know how to play a trumpet.

She ran lightly to the window and opened it, hoping to amplify the music's effect in the room next door, then sat at the keyboard and began to play. There was no music, so Lilah was forced to rely upon memory. This limited her repertoire, but no matter. She played the same two pieces, several times over, with gusto, then ran back and slammed the door to the music room a couple of times for good measure. Now *that,* she thought triumphantly, would wake a stone.

She tiptoed back to Drake's door and listened again, holding her breath. Nothing! Incredulous, she rocked back on her heels and stared at the doorknob as if her will alone could make it turn. The man must sleep like the dead. What more could she do?

There was a technique she had read about in a book. It was a work of fiction, but the idea sounded good. Determined to try it, she hurried back down the hall and found her way, by trial and error, to an outside door leading to the back garden. By careful counting, she divined which window belonged to Drake's bedchamber and trotted along the gravel path until she was beneath it. Then she bent and picked up a handful of gravel.

The window seemed much farther from the ground than she had thought it would be. Never mind. She leaned back, mentally calculated the distance, and threw. The gravel spattered against the plaster wall beneath the window. No good. She picked up another handful and threw harder. This time, the gravel pinged and rattled in a most satisfactory way against the glass.

She waited, hopeful. Surely Drake's head would appear in the window at any moment. Time passed. More time passed. Nothing! Lilah shook her head in disbelief. Did the man stuff cotton wool in his ears before retiring?

This time, she would wake him for sure. She picked up another, bigger handful of gravel, and threw it with all her might.

Four things happened almost simultaneously. Lilah realized she had inadvertently included a fair-size rock among the pebbles, the gravel hit the window, the rock broke the window, and someone grabbed her from behind.

Lilah screamed.

Drake's arms tightened around her like a vise. "What the devil do you think you're doing?" he thundered.

Lilah squirmed frantically, turning in his arms to face him. "Oh! Oh! You odious man," she panted, shuddering. "Look what you made me do!"

"I made you? I made you vandalize my aunt's home?" He seemed ready to strangle her. "Good God, what next will you accuse me of?"

Half mad with the horror of what she had done, Lilah beat her fist impotently against Drake's chest. "What are you doing here?" she cried. "You nearly scared the life out of me. I thought you were abed!"

"For God's sake, woman, it's nearly noon! I was taking a walk. What are *you* doing here? This had better be good, Lilah—I'm ready to hand you over to a constable!"

Lilah gasped. "I am not a criminal!"

"No? Then what in thunderation *are* you? Why are you standing out in the garden breaking windows?"

Tears of mortification pricked Lilah's eyes, but she blinked them back. She would not cry. Not again! "I am not breaking windows," she told him hotly. "Not deliberately, at any rate. I am trying to wake you."

His amber eyes widened with incredulity. "You're mad as a hatter."

"I didn't know you were already awake!"

"Obviously! But why not send a servant to

wake me? Or was that too easy?" He shook his head in disgust. "You always choose the most dramatic means you can think of, to accomplish the simplest of tasks. If a fly landed on your arm, you'd shoot a pistol at it."

"That's not true!" cried Lilah, stung. Her innate honesty compelled her to add, "Not entirely true, at any rate. I did try simpler ways, before I threw the gravel. But—" Her face crumpled. "Oh, this is terrible. I have broken the window. What will the Peabodys think of me?" She covered her face with her hands.

"Never mind," said Drake gruffly. He patted her awkwardly. "I'll tell them I did it. They are never surprised by anything I do."

Even in her distress, Lilah had to chuckle. She shook her head, however, dropping her hands from her face. "You are not to take the blame for my bad behavior," she told him staunchly. "Why should you? Although I appreciate the offer, of course."

She smiled up at him—and suddenly felt a bit shy. With a start, she realized she was gripping the lapels of his morning coat, and that his hands were linked behind her waist. It had felt so natural to be in his arms, she had thought nothing of it until this moment. Now she felt a blush heating her face.

He seemed to read the realization in her face,

and obviously sensed that she was about to pull away from him, for his arms tightened behind her. "Don't go," he said hoarsely.

Something in his voice made her feel all weak and shivery.

"Drake," she said, with an effort, "you know we agreed, last night that we mustn't be alone together." She took a deep breath. "We must be careful," she said unsteadily, addressing his neck cloth. She dared not look higher.

"Yes," he said. His voice still sounded strained. "You're right. There's no telling what might happen."

He had said the right words, but he hadn't let her go. Lilah peeped up at his face for half a second, and was caught. His eyes seemed to burn into hers, holding her captive, drowning her will. She stared helplessly at him. His face seemed to grow larger, filling the world, and she realized his head was bending down to hers.

"Damn," he muttered, in a voice of despair. And kissed her.

Oh, dear.

It was all wrong. But it felt so right. Some secret part of her had been longing for him to kiss her again, had been waiting for this very moment. That dark corner of her soul somehow overruled her sensible, everyday self. The everyday Lilah was too demoralized to make even a token protest; Drake's kiss was too important, too necessary, to her secret self. Thoroughly routed, her common sense surrendered without a whimper and clung to Drake with the rest of her, melting instinctively into his embrace as if she belonged there.

But she didn't belong there. Drake wanted to marry Miss Mayhew, and she had to help him. It was hard to remember why. . . . Things that had seemed important a few moments ago now seemed utterly insignificant. Confused, Lilah gave herself up to the moment. Now *this* . . . this was worth savoring. It wouldn't last forever. So she clutched Drake's lapels and held on, riding waves of sensation that somehow became waves of emotion, and she kissed him and kissed him and kissed him.

It was Drake who eventually broke away. He lifted his face from hers, growling as if in pain. "Stop it!" he ordered, apparently struggling for breath.

Lilah blinked dazedly at him. "Stop what?"

And then reality returned in a rush. She was standing on a garden path, in broad daylight, in full view of God alone knew how many windows, kissing Lord Drakesley for all the world to see. Horrified, she gave a frantic shove to Drake's shoulders. "Let me go!"

He did, and she stumbled backward. They stared at each other for a moment. Drake looked furious. "Let you go? With a good will, madam!

You may wipe that look of outraged innocence off your face. Who tempted whom?"

"*What?*" Lilah's voice cracked with incredulous wrath. "Don't you dare imply that *I* started that!"

"You damn well did."

"Oh! Oh, you—you—you *monster*! You coxcomb! I never knew such arrogance—such conceit—" Lilah fairly spluttered with rage. "I would never dream of throwing myself at a man! And if I did, you would be the last man on earth—"

"Oh, spare me," he said witheringly. "I was here, remember? You threw, and I caught. But, next time"—he shook his finger menacingly—"next time, Lilah, I will have my guard up."

Lilah felt her jaw drop. This was mind-boggling. She longed to box his ears. Or slap him. Or at least swear! Why couldn't a lady swear? "Hell's bells!" she shouted, and felt marginally better. "I did nothing! Nothing whatsoever! You came up behind me—"

"While you were hurling missiles—"

"—and grabbed me. You *attacked* me!"

His fists clenched. "The only reason I grabbed you, you crazy little harpy, was to keep you from breaking more windows!"

She advanced on him, quivering with fury. "I was only aiming at *your* window!"

"Oh, I see," he said sarcastically. "Once it lay

196

in smithereens, the others were in no danger. Pardon me! I failed to realize that."

"I will *not* pardon you," she cried. "You are sarcastic, and sneering, and contemptible! And you think *I* kissed *you*? How dare you?"

"You made the first move."

"I did not!"

"Yes, you did."

"Well, what was it?" she demanded, so angry she could barely speak. "What, exactly, do you think I did to provoke your—your *hideous* advances?"

"You held on to me," he snarled. "Like this." He seized her shoulders. "And then you *looked* at me. And *smiled*." He was apparently too angry to demonstrate this, judging by the ferocious glare that accompanied these words. "And then you . . ." Here, Drake seemed to lose his train of thought. He stared at her, a muscle jumping in his jaw. Lilah lifted her chin and gave him stare for stare, her eyes narrowed with fury.

"Yes?" she said icily.

He dropped his hands from her shoulders to her upper arms. His fingers caressed her flesh through the thin muslin of her morning dress, as if they had taken on a life of their own and could not help themselves. "Confound it, woman," he almost shouted. "You're doing it again!"

"I'm doing *nothing!*"

"Yes, you are." He looked half crazed. His amber eyes bored into hers. "You're being Lilah." His voice had softened, roughened. It turned her name into a caress. Lilah shivered with the shock of it; she could feel that whisper of her name all through her, like fire licking through her veins. It gave her gooseflesh, hearing her name on his lips like that, in such a voice.

And then he said it again. "Lilah," he whispered. "Lilah."

Madness seized them both. It was impossible to tell whether she had flung herself into his arms or he had crushed her into a bear hug, but there they were, against all odds, overcome with passion yet again. It was the most baffling, terrifying experience of Lilah's life—and the most exciting. This time, however, enough of her anger remained to cause her to pull her face away, gasping, "No! No! Good God, are you *insane*? Stop!"

But Drake continued to rain kisses on her face and hair. "There's nothing for it," he muttered despairingly. "I shall have to marry you."

"No," said Lilah sharply. She took his face firmly in her hands to stop him from kissing her nose. "For heaven's sake, control yourself! You do not want to marry me. You are going to marry Miss Mayhew."

"How can I? All I think about is you. Touching you. Kissing you. You're driving me mad."

"It—it will pass," said Lilah shakily. "It must. We don't even like each other, Drake."

"You don't like me?" He looked so comically wounded, Lilah had to bite her lip to keep from laughing.

"Oh, very well! I suppose I do like you," she admitted. "A little. But it doesn't matter, Drake. I could not live with you."

He sighed. For a moment, he rested his forehead against hers. "Right," he said. "Right. Then why do we keep having this conversation?"

"I don't know," she said in a small voice. She wished he would take his face away from hers; his nearness made her nervous. Or something. "Drake . . . please."

He sighed again, and let her go. Lilah took a deep breath. It was like coming into clear air after being underwater. Suddenly she remembered what it was that had sent her in search of Drake in the first place. Her eyes widened.

"Merciful heavens! What time is it? They'll be home from church at any moment—if they are not here already."

"Oh, did the Peabodys go to church? I assumed we had all slept through it."

"No, no—Papa went, with Miss Mayhew. I suppose they drove to Kensington, since that's where he has a house. Drake, did you know they are reading the banns?"

He looked as thunderstruck as she had felt upon hearing the news. "Banns! Already? *Banns*?"

"Yes, and they are being published today for the *second* time."

"The devil!"

He stood stock-still. She shook his sleeve anxiously, searching his face for some sign of what he might be thinking. "We've only one more week in which to act. Can you . . . would you . . . object to the banns?"

He stared down at her, consternation writ large on his face. "Stand up in church next week, d'ye mean? When they ask if anyone present knows of an impediment to the marriage?"

"Yes, that's right. I've never seen it done—"

"Nor have I!"

"—but the words must be there for a reason."

"I suppose so." Drake looked a little pale. He rubbed his chin, apparently trying to picture himself standing up at the crucial moment. "There must be more to it than simply raising an objection. What actual impediment is there? I can't say, 'This chap can't marry her because I wish to.' I'll look like an idiot."

Lilah hadn't thought that far ahead. She bit

her lip, crestfallen. "Oh, dear. What impediments *are* there, then, to two persons marrying?"

He looked doubtful. "Consanguinity is one. Good luck to us, trying to prove Sir Horace is Eugenia's long-lost uncle or something."

Lilah shuddered and changed the subject. "What about bigamy? I'm sure bigamy is considered grounds to bar a marriage."

He looked exasperated. "Is your father married to someone else? No? Well, neither is Eugenia, so we'll have to think again."

"You needn't sneer at me," Lilah snapped. "I am only trying to help."

"Help whom? It's *you* who wishes to stop their precious marriage."

Lilah set her arms akimbo and stared at Drake. "Oh, really? This is news to me! How do you propose to marry Eugenia if she marries my father first?" Her eyes narrowed, and she pointed a finger at Drake. "You're deliberately picking a quarrel with me. Aren't you?"

"No, I am not!" He ran his hand through his hair, as he always did when agitated, and the chestnut locks immediately sprang up into thick cowlicks. They glinted beautifully, red and brown and gold in the sunlight. "There's something about you, you little witch. You rattle me."

Lilah, absurdly pleased, returned her hands to her hips. It was deeply satisfying to know that she rattled Drake, since he definitely rattled her. "Hmph!" she sniffed, feigning disapproval. "I might have known you would blame me somehow. It's my belief you're queer in your attic."

She turned her back on him and marched toward the house. She was ashamed to admit it, but it gave her pleasure to hear his feet crunching on the gravel and know he was following her, cajoling and threatening and expostulating and . . . being Drake.

Seeing that the twosome were heading back toward the house, Eugenia and Polly drew hastily back from the library window. They needn't have bothered; Drake and Lilah were too focused on each other to spare a glance upward.

The women said nothing. They returned to their chairs and picked up the needlework they had discarded a few minutes ago, when the sound of breaking glass had sent them flying to look out the window.

Neither plied her needle. Both stared into space for a few moments. Eugenia's face was puzzled, but Polly looked merely reflective. A little smile played around the corners of her mouth. "Fascinating," she murmured at last.

Eugenia had the grace to blush. "Oh, Aunt! We ought not to have spied on them."

Polly waved a dismissive hand. "We're only

human. It was irresistible," she pronounced. "And besides, it was most instructive."

"Was it?" Eugenia looked dubious. "I confess, I don't understand what I saw. They fought with each other, then kissed, then fought, then kissed again, then fought again—why, it's ludicrous! But, of course, we were unable to hear their discussion. Perhaps their behavior made perfect sense, in the context of their quarrel."

"I doubt it," said Polly serenely. "I daresay the scene would have made even less sense, had we been able to hear it." She chuckled. "Words convey so little. They are frequently more a hindrance than a help, when the heart is overfull."

Eugenia shook her head, still mystified. "I hope, then, that my heart is never overfull."

"You have a placid nature, like mine. We are fortunate. Drake, poor boy, inherited the Harleston temperament. He is subject to storms of emotion that I daresay we shall never know."

"Yes. He has a strong personality." Eugenia picked up her embroidery hoop and studied the pattern. "That," she said in a faraway voice, "is why I never wanted to marry him. It must seem strange, that I would choose Horace over Drake—"

"Not at all," said Polly quickly. "Not to the family, my dear. We all love Drake—"

"Oh, yes! So do I."

"—but he would make you a poor husband."

Eugenia nodded. She set a tiny stitch, then glanced at her aunt, almost shyly. "I am glad you understand. I do not think Drake would make *every* woman a poor husband. But when Horace and I are together, I feel cherished and important. When Drake and I are together, I feel"—she smiled wryly—"invisible."

Polly glanced affectionately at her niece. "You were ever a sensible girl, Eugenia. I feel quite certain you have made the right choice. Drake values you, I believe—why, we all do!—and of course he doesn't mean to bully people, but he does tend to ignore the wishes of those who don't express themselves as forcefully as he does. And that group includes, unfortunately, nearly everyone." Polly tapped her chin, thinking. "I wonder . . ."

Eugenia looked up, a question on her face. Polly smiled slowly and nodded. "It seems to me," she said softly, "that Drake and Miss Chadwick are cut from the same cloth."

Eugenia's eyes twinkled. "She certainly seems willing to shout him down—which I never could, you know."

"Pooh! You are not a shouter. But Miss Chadwick . . . Miss Chadwick has a fine set of lungs."

Eugenia stifled a laugh behind her hand. "Oh, this is bad! We shouldn't try to play Cupid. Pray recall how vehemently they denied that there was any attachment between them."

"A little *too* vehemently, I thought."

Eugenia looked startled. "What! Did you think them insincere?"

"Not at all."

Eugenia set her embroidery hoop in her lap and stared at her aunt. Polly chuckled. "I do not profess to understand it any better than you do, my dear, but I have rather more experience of the world than you. I promise you, it is often thus, when two strong-willed persons have the misfortune to fall in love." She looked dreamily back at the window, as if recalling what they had just witnessed. "Yes," she mused. "I would not be a bit surprised if that is, in fact, what ails them."

"Really? I would be astonished," said Eugenia frankly. "Why would a couple who loved each other quarrel so much?"

Polly looked very wise. "Falling in love requires a degree of surrender. Those two"—her voice softened—"those two will resist surrender with every fiber of their beings."

"I see." Eugenia thought for a moment. "I hope you are right on one count. I hope Lilah will . . . resist surrender." She leaned anxiously forward, addressing her aunt in a low, hurried tone. "It seems to me that, whatever their opinion of each other may be, they share a—a mutual passion. Drake can be difficult to withstand when all he wants from you is a walk in the park or a button sewn on! I cannot imagine anyone having the fortitude to hold him at bay, were he pursuing something he strongly desires."

Polly looked troubled. "They will have to marry."

"But how are we to engineer such a thing? We cannot allow Drake to compromise her. Pray recall that Lilah will be my stepdaughter! I am, in a sense, responsible for her welfare. I cannot permit her to run into danger."

Polly choked. Eugenia saw that her aunt was struggling to hold back laughter. "Tell that to Lilah," said Polly in an unsteady voice. "If you dare."

Eugenia felt the corners of her mouth begin to twitch. And then, despite the seriousness of their conversation, the two women fell into a fit of helpless laughter.

"Oh, dear," said Eugenia at last, gulping air to control her mirth. "It's wrong to laugh. I really *am* responsible for Lilah—in a way."

"Rubbish. If Sir Horace cannot check her, how can you? You mustn't try to assert your stepmotherly authority, my dear. If you provoke her, she is liable to run directly counter to your advice—and, really, I could hardly blame her if she did, poor child. Her father's betrothal has been a severe shock to her."

"Has it? I was afraid of that." Eugenia sighed. "I did try to talk Horace into inviting her to London, so she could meet me and attend the wedding. But he thought it better to surprise her. The most I could persuade him to do was send a letter—and he refused to do even that much until the banns were being read."

Polly's lips pursed in cynical amusement. "It occurs to me, my love, that Sir Horace is a little afraid of his tempestuous daughter."

"Oh, no, Aunt. He loves her very much."

"I didn't mean to imply a lack of affection between them. But I have the distinct impression that Lilah rules the roost at Chadwick Hall." Her eyes twinkled. "It would be a very good thing, Eugenia, if you could marry her off to Drake. Otherwise, I very much fear you will never be mistress in your own home."

Eugenia, in the act of threading a needle, paused. Trouble flitted across her features. "You may be right," she said at last. "I have never played matchmaker before, however. I find such machinations repellent."

"I'm sure your sentiments do you credit, my dear. But in my experience, a little push never did any harm. If Drake and Lilah are not right for each other, your efforts will not bear fruit.

If, on the other hand, they are . . . then hurrying matters along may do a great deal of good."

Eugenia pondered this for a moment. "It would have to be done very delicately," she murmured, as if to herself. "They mustn't guess my object."

"Very true. Anything blatant will only anger them."

She thought for a moment more, then suddenly colored up, shaking her head as if startled from sleep. "Heavens! The notion is absurd. I have no power to make two people fall in love."

Polly was conscious of a strong sense of disappointment. "No," she agreed, then sighed. "But if you think of any way, my dear Eugenia, to make two people who have *already* fallen in love, come to their senses and realize it—I beg you will not hesitate to act."

13

"I have an idea." Drake's eyes held a wicked gleam.

Lilah looked up at him warily. "What is it?"

"You won't like it."

They were strolling in the garden—decorously, and side by side. Eugenia and Sir Horace had successfully evaded them thus far, much to their mutual frustration. Even at luncheon, when Drake and Lilah had been sure they would have a chance to arrange private conversation with the betrothed couple, the Peabodys had intervened and squelched their every manuever. On Polly's part, at least, this had seemed deliberate—and she proved maddeningly skillful at heading them off. Lilah strongly suspected that Miss Mayhew, or Sir Horace, or both of them together, had pleaded with their hostess to protect them from Lilah and Drake. Drake thought the same, and they had just spent a refreshing half hour roundly vilifying their family members.

Lilah tucked her head down to hide her smile. She was feeling in charity with Drake at the moment; he had, in fact, taken the blame for his broken window. It was an unexpectedly chivalrous move on his part, and Lilah was grateful for it. He would pay for the damage, and she would repay him out of her pin money, and no one would be the wiser. She had an uncomfortable suspicion that nobody had believed Drake when he said he broke it. Despite his assurance that his family thought him such an odd duck, Polly Peabody and Miss Mayhew had both appeared surprised when he "confessed."

She twirled her parasol and looked back up at him. "Very well; I have been warned. Tell me your bad idea."

"First, an observation. I think you will agree that our confrontation last night had little effect."

"None whatsoever! But we haven't actually presented our arguments. We had no chance."

"Nevertheless, there is no time to waste in wearing Sir Horace and Eugenia down. We'll have to try something more drastic." He shot a keen glance down at Lilah. "What was it that brought you hotfoot to London?"

"Papa's letter."

He shook his head and corrected her. "Emotion. Fear, to be precise. Strong emotion is the only thing that spurs a person to swift action."

"Oh, I see." She frowned. "But what is your point? We cannot frighten Papa and Miss Mayhew into calling off their engagement. How could we?"

"I can't speak for your father. But I think we can frighten my Jenny a little."

Lilah raised an eyebrow and started to say something, but Drake held up a warning finger. "Let me finish. You know she declined my offer last night. But we agreed, after the fact, that she may have felt pressure to do so. I think I know a way to discover her true feelings. Speedily." His eyes met hers, his expression an odd combination of dogged determination and sly mischief. "Let's pretend that you and I are falling in love."

Lilah stared at him. A very queer feeling churned inside her, and alarm bells seemed to ring out a warning along all her nerves. *Danger!* Several seconds passed before she could trust herself to reply. Then she took a careful breath, and spoke.

"Well. If that's your idea, you are absolutely right," she said cordially. "I don't like it."

His rare grin flickered. "Remember, I can personally vouch for the power of jealousy. I had only the vaguest notion that I might marry Eugenia one day, until I learned she was on the brink of marrying someone else."

Lilah looked at him in a fascinated way. "So

you think that if Eugenia believed you were on the brink of marrying someone else, she would instantly realize she had made a terrible mistake, break off her engagement to Papa, and fall at your feet."

"That's right." He winked at her. "We'll fight fire with fire."

Lilah's chin assumed a stubborn tilt. "Those who fight fire with fire get doubly burned. No, no, and no. I won't do it."

Anger sparked in the back of his eyes. "It's the best plan we've come up with yet."

"It's the only plan we've come up with yet. There must be a better way."

"Since we haven't thought of another, why not try this one?"

"Why *not*?" Lilah shuddered. "Because it's dangerous. And it's ridiculous! You can't play with people's emotions like that; such schemes only work in fiction. In real life, people are completely unpredictable. There's no guarantee she will fall on your neck just because she thinks she can't have you. What if Miss Mayhew turns out to be a rational creature, not subject to fits of jealousy? That's just remotely possible, you know."

Lilah's sarcasm evidently did not offend Drake. "Blast," he muttered, looking chagrined. "It's more than possible. It's probable. Eugenia was always the sensible type."

"There, then!" said Lilah triumphantly. "Besides, it would be extremely difficult to pretend to fall in love. I daresay we wouldn't fool anyone."

She had to look away when she said that, to give it the proper airy tone. It still sounded oddly unconvincing. She wished she hadn't brought up that particular objection. There were some things better left unsaid, and this was one of them. Mentioning how hard it would be to pretend to fall in love had immediately made her picture how *easy* it would be, if the supposed object of her affections were Drake.

She felt his touch, warm against her glove. He pulled her hand up and tucked it in the corner of his elbow, covering it with his. "Would it be that difficult for you?" he asked. His voice was low and rough. "I think I could do it."

Lilah, as usually happened when he touched her, had to remind herself to breathe normally. "I was never any good at pretense," she said, willing her voice to not shake. "I know you think me overly dramatic, and I suppose I am. I must be; everyone accuses me of it. But that's not the same thing as acting a part."

"I've no talent for playacting, either." He gave a short, mirthless laugh. "But all I need do, to behave exactly as if I'm in love with you, is turn off my brain."

Lilah choked. "And *that*, I suppose, comes

naturally to you," she remarked. "Alas, I am not accustomed to turning off my brain, and cannot promise that I would make a convincing nincompoop."

"You're extremely convincing," he said encouragingly. "In fact, I believed you were a nincompoop the first time I met you."

She looked daggers at him. "Nevertheless, I suggest we try an alternate method."

"Is there one?"

"Rather! Remember, we haven't yet done what we set out to do. There's no reason to think our original plan won't work. We never had an opportunity to try it."

"I've forgotten. What was our original plan?"

"Turn your brain back on," suggested Lilah. "Our original plan was simply to persuade Papa and Miss Mayhew, singly or together, to break their engagement. Miss Mayhew will then be free to wed you—if she so chooses, although I cannot hold out much hope that such a sensible creature will have you—and Papa will be free to seek a more suitable partner, a lady closer to him in age."

Drake looked glum. "It all sounded perfectly reasonable a couple of days ago. I confess, my optimism has faded."

"So has mine," Lilah admitted. "But if we do not try, we may regret it all our days."

They reached the end of the Peabodys' avenue

of oaks and turned to promenade back toward the house, Lilah's hand still tucked in Drake's arm. Drake glanced down at Lilah. "It occurs to me—having turned my brain back on—that we still have one element of surprise left to us."

"Do we? How so?"

"They are clearly avoiding us because they know we are itching to make our case, and they don't care to hear our arguments. Eugenia expects to hear from me. Your father will, likewise, expect to hear from you—doubtless at great length and with elevated pitch and volume."

Lilah had learned, by now, that it was a mistake to react when Drake needled her. She sighed in a long-suffering way, but did not rise to his bait. "Your point being—?" she prompted him.

He chuckled, showing that he was well aware of the restraint she was displaying. "I think," he said mildly, "that you and I should switch targets."

Lilah cocked her head, regarding him approvingly from beneath the brim of her bonnet. "That's not bad," she told him. "If you mean that I should speak with Miss Mayhew and you should approach Papa."

"That is exactly what I mean."

Lilah thought for a moment. "It could work," she said. "I must say, Papa has grown inured to my tactics over the years. A fresh voice, a fresh style, might be more persuasive. And, of course, he will not like to contradict you—something he has no compunction about when it is only his daughter making the argument."

"Precisely. Eugenia, similarly, has acquired a distressing habit of humoring me rather than actually listening to me. I am hopeful that she will show you more courtesy."

Sudden doubt shook Lilah. "But, surely—you do not expect me to act as a go-between? I couldn't possibly propose marriage to Miss Mayhew on your behalf."

Drake's shoulders shook. "I'd love to be a fly on the wall while you tried it! But no, I don't think that will be necessary. I proposed to her last night, you will recall. All I need you to do is sow a few doubts about the wisdom of her present course, plead my case a little, and let the idea simmer for a while. Meanwhile, I will try to explain to your father why the most chivalrous course for him would be to give Eugenia up—nobly, you know, so she might marry the better man."

Lilah shrugged one shoulder pettishly. "I wish you would disabuse your mind of this silly notion that you are a better man than my father. You are a younger man, and you outrank him, but you are not *better* than Papa."

She wasn't sure why she was feeling cross and unsettled. Drake seemed to understand, however, which surprised her a little. He halted on the gravel path, forcing her to stop and look up at him. His hooded eyes gleamed down at her, their expression serious but unreadable.

"It's not my intent to disparage your father," he said. "It would have been, two days ago. Not today. It's easy to vilify a man you've never met. It's easy to blame others for your own shortcomings, when you've never had to face your shortcomings. I'm facing them now, Lilah, and I'm no longer sure of anything. I'm not even sure that I'm the best man for Eugenia to marry." His hand covered hers again, and his eyes darkened. "I'm not sure I'm right for Eugenia, and I'm not sure Eugenia is right for me. And if anyone had told me two days ago that I could become this unsure, this quickly, about something I have always been so sure about . . ." He shook his head, seeming both angry and bewildered.

As if moving of its own volition, Lilah's hand turned and clasped Drake's. "I understand," she said in a low voice. "But I think at times like this, when we know we are not behaving rationally, all we can do is hearken back to the time when our minds were clear—and follow the course we set then."

His eyes searched hers. "I hope you are right," he said hoarsely. "Because that is what I think, too. We must try to accomplish what we set out to accomplish. We must try to achieve

217

the goals we set when we could think straight. As God is my witness, I want nothing more than to chuck it all. But I know I'm not thinking straight . . . because all I can think about is you."

Lilah gave a shaky little laugh. "If you are thinking of nothing but me, then you are definitely a bit addled. I know, because all I ever think about is you, and it's driving me completely round the bend."

Miss Mayhew proved remarkably difficult to move. For such a plain Jane, she certainly held a good opinion of herself. Lilah lured her into a private audience on the pretext of wishing to become better acquainted, then launched into an assault on the pairing of younger women with older men. She tried charm, then flattery, and finally a tearful plea calculated to appeal to Miss Mayhew's sympathies. Miss Mayhew's poise remained unshaken. At the end of Lilah's carefully crafted presentation, Miss Mayhew still sat serene, regarding her with calm and friendly attention. Lilah's impassioned words had evidently had no effect whatsoever.

She dropped into a nearby chair, exhausted. Miss Mayhew smiled kindly at her. "I hope you will not think me stubborn," she said. Her voice had a soft, diffident quality. "I believe I understand what your feelings must be, and I am heartily sorry to be the cause of your distress.

But I cannot alter such a momentous decision merely to please you."

Lilah eyed her with hostility. "What of Drake?" she demanded. "You could alter your decision to please Drake."

Miss Mayhew's eyes slid away in a manner that struck Lilah as furtive. She gazed out the window in a meditative way. "I could," she agreed. "But it would be rather silly of me, don't you think?"

"Not at all," countered Lilah, sitting bolt upright. "Throughout the ages, women have made life-altering decisions based on the preferences of the men they love."

Miss Mayhew's mild eyes returned to Lilah, studying her. "Indeed they have. And I'm very fond of Drake. But what of your father's preferences? Am I not to consider those? I think I should." Humor lit her features. "Particularly when his preferences march so well with mine."

The woman was infuriating. Lilah scowled at her. "I do not understand you," she complained. "How can you—how can any woman—wish to ally herself with a man old enough to be her father?"

Miss Mayhew colored. "Oh, come now. Hardly that. The disparity in our ages is only nineteen years."

"*Only?*" Lilah flew out of her chair in her agitation. "It is a lifetime! Not to mention that you will have a stepdaughter who is nearly your own age. How can you bear it?"

"Easily, I hope," said Miss Mayhew. Was that laughter quivering in her voice? "I have been looking forward to it with great pleasure. Lilah—may I call you Lilah?"

Lilah nodded mutely.

Her smile warmed. "And I hope you will call me Eugenia." She leaned forward in her chair, looking very earnest. "You must know little about my life, or you could not wonder at my attitude. I was orphaned at the age of eleven. My parents left me quite penniless, I'm afraid. The dowager Lady Drakesley was my father's second cousin, and it was she who offered me a home. Her son, Adam—Drake, you know— was my only companion—indeed, my closest friend—from that day until this. Whenever he was away at school, or off on his wanderings, I was desperately lonely. I have always secretly longed for a sister." The color had risen in Eugenia's cheeks again, but her eyes never left Lilah's face. "When your father told me of your existence, I rejoiced," she said softly.

A lump formed in Lilah's throat. Eugenia's brief history, so simply told, and ending with such a naked plea for friendship, could not but move her. She had to look away for a moment. "I am sorry," she said, hoping she did not sound too gruff. "I should not have . . . badgered you. I am only trying to comprehend your motives. So far, I'm afraid they escape me."

Eugenia folded her hands quietly in her lap. "Marriage is a contract. It is more than that, of course, but a contract it surely is. Your father and I are entering into an alliance that will, we hope, benefit both of us. Do I seem mercenary to you?"

At least the lady did not mince words. Relieved, Lilah faced her squarely. "No," she said levelly. "That is what I do not understand. If you were marrying for money and position, you would choose Drake."

"Not necessarily." Humor lit Eugenia's eyes again. "It is important, when marrying for position, that a lady know the position to which she is best suited. I would make a poor countess, I think. But mistress of a snug little property in Wiltshire? I confess, that life appeals to me strongly."

Lilah flung her arms wide. "But it's nonsensical!" she cried. "The life of a countess is far superior to that of a mere baronet's wife! My mother was a great lady in the neighborhood, but her sphere was woefully small. Think, Eugenia! You have lived among the aristocracy. Your life as Lady Chadwick will seem sadly flat compared to the life you have witnessed Drake's mother lead."

Eugenia laughed and wrinkled her nose.

"Important duties, vast responsibilities, arranging enormous parties and then having to play hostess at them—feeling all eyes upon you everywhere you go, your every utterance weighed and judged and repeated and occasionally finding its way into the gossip columns! No, thank you. Everyone around Lady Drakesley jockeys for position and tries to curry favor, until the unfortunate woman scarcely knows who her real friends are. I've no desire to lead a countess's life. In fact, I would hate it."

Lilah struggled to see Eugenia's point of view, and failed. How could any woman turn down a life of never-ending excitement, glamour, and high drama? A life where she would hold the reins, wielding power over a large and complicated household? A life where she would be forever the center of attention?

"Well," said Lilah frankly, "perhaps I am a shallow creature, but I would absolutely love it."

Eugenia's smile was suspiciously demure. "Mayhap *you* should marry Drake," she suggested, as if the idea had just occurred to her.

Lilah was not fooled. Eugenia's expression was just a shade too innocent. She glowered at her. "No," she said flatly. "I should not."

"Why not, pray?"

Lilah began flitting restlessly around the

room. "Well, for one thing, he wants to marry you," she said roundly.

"Oh, pooh." Eugenia pulled a face. "I wouldn't let a trifling thing like that stop me."

"But that's not all," exclaimed Lilah, exasperated. "Drake and I fight constantly. We can't seem to help it. We just naturally rub up against each other." That was an unfortunate image. Lilah corrected herself hastily. "What I mean is, we are too much alike."

"I have noticed that," said Eugenia thoughtfully. "It's really quite remarkable. You and Drake are like two sides of the same coin."

"I daresay we are. Unfortunately, two sides of the same coin can never see eye to eye," said Lilah firmly. "I've no desire to spend my days fighting over every little thing."

"Interesting," Eugenia commented. "Most people search for common ground in a life partner. But you seem to believe, as Drake does, that you would be happier with someone who is *unlike* you."

"Oh, yes. Of course I would! I saw such a match work well for my own parents, you know—a pairing of opposites. My mother was a lively, brilliant woman, but . . . volatile. My father is self-effacing and mild. He is never the brightest light at the dinner table, but he is utterly reliable. One can depend upon him."

"Yes," said Eugenia softly. "That is the quality that first drew me to him."

Lilah was suddenly aware that she was failing to make a case for Drake. "Drake has fine qualities, too," she reminded Eugenia desperately. "I do not think you should dismiss his suit out of hand."

Eugenia chuckled. "You would."

"That is an entirely different matter," said Lilah, annoyed. "Drake and I do not get along. That's not the case where you are concerned. He tells me you never argue with him at all."

"I do not enjoy confrontation."

Spineless, thought Lilah in disgust. It was clear from the look of reserve on Eugenia's face that she had frequently disagreed with Drake but had never asserted her own opinion. She disliked confrontation so much that she would rather knuckle under than oppose a more forceful personality. Just like Papa!

Still, Lilah would try to be diplomatic. "No one enjoys confrontation," she said soothingly. "But people like you—and my father, for that matter—are suited by nature to avoid it. Drake and I cannot control our tempers and must, therefore, marry someone who can."

Eugenia's lips tightened. "How pleasant it must be," she said tartly, "to have that luxury."

Lilah was startled. Perhaps Eugenia had some spirit after all. "What luxury do you mean?"

"Do you feel no obligation to consider the

feelings of others? I call that a luxury. I, for one, cannot afford it. I have never had the privilege of living with my will unopposed, my opinions unchallenged, and my every whim indulged."

Lilah sank back into her chair, intrigued. The worm, it seemed, was turning. "Is that the way Drake and I seem to you?" she asked.

"Frankly? Yes," said Eugenia. Her voice was still well modulated, but two spots of color had appeared high on her cheekbones and her backbone was very straight. "A man who has enjoyed high rank since infancy, and a cherished only daughter, are apparently reared with similar notions of their own importance."

"That may be," said Lilah, nettled. "Or it may be that we are born with our temperaments and cannot change them."

"Forgive me, but I think you choose to believe that, to soothe your conscience. After all, if you cannot change, you needn't try."

Lilah frowned. She must not let Eugenia goad her into losing her temper. "We are wandering rather far from the point," she said crisply. "Whatever the reason, whether a forceful personality is natural or induced by childhood indulgence, I think you will agree that some people *are* more fiery than others. More impulsive. Less controlled. But that is not to say that they are monsters. I have not known Drake long, but I see many virtues in him."

Amusement relaxed Eugenia's features. "By all means, let us talk of Drake," she offered. "What virtues do you see in him? Tell me, and I will let you know if you are near the mark or not. I have known him all my life."

Lilah smiled a little. At last, the conversation was heading in a direction she could steer. "I am not convinced that long acquaintance makes you see him more clearly," she said, assuming a worldly-wise expression. "In fact, I would not be a bit surprised to find that it has blinded you to his best features." She studied Eugenia for a moment, head cocked to one side. Eugenia was a little too sure of herself, Lilah decided. A little too placid. A little too remote. "Would it surprise you to learn that you have overlooked his virtues? You might very well be carrying about, in your head, a picture of Drake formed in your childhood—a picture he no longer resembles at all."

"A case of familiarity breeding contempt?"

"Something like that," said Lilah, pleased that Eugenia understood her. "For I cannot imagine a young woman who wishes to marry, wishing to marry my father when she could have a man like Drake."

Eugenia appeared surprised. "Does Drake seem to you a superior choice?"

Lilah's eyes widened in amazement. "Vastly superior! Beyond comparison. Eugenia, for heaven's sake, you are not blind! All other things being equal—which they are not!—surely you would rather marry a young and attractive man."

A very odd look descended on Eugenia's face. "You think Drake is attractive?"

On this subject, Lilah could speak with authority. "Excessively attractive," she said fervently. "Extraordinarily attractive." Eugenia's expression was so strange, Lilah felt she should elaborate. "I know my father is reckoned a handsome man, but he cannot compare to Drake! Drake must turn heads wherever he goes. I can't imagine women seeing him without being struck by it. His style is distinctive. Unique. His features are strong and powerful—but aristocratic, too. There is nothing coarse or common about him. One can tell at a glance that he is a man of breeding. His coloring, too, is so striking—that marvelous chestnut hair! And there is something so compelling about his face—"

"You would not call his features harsh?"

"Harsh? By no means! He scowls more often than he should—"

"More often than not, some would say," mused Eugenia.

"But his eyes . . ." Lilah shivered. "Those deep-set amber eyes. In some lights they look golden. His eyes are unforgettable."

"They are certainly unusual," Eugenia admitted.

"And there is something about a very large man that appeals to one," Lilah confided. "On some primal level."

"You do not think his size is intimidating? A bit overwhelming?"

"Certainly not. He is not a *giant*," said Lilah indignantly. "And you are taller than I, so if he does not strike me as too tall he should seem just right to you."

"Logic rarely applies in these matters," Eugenia murmured.

"But Drake's qualities go far beyond his physical attributes. He is more than merely handsome. And I am not speaking of material considerations, such as rank and fortune! I am speaking of the man himself." Lilah's eyes glowed with enthusiasm. "It is rare to meet a man of such keen intellect, don't you think? He has strong passions, sharp intelligence, a sense of humor—and, I think, high principles. Pray correct me if I am wrong." She raised an eyebrow in challenge.

Eugenia shook her head. "No, you are quite right. Drake is all these things and more. He does, in fact, have a strict sense of right and wrong and is a bit of a stickler for principle. In his way. And he does follow the rules . . . so long as the rules are of his own making."

"Admirable," said Lilah promptly. "All admirable. After all, nobody respects a man who slavishly follows the rules of others." She began ticking points off on her fingers. "He can be elegant—when the occasion warrants—but he is never overdressed or fussy. He is extremely observant. Witty. An excellent conversationalist."

"Oh, yes," Eugenia agreed. "Drake is never at a loss."

"And *there* we come to the crux of the issue." Lilah feared she was gushing like a dreamy-eyed schoolgirl, but could not help it. How else could she make Eugenia see Drake as he really was? "Drake is the most exciting person I have ever met. Whatever difficulties might arise in your married life, you would never, ever, be bored! Perhaps you do not appreciate this about him, having known him so long, but he is truly a remarkable man. It is rare indeed to meet with such stimulating company."

Eugenia's expression had become thoughtful again. She seemed to be studying Lilah with great interest. "I had not realized," she said mildly, "that Drake's entertainment value might prove an asset to married life. Might it not be exhausting, to be forever in the company of such an exciting person?"

"Oh, no!" said Lilah impulsively. "It would be wonderful."

"Even if he continually tried to assert mastery over his wife?"

"He wouldn't mean anything by it," Lilah assured her. "It's just his way. He tries to assert mastery over everyone. Just put him in his place from time to time. It's good for him."

"I see." Eugenia seemed to be biting back laughter. "Well! Thank you, Lilah. You have given me something to think about."

14

*L*ilah flew down the passage, eager to share the news with Drake. She had made Eugenia think! That was progress. She hoped he had had similar luck talking to Papa. If Eugenia reached a point where she was willing to break the engagement but Papa was unwilling, the situation could become even more complicated than it now was.

When she reached the entrance hall, still running, she collided with her father. Lilah gasped and grabbed at his coat. Despite her surprise, Papa's guilty look did not escape her. Neither did the fact that he was dressed for travel.

"Papa! Where are you going?"

"Hallo, hallo, Lilah," he said hurriedly. "No time to discuss it, I'm afraid. Must be off! Pressing matters, my dear. Pressing matters. I'll see you again in a day or two."

"What! Am I to stay here without you?"

"Only for a couple of days, kitten." He patted her anxiously. "Miss Pickens will take good care

231

of you, what? And Mrs. Peabody, of course. An excellent hostess; most attentive. Yes, yes, you'll be fine. And I won't be gone long, my dear. I promise you that."

Lilah's expression darkened ominously. "Papa"—she placed her fists on her hips—"I have a few things I *particularly* wish to say to you!"

Sir Horace blanched. "Yes, of course, dear child. I'm sure you do," he said earnestly, backing toward the door. "Later!"

"But, Papa—"

"Can't keep the horses waiting, what? We'll talk when I come back. You can say whatever you wish to say, then; we'll have a nice long chat. But not now!" He dashed toward the door, then halted, turning round to point an accusing finger at her. "And mind, now, Lilah—behave yourself while I am gone! I do not entirely trust Lord Drakesley. He seems a most peculiar young gentleman. Making advances to my Eugenia directly after pawing you—which I saw him do with my own eyes! I didn't care to say anything in front of the Peabodys—he's a near relation of theirs, you know—but I shouldn't wonder if he's deranged."

And with that Parthian shot he was gone, racing outside like a rabbit fleeing hounds. Lilah stared after him, mouth agape.

She had never seen her father in such a state.

On the other hand, Papa had never done anything like this before—contract an engagement and keep it secret from her! Knowing how he shrank from confrontation, she supposed he must be quaking in his boots at the thought of the fireworks in store for him—if Lilah ever got him alone. No wonder, then, that he was going to extraordinary lengths to keep his distance from her.

Behind her, Drake suddenly dashed into the hall. His scowl was black as thunder. "Was that Sir Horace going out the door?" he demanded.

"Yes, it was." Lilah was fuming. "Only fancy! He is leaving us for a few days. Did you ever hear anything like it?"

"Blast!" Drake strode past her and flung open the door. Lilah joined him. Together, they watched her father's berline bowling swiftly down the drive. "I've been chasing your wretched father all over the house," said Drake grimly. "He's too fast for me."

Lilah gave a little cry of dismay. "Then you haven't had speech with him at all?"

"No, confound the man! Not a word."

"Kindly watch your language," said Lilah stiffly. "It is my father you are abusing."

"Sorry! But of all the crazy starts I ever witnessed—"

The Peabodys' butler stood on the steps below them, having just closed the carriage door on

233

Sir Horace moments before. He now coughed discreetly. Two pairs of angry eyes swiveled to look at him. He bowed. "May I be of any help, my lord? Miss Chadwick?"

"No," Drake growled. "It seems you've done enough."

"Very good, my lord." The butler moved to go back in the house.

"Hold a moment! There may be one thing you can do for me, Higgins." Drake bent a fierce glare on him. "Do you know where Sir Horace has gone?"

Higgins cast his eyes discreetly down. "I'm sure I couldn't say, my lord."

"Hell and the devil blast it!" Drake pulled out a coin and tossed it to the butler, who deftly caught it. "Information, man! And quickly."

The butler palmed the coin without looking at it, as if the exchange of sordid cash for his services offended his delicate sensibilities. He fixed his disinterested gaze on the middle distance. "It is my impression, my lord, from a word he dropped to the driver, that Sir Horace is en route to Uxbridge."

Drake stared blankly at the butler. "Uxbridge. What the devil for? What's in Uxbridge?"

"His sister lives in Uxbridge," supplied Lilah, tugging insistently on Drake's arm. "For heaven's sake, let him go! What are we to do—send runners after him? We will have to wait, and speak to him when he returns."

Grumbling, Drake returned to the house with her. "I've no wish to keep ragging on your father, Lilah, but—" He clamped his mouth down as if biting back the end of his sentence.

"I appreciate your restraint, but I assure you it is wasted on me," she said darkly. "If you are thinking what I am thinking, we are in perfect agreement. This trip to Uxbridge arose rather suddenly, did it not?" She shook her head in disgust. "Aunt Jane will welcome Papa without question, whether he warns her of his arrival or not. It's my belief he is running away. What did you do to frighten him?"

"Nothing, upon my honor!" He raked his hand through his hair. Lilah was becoming rather fond of the gesture. "I asked if I could speak to him privately for a moment. On a matter of grave importance."

"Did you glower at him while you said it?"

"What do you mean?"

Lilah stifled a laugh behind her hand. He was glowering at her now, with his hair standing all on end like a maniac. She could just imagine the terrifying effect he must have had on poor Papa. "Never mind," she said kindly. "You cannot help terrorizing lesser mortals. At least I was able to make a little progress with Eugenia."

He shot a keen glance at her. "Were you, by Jove? What happened?"

She folded her lips demurely. "The correct response is, 'Thank you, Lilah. You're a wonder.' "

"That remains to be seen." His grim tone was belied by the glint of amusement in his eyes. "Did she agree to marry me?"

"Not quite," admitted Lilah. "But she said she will think on it."

Drake looked skeptical. "Sounds to me like she fobbed you off."

"No such thing! I sang your praises, and she told me I had given her something to think about."

He looked both startled and appreciative. "You sang my praises? I'd have given a monkey to hear that. What did you say?"

Lilah felt her color change and looked away from him, trying to hide her face from his scrutiny. "For heaven's sake, try for a little conduct," she scolded. "What I said to her is neither here nor there. The point is, I made her think."

Drake scratched his chin, pondering this. "Well," he said at last, "I hope that indicates progress. Eugenia's a dark horse, though. She's often told me she'll think about something, but I've learned that unless she tells you *what* she's thinking, you generally discover at the end that your arguments have had no effect on her."

Lilah frowned. "Really? How vexatious. In fact, I call that a bit filthy."

"It's no more filthy than bolting off to Uxbridge," he said cynically.

Lilah sighed. "That's our problem in a nutshell," she agreed. "To be perfectly frank, Drake, we are dealing with two persons who are afraid of us. One hesitates to put it as baldly as that—"

"No, one doesn't. Not this one, at any rate. You're quite right. And they're winning the game, brat." He almost grinned. "Their avoidance of disputes is so alien to you and me, we are finding it hard to anticipate their next moves."

Lilah decided to overlook his choice of epithet, since he said it in such a friendly tone. She regarded him, chin tipped sideways. For a man who had been thwarted in love, he appeared remarkably relaxed. "You speak of defeat, but I am not deceived," she remarked. "You expect to win."

"I do indeed."

For some reason, this annoyed her. "Well, then?" she said challengingly. "Why don't you go and speak with her? Papa is out of your way now. It seems to me the time is ripe."

He raised an eyebrow. "Don't you think I should let the ideas you planted in her brain take root?"

"To what purpose? You have already told me

that arguments have little effect on her. If she is inclined to accept you, she will accept you now." She looked at him from under her lashes. "Are you afraid?" she purred.

The provocation in her voice made him look at her. Their eyes met and clashed, and, to Lilah's dismay, sudden heat flashed and simmered between them. He actually moved to touch her, and she was sure, for half a heartbeat, that he was about to take her in his arms. He immediately seemed to recollect himself, however, and she saw his fists clench at his sides. "I would dearly love," he said evenly, "to take you over my knee someday."

His words were shocking enough on their own merits. The hidden meaning she sensed behind them made gooseflesh rise on her arms— whether from anger or something else, she did not know. "If you ever so much as *think* of such a thing," she said through her teeth, "I'll make you rue the day."

He leaned over her, so close she could feel warmth radiating from his body. "I have thought of it," he informed her, "almost continually since the moment we met. And I do, in fact, rue the day."

She bristled. "You rue the day you met me?"

"Does that surprise you?"

"I never heard anything more uncivil! If

merely being acquainted with me is such a thorn in your side—"

"It is. Believe me, it is."

"—I suggest you propose to Eugenia without delay. If she takes you, you can hide behind her skirts. Marriage to a plaster saint ought to cure you of your uncontrollable urges. Of every kind."

Soundless laughter shook him, but there was anger in his face. "You little witch. That's exactly what I'll do. I'm sick to death of uncontrollable urges." And then, with three quick strides, he was gone.

Lilah stood in the hall and stared at the doorway through which Drake had vanished, furious. How dare he threaten her with bodily harm? How dare he threaten her with humiliation? A spanking, no less! As if she were a naughty toddler!

She realized she was breathing through her teeth, panting with rage. She struggled to calm herself, pressing one hand against her rib cage and breathing deeply.

Enough. He was gone. He would propose to Eugenia. Eugenia would accept him. She and Drake were on the brink of success. And once they achieved their goal, they need have nothing more to do with each other. She could go home and return to her ordinary life with Papa. That would be good. *Good,* she told herself firmly, wondering why the word rang hollow.

Lilah walked down the passage toward the library, pondering the afternoon's events. So far, she reminded herself, everything was speculation. No need to feel elation, no need to feel despair. Yet.

Funny. The suspense she was in was bound to end at some point soon, with one of two outcomes. Either Drake would marry Eugenia or Papa would. One outcome guaranteed relief, the other, misery. But the odd thing was, Lilah was no longer certain which outcome would produce which.

She felt a headache beginning.

Eugenia was peacefully writing a letter at the tambour-topped desk in Mrs. Peabody's morning room when the door burst open. It was Drake, of course, who strode into the room unannounced. Eugenia set down her pen.

He looked as if he had just been dragged backward through a bush. His hair stood on end and his clothing was rumpled. Dear old Drake. Whatever his faults, he certainly wasn't vain. He probably hadn't glanced at a mirror since dressing this morning.

"Jenny, I must speak with you alone," he commanded without preamble.

Eugenia braced herself. She had known, the instant she refused Drake's proposal, that she had not heard the last of it. Drake was incapable of taking "no" for an answer. Under the circumstances, however, that was just as well. Eugenia had had some time for reflection, and she had also had a very illuminating conversation with Delilah Chadwick. She was prepared for this interview. Or so she hoped.

"Very well. What is it?"

"Lilah tells me you are reconsidering your refusal," he blurted with typical brusqueness. "Good girl! I knew you wouldn't let me down."

"No, never that," murmured Eugenia. She smiled. "I suppose you have come to tell me that my time has run out. Are you about to renew your offer?"

"Yes! With all my heart." He moved swiftly toward her and sat on an ottoman at her feet. It wasn't as romantic as kneeling, but it served roughly the same purpose. Instead of towering over her, he now had to look up to meet her eyes. The novelty of looking down on Drake, she had to admit, was rather enjoyable. He seized her cool hands in his large, warm fists and gazed beseechingly up at her. "Come on, old thing. You know we were meant for each other."

"Were we?"

He looked a bit sheepish. "I can't make you a pretty speech," he said gruffly. "You know me too well. I'd feel like a perfect gudgeon."

Eugenia did not think that their long acquaintance was the reason why Drake couldn't make her a pretty speech, but she decided not to comment on this. Sir Horace, she reflected, was even less a speech maker than Drake . . . yet he had found words to do justice to the occasion. In Eugenia's admittedly limited experience, a heartfelt proposal did not include endearments such as "old thing." Still, she held her tongue and waited patiently. She would give Drake a chance to say what he wanted to say, in whatever words he chose.

He still held her hands. Now he wagged them back and forth in a friendly manner. "Well? What do you say?"

Eugenia decided there was no point in making this easy for him. She summoned a puzzled look. "About what?"

He frowned. "About marrying me. Say yes, Jenny. You've nothing to fear. I'll help you face down Sir Horace and we'll break you out of that entanglement. I'll protect you from the gossips and backbiters, if that's what worries you."

"I own, it is something of a concern," she admitted. "And you say you will help me break the news to Horace?"

"If you like," he said, with a careless shrug.

"I daresay the news will come as no surprise to him."

"Really? Why wouldn't it?"

Drake gave a crack of rude laughter. "Because he knows I've entered the lists, poor chap. Why should you marry some country squire when you could have me? Now, I don't mean to sound like a coxcomb. I know I'm not the greatest prize in creation—"

"Nonsense. You know you are among them, at least," said Eugenia, taking a perverse delight in contradicting him for once. "The matchmaking mamas have been thrusting their daughters in your path for the past ten years. I have wanted to ask you something for a long time, Drake. Why haven't you married one of them?"

Drake's mouth twisted in disgust. "Because I've encountered only two kinds of women. Those who throw themselves at a man and those who do not. Those who do are repellent. Those who don't are boring." He caught himself, then, seeming to remember whom he was with and what he was trying to accomplish. With an obvious effort, he relaxed his frown and tried a more ingratiating manner. "And then there is you," he said in a congratulatory tone. "You fall into neither category."

"I am a friend."

"That's right," he said, seeming pleased by this clue that she understood him. "You are my friend. And you're the only woman with whom I could possibly share my home. I'm used to you, Jenny, that's the thing. You've always been there. If I marry you I won't have to change my ways, or rearrange my house, or alter my habits, or do anything new. I'm already accustomed to having you around."

Eugenia's smile was enigmatic. "I see," she said encouragingly. "I'm as comfortable as an old pair of slippers at the end of the day."

He looked relieved. "That's it. Exactly."

Eugenia had to glance away to keep him from seeing the mixture of laughter and vexation in her eyes. She had already made up her mind what to do—but now that it was time to give him her carefully rehearsed answer, she found it unexpectedly difficult.

"Well, Drake," she said serenely, "I have been pondering this question all day, and I do think you are right. You and I get along splendidly, and I have always been very fond of you." She forced herself to meet his eyes again, keeping her expression tranquil. "My answer is yes."

To her secret delight, Drake looked absolutely thunderstruck. "Yes?" he said numbly. He licked his lips as if they had suddenly gone dry. "You mean—you will marry me?"

"Yes, Drake," she said simply. "I will."

She could have sworn he turned pale. "You

will," he repeated, still with that stunned, horror-struck expression. "You will marry me."

"Yes. Although . . ." She hesitated delicately. "I do feel awkward about one thing."

A wild hope flickered in his eyes. She had to cast her gaze modestly down at their linked hands to keep from laughing aloud. "We mustn't announce our engagement, Drake," she said demurely. "Not until we have had a chance to speak to Horace. We must tell him face-to-face. It's the honorable thing to do."

"Oh. Oh, that. Honorable thing. Quite right." He cleared his throat. "Sir Horace has gone to Uxbridge."

"Yes. He wanted to consult his sister about our plans and borrow some jewelry she inherited from their mother. For our wedding, you know." Having mastered her impulse to laugh, she lifted limpid eyes to his. "It would be cruel, Drake darling, to let word reach him through idle gossip that I am breaking my promise to him and planning to wed you. We must keep my decision secret for a few days."

"Right." He blinked dazedly at her. "Right."

Feigning nonchalance, she watched him carefully. "I will write him immediately, of course, in care of his sister in Uxbridge. In the meantime, I suppose we can tell the family here," she suggested. "Aunt Polly and Uncle Nat. And Lilah, of course."

The hands that were holding hers jerked spasmodically. "Lilah," he muttered, sounding pained. "Yes, we must tell Lilah. She . . . will be glad."

"I hope so," said Eugenia in dulcet tones. It was the second falsehood she had told him. She trusted that Providence would forgive her. Providence—and Horace—would also have to forgive her for kissing Drake, she soon discovered. He pulled her to her feet and into his arms before she knew what he meant to do. The kiss was brief, however, and he immediately let her go. It seemed more a matter of form than an expression of passion.

He soon left, and she enjoyed a long, albeit muffled, laugh. Poor Drake! Really, she was not cut out for the Machiavellian life. She felt too much pity for the victim. She could only hope that, when all was said and done, Drake would come to appreciate the joke himself.

After she had wiped her streaming eyes, Eugenia sat back down at the desk, still chuckling, and penned the last lines of her letter to Horace. *Drake has renewed his offer of marriage, as I warned you he would, and I have accepted him.* Her smile broadened. *I wish you could have seen his face.*

15

The family's habit was to gather in an upstairs drawing room early in the evening
and wait for Higgins to announce that dinner
was served. When Lilah walked in, the Peabodys were already present. Polly greeted her
warmly and inquired very kindly about her day,
and Nat ushered her to a chair by the fire with
great punctilio.

Polly told her she had spent a good part of
the day with Miss Pickens and had enjoyed her
company very much, although the quick trip
from London to the Abbey had not agreed with
Miss Pickens's constitution. When Miss Pickens
confessed to a lingering headache, Polly had insisted that she take to her bed. She also had
arranged for special delicacies to be prepared in
the kitchen and carried to Miss Pickens on a
tray. Nat assured Lilah that their cook's tisane
worked wonders and he had no doubt Miss
Pickens would be better by morning. Lilah was
touched; their warm, unquestioning acceptance

of two strangers thrust into their midst, and their generous attention to her old governess, struck her as sincere. One had to admire such bone-deep kindness.

Unfortunately, Lilah's early arrival in the drawing room placed her at a disadvantage. In chatting idly of the day's events, she unwittingly broke the news to the Peabodys that Sir Horace had left. Lilah had, naturally, assumed that her father had informed his hosts before departing. She was vexed and mortified when she saw that the Peabodys were mildly startled to learn that one of their guests had unexpectedly departed for Uxbridge.

"Dear me," said Polly. "Did he tell us he was going to Uxbridge? I don't recall him mentioning it. Do you, Nat?"

"No, my love. You'd think we'd recall it, wouldn't you? Very odd, very odd indeed."

Lilah was pink with embarrassment. "I'm so sorry. It's really most unlike him. I hope you won't think less of Papa . . ."

"Oh, heavens, no," said Polly comfortably. "It's entirely possible he mentioned his plans to us a dozen times or more. We've been at sixes and sevens, you know, with the masquerade last night and all this furor about Eugenia's betrothal. I daresay he told us he was going to Uxbridge, and we simply forgot."

"Happens all the time," Nat assured Lilah.

"No need to color up, Miss Chadwick. We never stand on ceremony here. If your father needs to pop off to Uxbridge, why shouldn't he? We're happy to have him; we're happy to let him go. And when he comes back, we'll be happy to see him again. Won't we, my love?"

"Naturally," said Polly immediately. She reached over and gave Lilah's hand an affectionate pat. "I hope you know, dear child, that we have already grown very fond of your father."

Nat beamed. "Oh, aye! Very fond. He's an excellent fellow, what? A most admirable chap. Liked him at once."

Lilah was ready to weep with gratitude. The Peabodys, she thought, for all their informality, displayed the truest form of good manners—the natural tact of caring hearts.

Just as she was stammering out her thanks, the door opened to admit Drake. Eugenia was on his arm, looking as calm and collected as ever. Lilah was chagrined to discover, from the pang that shot through her at the sight of Drake and Eugenia together, that she was not immune to jealousy. She was so occupied in quashing her impulse to scratch Eugenia's eyes out, it took her several seconds to realize that Drake was wearing an expression she had never seen on him before. He looked like a caged thing— wild and miserable.

The reason for this soon became clear. After

exchanging perfunctory greetings with the Peabodys, Drake said, in his blunt way, "No point
in postponing the inevitable. May as well tell
you now. Eugenia's accepted me." The blank
stares that greeted this announcement caused
him to add, in a decidedly snappish tone, "You
must know what I'm talking about; you were
all present! I offered marriage. She's accepted.
That's all."

Nat chuckled good-naturedly. "You must be
mistaken, dear chap," he told Drake. "Eugenia's
accepted Horace Chadwick. Can't marry you
both, what? Must have misunderstood her."

"No, Uncle," said Eugenia, displaying no
more emotion than would be suitable for a discussion of the weather. "Drake understood me.
We must keep this news secret for the time
being, until I am able to explain it all to Horace
face-to-face, but Drake has persuaded me that
my prior engagement was a mistake and that I
will be happier as Lady Drakesley." She turned
courteously to Lilah. "I hope you will forgive
me, Lilah, for any pain my decision may cause
your father."

"Certainly," said Lilah faintly. A fog of unre-
ality seemed to have descended upon the room.
There was something unnerving about Eugenia's apparent apathy while making such a sensational announcement. "I understand your
reasons. I think."

Eugenia inclined her head in gracious ac-knowledgment. "Thank you. I hope Sir Horace will be equally understanding."

Lilah shivered with a sudden chill of dread. Saints above! She hoped so, too.

Until this moment, she realized in dismay, she had not really believed Eugenia would cry off— and had therefore not seriously pictured what her father's reaction might be if she did. Her notion that Papa would feel relief at the news now struck her as self-serving and improbable. He would be upset. The only question re-maining was, how upset? Would he be angry at the insult to his pride? That, certainly. But what was causing Lilah to suddenly feel a bit clammy was the fear that Papa's pain might go deeper than that.

What if Papa truly loved Eugenia? This news would break his heart. And she, Lilah, had had a hand in it. Oh, it did not bear thinking of. She might have brought unnecessary grief to her beloved father, who had already suffered so much through losing Mama. Eugenia might have been his last chance at happiness. Guilt and remorse swept through Lilah like a strong tide, overwhelming her. Too late!

Meanwhile, Nat Peabody was swelling like a flustered frog. "Now, see here!" he exclaimed. "If I didn't know better, Eugenia, I'd think your wits had gone begging! You can't go about, accepting every proposal you receive. You must pick and choose, girl! You must settle on one, and decline the others!"

"Yes, Uncle," said Eugenia submissively, although amusement quivered in her voice. "I do realize I must break my engagement to Horace before I may wed Drake."

Nat clucked and blessed himself and appeared extremely agitated. Polly was watching Eugenia with sharp eyes. When she finally spoke, it was to Nat. "Never mind, my love," she said soothingly. "We must trust Eugenia to do what's right."

Higgins entered and announced that dinner was served. The company gathered itself for the short walk to the dining room, and Lilah was placed behind the Peabodys. She could not help but overhear their conversation as they paced down the passage ahead of her.

Nat leaned down to his wife, obviously deeply troubled. "Such a good man," he muttered distressfully. "Hate to see her give him the go-by. Horace, you know! Fond of him. Thought he was just the chap to make her happy."

"Yes, dear," said Polly, patting her husband's hand affectionately. "I like him, too. But we mustn't interfere. Eugenia is the best judge of what will make her happy. Pray recall that we are fond of Drake as well."

"Aye," said Nat gruffly, apparently struggling

to control his emotions. "Drake's always been a prime favorite of ours, there's no denying that. I just can't picture him making Eugenia happy. Or she keeping him content, either. Well! Could be worse. Could be worse. She might have chosen Hatfield, eh? Didn't care for him at all."

It was a miserable meal. Lilah tried very hard to behave normally, since she knew she had behaved badly at breakfast—what *would* the Peabodys think of her?—but it was extraordinarily difficult to make small talk while suffering the torments of the damned.

This was not the first time she had acted on impulse and lived to regret it, but it was surely the worst. No wonder Papa had waited until the last possible minute to write to her, trying to hold her at bay! He must have known she would fly off the handle and do something crazy. Well, she had, and now the deed was done. She had meddled in something serious, a matter that did not truly concern her, and wreaked havoc in the process. Now she had to face the unpalatable fact that she might have done lasting harm to her beloved father. Surely she was the most wretched of mortals.

After dinner, the three women withdrew to the cozy drawing room again. Lilah, drained by her efforts at normalcy during dinner, perched unhappily on a low chair near the fire and stared silently into the flames. Polly and Eugenia talked in low tones on the sofa behind her, but she made no effort to hear what they said. She felt unable to hold up her end of a conversation anyhow. The emotional toll taken on her by the past few days was proving difficult to bear.

It was a relief when Nat and Drake joined the ladies just a few short minutes after they had withdrawn. Nat still looked perturbed, and Drake morose, but Lilah felt that almost any addition to the company would improve the evening. If she had to spend it in quiet conversation with Eugenia and Mrs. Peabody, she thought she might go mad.

As Drake hesitated inside the door, eyeing the room, Nat walked over to join his wife and Eugenia. He sat on the settee facing them and immediately leaned forward and took Eugenia's hand, speaking to her in a low and earnest tone. Drake frowned, appearing uncertain of his welcome among that threesome. Eugenia, concentrating her attention on Nat, did not look up to invite him over, so he hovered near the door for a few seconds, fidgeting, and then went to join Lilah. He dropped moodily into the chair beside hers and stretched out his long legs toward the blaze.

"My engagement to Eugenia is receiving a rather lukewarm reception in the bosom of my family, don't you think?" he muttered. "Nobody seems to be breaking out the champagne or falling on my neck with tears of joy."

"You must make allowances for them," said Lilah, trying to reassure him. "A surprise of this nature is unsettling. When they become used to the idea, they will see that it's all for the best."

She glanced sideways at him. His mood had not visibly lightened. He was staring into the fire, frowning. The firelight edged the somber planes of his face in gold. "It *is* all for the best, isn't it, Drake?" she asked, a catch in her voice.

He looked at her, his expression bleak. "I hope so. There's no turning back, Lilah. She's already written your father to give him the news."

Her heart sank. "Oh." Her hands twisted in her lap and she shivered again. "In that case, Drake, congratulations. I . . . I wish you happy." She forced a smile, but he did not return it.

"Thank you," he said tonelessly. His eyes met hers. The firelight leaped and burned, turning his eyes to molten gold, mesmerizing her. A strange ache formed at the core of Lilah's being, tightening her throat as if with unshed tears. A profound sense of loss gripped her. If only things had been different. If only she and Drake could get along. If only . . .

But Nat Peabody's good-humored voice broke into their tête-à-tête, calling out a suggestion

that the company put together a game of commerce. Lilah was loath to offend her genial host,
so she turned courteously and feigned enthusiasm for the idea. Drake's negligent shrug was
interpreted as his having no objection, so servants were called and a round table set up.

Lilah was careful to avoid sitting beside
Drake, fearing that the temptation of his nearness might cause her to touch him more often
than was necessary. She chose a place between
Polly and Eugenia. Drake and Nat sat facing the
women, and the game began.

Lilah did not expect to derive any real pleasure from a silly game of commerce. She was
not in spirits, and braced herself for a tedious
hour of pretending an enjoyment she did not
feel. It was plain that Drake felt the same way
she did, because he, unlike Lilah, took no pains
to hide his surly mood. Eugenia dealt the cards,
and Drake, barely glancing at his hand, knocked
on the table.

"What are you doing?" demanded Lilah,
annoyed.

He raised an eyebrow. "That's how the game
is played."

"We haven't played yet," Lilah pointed out.
"You can't knock on the table until you have a
winning hand."

"I was dealt a winning hand."

Lilah rolled her eyes. "You always think that," she said provocatively.

Drake leaned forward, his eyes gleaming. "Fortune favors me. Or haven't you noticed?"

"It won't favor you this time," Lilah told him sweetly, studying her own cards with a knowing smirk. When the play came round to her, she bartered a card and waved it triumphantly.

Drake cupped a hand behind his ear. "I don't hear you knocking."

"Just you wait," promised Lilah.

What followed was the most entertaining game of commerce Lilah had ever played. The cards flew thick and fast, with much shouting and laughter. Formality disappeared immediately; within ten minutes Lilah was calling the Peabodys Aunt Polly and Uncle Ned, as Eugenia and Drake did, and they were calling her Lilah. Eugenia smiled more often than she laughed and therefore kept her dignity throughout the game, but the Peabodys were as noisy as children. Their merriment was infectious, and Lilah and Drake's competitive natures further enlivened the table with a bloodthirsty spirit that added tremendous excitement to the game.

It seemed that Drake, like Lilah, was constitutionally incapable of losing gracefully. Although they were playing for pennies, both played with a cutthroat intensity more appropriate for matters of life and death. Fortunately, they coupled this tendency with a lively sense of their own ridiculousness, so that their table pounding and fist shaking and cries for vengeance caused hilarity rather than ill will.

When the servants entered with the tea tray, the players were startled to discover how late it had grown. The game broke up, tea was drunk, and everyone went to bed pleasantly tired.

After the candle was blown out, Polly leaned over and patted her husband's shoulder in the dark. "Nat, dear. Thank you for not making a fuss over Eugenia's change of partners."

Nat grunted. "Can't say I approve of it, for I don't. Never thought Eugenia would use a fellow so ill."

"No," said Polly thoughtfully. "It's very unlike her. But that's what gives me pause. I wonder if she's playing a deep game."

"Hey?" Nat opened one eye. "Shouldn't be playing a game of any sort. That's my point."

"And a good one it is," agreed Polly. "But, still . . . I couldn't help but notice . . ."

"Notice what?" asked Nat sleepily.

"Never mind, my love. Go to sleep." Polly smiled into the dark. It would be cruel to keep Nat from his slumbers to discuss romantic entanglements, a subject he followed with difficulty when wide-awake. But she had noticed that Drake and Lilah had eyes for no one but each other. And that Eugenia faded into the woodwork in their presence, seeming to allow it. Eugenia was not in the least ruffled when her supposed fiancé neglected her entirely for several hours, never even glancing her way because his attention was completely riveted on another woman. This was strange. In fact, it was unnatural.

Eugenia must have something up her sleeve. Polly drifted off to sleep wondering what it was . . . and hoping that, whatever it was, it would cause a minimum of scandal.

16

L ilah tapped the edge of her pen against her cheek, frowning. The sheet of foolscap on the desktop before her contained only the words, "Dear Jonathan." She had never written to Mr. Applegate before in her life, which made the composition of this particular missive rather difficult. It was odd to begin a correspondence at such a critical juncture in their relationship. It was rather like starting a play with Act III.

In fact, it had taken her ten minutes to get past the "Dear," since she wasn't quite sure whether she should address Jonathan by his Christian name. Using Christian names was all very well in conversation, but there was something frightfully cheeky about putting it down in writing. She hoped, if he kept the letter, his future wife would not discover it and draw erroneous conclusions about their friendship.

Then, with a start, she remembered that *she* planned to be his future wife. In fact, that was the whole purpose of her letter. With a flush of annoyance at her mental lapse, she put pen to paper again. She had sat cogitating for so long, however, that the ink had dried.

Really, this wasn't going well at all.

Delicacy had never been her strong suit. This task required a light, deft touch, a smidgen of diplomacy. Lilah's talents in this area were nil. Still, she had to try. She must put words together in just the right way to convince Jonathan to leave his post immediately and fly to her side—without, of course, alarming him unduly. Once he arrived, she was certain that everything would fall into place. Getting him here was the hard part.

Dear Jonathan. Hmm. What should follow? *I need you.* No; that would scare him away. *Papa needs you.* No; he was too clever to fall for that trick. If Papa needed him, Papa would write the letter. *My life is careening out of control and I am writing to you in a complete panic.* Her lips twitched. She didn't dare write that, of course, but it had the advantage of being true.

She was becoming obsessed with Lord Drakesley. She needed a distraction, and she needed it now. High time she forced the issue. High time she weaseled a promise of marriage out of the elusive Mr. Applegate. For heaven's sake, how could he object? Securing the hand of Delilah Chadwick would be a stunning achievement for a landless younger son—even if she did say so herself. As the world viewed such matters, all the advantage of the match would be on his side. People would wonder why a rich young gentlewoman—his employer's only child, no less—would agree to marry an obscure, gangly young man of scholarly habits and few personal gifts.

For a few confused moments, even Lilah wondered why.

It would help if he had ever given her overtures the slightest encouragement, but Jonathan Applegate was a pretty slippery fish, and difficult to land. He dodged, with great good humor, her every attempt to flirt with him. Now, *that* took diplomacy. But it left Lilah without a single string to pull, even in an emergency like this.

By the time Miss Pickens's timid knock sounded on Lilah's bedchamber door, she was in a rare temper. She had tossed several wadded sheets of foolscap into the grate, hurling them with increasing force as her frustration level rose, and was no nearer completion than she had been an hour ago. "Come in!" she shouted. Her pen promptly snapped in half. She flung it down in disgust.

Miss Pickens peeked around the edge of the door, trepidation written across her features. "Gracious. Have I chosen a bad time?"

"No," said Lilah shortly. "Sorry. It's this wretched pen. Good riddance to it, I say." She remembered her manners then, and waved Miss

262

Pickens in. "Pray come in, Picky. Are you feeling better this morning?"

Miss Pickens's thin face brightened as she closed the door behind her. "Never better, thank you. I slept very well last night. A delightful spot, isn't it? And I must say, Mrs. Peabody is the kindest creature imaginable. She showed me all through the oldest portions of the abbey yesterday. Insisted on doing it herself; fancy that! As if she had nothing better to do than dance attendance on a stranger."

"The Peabodys are amiable souls," Lilah agreed, still feeling cross as crabs. A dot of black ink had spattered onto her wrist. She rubbed it absently with her handkerchief. "Did you go down to breakfast?"

"Yes, indeed. When you did not appear I thought I had better check on you. You are feeling all right, aren't you, Lilah?" She peered anxiously at her former charge. "I must say, you don't look quite yourself."

Lilah rose and paced restlessly. "I don't feel quite myself," she admitted. "Perhaps I have a touch of influenza."

Miss Pickens blinked doubtfully. "Do you really think so, dear?"

Lilah imagined long days in bed, sweltering under piles of comforters and choking down endless basins of gruel. It would remove her from Lord Drakesley's path, but at what cost?

She loathed being ill. "No," she said at last, feeling crosser than ever.

"Well, I am relieved to hear you say so. The Peabodys have made a charming plan for the day's entertainment, and it would be a pity if you missed it. A drive to see some very interesting Roman ruins, followed by a picnic luncheon! All very elegant, I daresay, as well as educational. I own, I am looking forward to the day with no small degree of pleasure."

Lilah hid a smile. She suspected that Miss Pickens's passion for history had influenced Aunt Polly in choosing the picnic destination. "I never saw you look forward to jouncing about in a carriage," she teased.

Miss Pickens gave a tootling little laugh. "Oh! You are jesting, my dear. I never have any trouble in an *open* carriage."

This, indeed, proved to be the case. Miss Pickens, almost incoherent with delight, was seated facing forward in the Peabodys' barouche. It was a large barouche, seating three persons on each well-padded bench. The Peabodys shared the seat with Miss Pickens, leaving Drake, Lilah, and Eugenia to face them, riding backward. Uncle Nat made some jocular remark about the men's luck, each being placed between two lovely ladies, but none of the young people gave him more than a strained smile in response.

Emotions on the backward-facing bench ran high.

Lilah was grateful, for once, for Miss Pickens's inexhaustible supply of small talk. Her old governess was so happy, included in a congenial party of persons she insisted on thinking of as her "betters," riding with stately slowness, in the open air, toward a destination of historical interest, that she prattled and chirped like a canary in sunshine. Her joyous chatter filled what otherwise might have been an awkward silence. Lilah, for one, found conversation quite beyond her. She was acutely, almost painfully, aware of Drake's long body pressing against her from shoulder to knee. Her fingers trembled on the handle of her parasol, causing it to flutter over her head in a way that the breeze could not quite account for.

She fixed her eyes, a bit glassily, on the road unwinding behind them. She dared not look to her left, where Drake sat. The sight of his thigh, encased in skin-tight pantaloons and just visible at the corner of her eye, was overpowering enough. She had difficulty following Miss Pickens's remarks, but Eugenia and the Peabodys chimed in from time to time, so there was no need for Lilah to speak up. Thank heaven.

Drake was as silent as she. Did he share her agony? She thought he might. The idea was unbearably exciting. Feverish fantasies rippled through her mind, unbidden. If they were alone, she would turn to him. He would look down at her with those hot, golden eyes. His arm would slip behind her back. She would lift her face, daring him, and he would not resist her. His head would bend down to hers . . .

Merciful heavens. She was fantasizing about a man who had just become engaged. Not to mention, she reminded herself sternly, a man whom she did not like. Much. Oh, why did he have this effect on her? It wasn't fair. Jonathan had never turned her all hot and cold and shaky just by sitting beside her in a carriage.

The drive seemed interminable . . . and much too short.

The Roman ruins were just like every other set of Roman ruins, as far as Lilah could tell: incomprehensible mounds of rubble strewn about in a field. Miss Pickens, however, was transported by the sight. The instant she was handed down from the carriage she began quivering like a spaniel scenting game. Within seconds, she was trotting from hillock to hillock, magnifying glass and sketchbook in hand, apparently thrilled to the core of her being.

The others stood at the edge of the field for a few minutes. Polly watched Miss Pickens's gyrations with an indulgent smile. "I do like to see Miss Pickens enjoying herself," she remarked. "I fancy her preferences are not often considered, in the general way of things."

Lilah immediately felt guilty. "She never complains," she said quickly. "And we do try to accommodate her at home. Or, at the least, we inconvenience her as little as possible."

"Oh! I wasn't criticizing you, my dear," said Polly. "I was only observing that a governess's life—or the life of any indigent gentlewoman, for that matter—is no bed of roses. I like to pamper such women when I can."

"Quite right, my pet," said Nat approvingly. "I daresay it won't harm us to view a few ruins, eh? Not my cup of tea, but I've no objection to obliging Miss Pickens. Very fine weather for it, too." He offered his arm to his wife and they strolled off, their heads together as they chatted.

"What a dear old couple they are," said Lilah impulsively. "It is impossible not to love them."

"Yes," said Eugenia's soft voice, on the other side of Drake. "There is much we can learn from their example of loving-kindness."

Lilah felt a stab of irritation. She had forgotten Eugenia's existence for a moment, yet here she was, holding Drake's arm and making pious remarks. And spoiling everything. Why couldn't she have gone off with Uncle Nat and Aunt Polly? The woman would have Drake all to herself soon enough; surely there was no need to monopolize him now.

Eugenia tugged gently on her escort's sleeve. "Drake, darling. May we explore a little?"

Was it Lilah's imagination, or did Drake flinch when Eugenia called him "darling"? He seemed to collect himself with an effort, then look down at his fiancée as if bemused by her presence at his side. "Certainly," he said. He then added, a bit lamely, "my dear."

What *was* the man thinking? Lilah felt another twinge of annoyance. Did he want to marry Eugenia, or didn't he? Did he love the creature, or didn't he? And why on earth would he put everyone through this nonsense if he didn't?

Drake and Eugenia headed out into the lumpy grass. Feeling decidedly put-upon, Lilah trudged discontentedly in their wake. *If Jonathan were here*, she thought resentfully, *I wouldn't be walking alone. If Jonathan were here, I'd show Drake how it feels to be ignored. If Jonathan were here—*

Lilah squeaked aloud as her thin-soled shoes slid on the wet grass and she stumbled. Drake was at her side in a flash, pulling her upright with his strong arms, steadying her.

"My hero," she declared weakly. She was trying to make a joke, but nobody laughed.

"Are you hurt?"

"No. No. I just—" She swallowed hard. "I just twisted my foot a bit."

It wasn't pain that was causing her to cling to

him. It was need. He was holding her, his eyes searing her, the heat radiating from his body turning her dizzy and faint. Oh, this was ghastly. Eugenia was standing right over there, watching them. She would guess soon, if she hadn't already, the powerful force drawing Lilah to Drake. She must get a grip on herself, she really must.

She tore her eyes from Drake's and jerked out of his arms, pointing a shaky finger at the parasol she had dropped. "If you please," she said. Her lips felt stiff as she struggled to hide her emotions.

Drake picked up the parasol, shook it out, and handed it to her. "Here you go," he said gruffly. "No harm done. You're sure you weren't injured?"

Before she knew what he was about, he had dropped to one knee and taken her foot in his hands. She gasped with surprise, then had to grab his shoulders to keep her balance as he lifted her foot and placed it on his thigh, gently probing it with his fingers.

She blushed. She couldn't help it. She was terrified that Eugenia would see how Drake's touch affected her. There was something astonishingly intimate about the way he ran his thumbs across the top of her foot, over and under her ankles, and back along both sides of the arch. It felt so wonderful, she longed to tell him that something hurt, just so he would go on touching her.

But she didn't tell him that anything hurt, and he still went on touching her.

Scarlet-faced, Lilah eventually gritted her teeth. "Put my foot down."

His hands stilled. "There's nothing broken," he said, his voice sounding strained.

"Of course there is nothing broken. I told you I wasn't injured." She knew she shouldn't snap at him, but anger was all she could cling to in this impossible situation.

He flushed a dull red. "I'm not taking liberties, if that's what you think," he said sharply. "I have a little knowledge in this area."

"From diagnosing horseflesh, no doubt." She tossed her head with a sniff. "I am not one of your fillies, to be handled at your whim."

He returned her foot to the ground and rose, his fists clenching at his sides. "I don't know why I tried to help you," he said disgustedly. "I should have known you'd bite my head off." He leaned over her, eyes gleaming. "I wish you were my filly. I'd break you to bridle, and that right speedily."

Lilah gave him an oversweet smile. "If I were your filly, I'd run away."

The gleam in his eyes burned hotter. "I'd offer you sugar and you'd come to me sweetly. You wouldn't suspect a thing until it was too late. I'd have the halter on you in no time."

Lilah's chin came up. "Nonsense. I'd see right through you," she said softly. "You'd not get near enough to lay a hand on me."

"Drake," interposed Eugenia's calm voice. "Offer Lilah your other arm. She should not be walking on this uneven ground unsupported."

Drake straightened hastily. It seemed that he, like Lilah, tended to forget Eugenia's quiet presence. "Right," he muttered. He held his right arm toward Lilah—a bit stiffly. She took it—a bit warily. Eugenia took Drake's left arm, and the threesome strolled forward again. Slowly.

The ground really was uneven, and the thick grass was deceptive. One never knew when one's foot might land in a hole or hit a hidden rock. Conversation flagged while they minded their steps. "Heavens," said Lilah at last, "I call this dangerous. No wonder the owner has left it to his flocks. One couldn't possibly plow this field."

"Oh, stop grumbling," said Drake. "Don't you hear the siren call of history?"

"Is that what it is? Sounds like sheep bleating."

His shoulders shook. "You find fault with everything. I never saw a more fascinating place in my life. This field is chock-full of antiquities."

Lilah tried not to laugh. "I knew it was chock-full of something. I can smell it."

Miss Pickens's voice called excitedly from the other side of a series of hillocks. "I have found a denarius!" She held up a small object pinched between her thumb and forefinger, waving it with enthusiasm. "Do you suppose I might keep it?"

"If it doesn't bite," murmured Lilah.

Drake almost grinned. "A denarius is not a creature. It's a coin."

Lilah peeped up at him, feigning intense admiration. "How wonderful it must be to have a classical education."

At that, Drake laughed out loud. This pleased Lilah enormously. Really, it was marvelous to have someone to joke with. She would miss him when she went home with Papa.

That turned out to be an unfortunate thought. Home had never seemed less inviting. Plunged into gloom, Lilah fell silent. She had just recognized the source of her crankiness. When Eugenia's letter brought Papa hurrying back from Uxbridge, there would be a frightful row. She didn't mind the row so much, but she knew it would end with her immediate departure from Wexbridge Abbey.

Papa would drag her back to Chadwick Hall—a place that, until now, had always been her favorite place to be. Now, her beloved home would seem sadly flat. She very much feared that her thoughts would turn to Drake far more

often than was good for her. In just a few short
days, she thought resentfully, the exasperating
earl had completely cut up her peace.

Her mood did not improve. Wandering
through the ruins, admiring the view, peering
at weathered stones while assuming an interest
she did not feel, Lilah was, by turns, exhilarated
and miserable. When engrossed in conversation
with Drake she tingled with awareness of him,
forgetting everything but his exciting nearness.
When rudely recalled to the present, usually by
Eugenia intruding some remark that reminded
Lilah of her existence, Lilah's heart sank into her
shoes. It was the most unsettling morning Lilah
had ever spent.

She welcomed the call to luncheon with relief,
hoping it would provide a break from her emotional turmoil. It did prove more interesting
than the Roman ruins. The Peabodys' idea of a
picnic was a lavish spread of dainty edibles,
trucked in by cart and served by members of
their staff. The party sat on pristine linens
spread on the ground beneath a tree, and ate off
china plates handed them by footmen. The fine
weather held, and a pleasant breeze kept flies at
bay. All in all, the meal was a huge success.

The only difficulty was, Lilah grew increas-
ingly nervous as the meal wore on. She feared
that her attraction to Drake, and his to her, was
becoming glaringly obvious. Try as she might,

her attention was drawn to him again and again. He would keep staring at her, and it seemed that every time she lifted her eyes they met his. She was uncomfortably aware that Aunt Polly was watching them with a sphinxlike expression that gave no clue to her thoughts.

She dreaded speaking with him alone, fearing that it would only add fuel to the fire, but his marked attention to her was making her frantic with embarrassment. While the servants were gathering up the gear, Eugenia and the Peabodys moved away to give them room and Lilah seized her chance, plucking urgently at Drake's sleeve.

"You must stop looking at me," she told him in a furious whisper. "It's impolite. And besides, you're embarrassing me."

"I'm not looking at you," he snapped. "You're looking at me. Every time I glance in your direction, I catch you watching me. What the devil do you mean by it?"

The injustice of this remark fairly took her breath away. "Oh! You—you—why, I don't know a name bad enough to call you! How can you sit there beside Eugenia and stare me out of countenance? I hardly knew where to look. It's rude to *both* of us. It's more than rude, it's vulgar!"

She saw the muscles jump in his jaw as he fought for control. "Was I looking at you?" he said through gritted teeth. "Very well; I was! If you don't like it, then stop being so bloody interesting."

"*What?* How dare you use such language—"

"If you don't want me to stare at you," he interrupted, "I suggest you keep out of my sight. For whenever you're in view, I swear by all that's holy, I *cannot* tear my eyes away."

She stared at him, completely flummoxed. In another man's mouth, that assertion might have sounded flirtatious. Drake sounded enraged, as if her mere presence had goaded him past endurance. He was motionless beside her, but his stillness somehow gave the impression that he was holding himself on a very tight leash. There was a tenseness about his body that suggested restraint. And his eyes burned like a madman's as he gazed down at her.

"You are driving me insane," he told her, still through clenched teeth. "I am counting the moments until your blasted father takes you away from here. If I am to survive until then, you are going to have to keep your distance. For God's sake, Lilah, have a little mercy. Stay away from me."

"How can I?" demanded Lilah, stung. "It's impossible. We are guests here. We must endure each other's company as best we can. Besides, what is the matter with you? You told me you wanted to marry Eugenia. Now that she's accepted you, you're ignoring her—and, if you ask me, behaving very oddly."

Drake looked ready to explode. "Of course I am behaving oddly!" he exclaimed. "I can't keep my eyes off you—I can't think about any-one but you—I try to escort Eugenia like a duti-ful fiancé and *you* end up on my other arm. I can't win!" As usual, he thrust his hand wildly through his hair, careless of the destruction he wrought. And, as usual, the gesture tugged pe-culiarly at Lilah's heartstrings.

"Don't do that," she ordered, distracted. "It makes you look a fright." Without thinking, she reached up and smoothed his hair back into place.

Oh, dear. She should have worn proper gloves instead of these lace mitts. Her bare fin-gers were in his hair, and the sensation was sin-fully delicious. Drake's hand shot up and caught her wrist, holding it in a grip that was almost painful. "Lilah," he said hoarsely, as if goaded almost beyond endurance, "I'm begging you."

He didn't need to finish the thought; she knew what he meant. Lilah discovered that she was trembling. She took a ragged breath and tried to smile. "Sorry," she whispered. Her throat had suddenly gone dry. "I wasn't thinking."

Aunt Polly's prosaic voice cut into the mo-ment, causing Drake and Lilah to jump like startled hares. "Time to go," called Polly cheerily. "I rather fancy a storm is coming."

The darkness on the horizon had nothing to do with the electricity jolting through Lilah. As far as she was concerned, the storm was already here. And raging.

17

This night's after-dinner gathering was far more sedate than the previous evening's had been. Part of the reason was that the vicar and his wife were present, so a noisy game of commerce seemed vaguely unsuitable. And part of the reason was the weather. The wind whistled and moaned, rattling the shutters and blowing occasional gusts of smoke into the room from the fireplace. This seemed to subdue the spirits of everyone save Lilah. She actually felt calmer and more cheerful than she had earlier. The weather matched her mood, making it seem as if Mother Nature herself sympathized with Lilah's plight. She felt less necessity to vent her feelings while the storm expressed them for her.

Wexbridge Abbey, like many old buildings, was exceedingly drafty. On a night such as this, inexplicable breezes blew and eddied in the rooms. This was uncomfortable for everyone, but torture for Miss Pickens. The unfortunate woman believed in spirits. Despite her best efforts to hide it, she grew more and more skittish as the wind worsened. Several times during the course of the evening she whirled fearfully round, clapping one hand to her neck as if feeling ghostly breath upon her. Shortly after the clock chimed eleven, the candle on the table beside her suddenly went out. Miss Pickens gave a terrified gasp, her hand clutching wildly at her throat.

" 'Tis the wind," said Lilah soothingly. "Naught but the wind."

"Oh! Of course. So silly of me," said Miss Pickens, trying to laugh. "There is no earthly reason for a Christian woman to be fearful on a night like this, is there?" She glanced nervously at the vicar.

He gave her a thin, disapproving smile. "None whatsoever," he said repressively. "I am always a little astonished at the power of a mere rainstorm to overset the nerves of suggestible persons. We ought to know better, oughtn't we? We are not children."

Miss Pickens flushed to the roots of her hair, too ashamed to reply. Lilah's eyes sparkled with anger as she lifted her chin at the clergyman. "People of all ages dislike storms," she said coolly. "I am not overfond of them myself."

Drake was sitting across the room, studiously avoiding contact with Lilah. But she saw a flash of approval in his eyes, and a grim smile lifted the corners of his mouth. "I don't like them, either," he said shortly. "Never have."

Lilah's heart warmed. It was good of him to champion Miss Pickens. She knew perfectly well that weather was a matter of complete indifference to him; in the short time she had known him, she had seen him out in weather of all sorts. His remark must have been motivated by pure kindness.

Beside her, Miss Pickens breathed more easily and her embarrassed flush faded. She slipped a grateful arm beneath Lilah's and squeezed it. "Thank you," she said softly. "Perhaps, as I am not entirely myself this evening, I should go early to bed."

"I'll walk with you," said Lilah stoutly. She knew Miss Pickens must dread going down the dark and drafty passages to her bedchamber alone. She also knew that her old friend would be heartily embarrassed to let a servant see her to her room, since she would hate for a stranger to witness her fear.

Polly looked up. "Miss Pickens need not stay if she doesn't feel up to it. But, Lilah dear, must we lose you so early?"

"I will return," Lilah assured her, smiling. "But if I do not see Miss Pickens safely to her door, I will spend the rest of the evening fretting about her."

Drake rose lazily out of his chair. "I'll escort

you." Lilah must have looked as startled as she felt, for he added, "To see you safely back to the drawing room, Miss Chadwick."

"Oh," said Lilah, nonplussed. She could hardly argue with him in front of the vicar and everyone, but it seemed strange that he would offer his escort. He had been avoiding her ever since their brief argument at the picnic spot. "Very well," she said at last, not wishing to appear ungracious. She gestured to the table beside him. "You might bring that lamp."

They formed a well-lit group as they walked toward Miss Pickens's bedchamber; Drake carried the lamp and the women each held a candle. The strong light, and being flanked by two supporters, seemed to ease Miss Pickens's jumpiness. "Thank you," she said in a low, embarrassed voice. "I know I should not be afraid of storms, but I cannot seem to help it. It was on a night like this that I saw—" She broke off with a shudder. "Well! I had better not think of that experience. I shan't sleep a wink as it is."

Drake raised an eyebrow. "What! Did you see a ghost?"

Miss Pickens gulped and nodded. "I was a mere child," she said faintly, "but I never shall forget it. A white shade, floating across the lawn. Horrible!"

Drake's eyes met Lilah's over Miss Pickens's head. She looked a warning at him, and he quelled his amusement. Instead, he looked down at the governess on his arm and said bracingly, "If I saw something floating across the lawn tonight, I'd think someone's laundry had blown off the clothesline. A nightshirt, or a pillowslip, or something of that sort. But that's the advantage of seeing through an adult's eyes. Daresay a child wouldn't even think of that explanation."

Doubt and surprise flitted across Miss Pickens's features. It was clear that that explanation of what she had witnessed had not occurred to her—then, or at any time since. "Gracious!" she murmured, looking dazed. "Do you suppose . . . No, no. There was something indescribably eerie about what I saw." She shuddered again. "I have been afraid of ghosts ever since."

Drake assumed a philosophical air. "Well, if you see any shades tonight, Miss Pickens, you may send 'em along to me. I'm three doors down the hall from you. They are welcome to float across the lawn, or rattle my shutters, or whatever takes their fancy. Won't bother me a bit."

Miss Pickens actually smiled at this. "It does sound foolish, doesn't it? To be afraid of something that merely floats across a lawn."

Drake's eyes crinkled slightly as he looked at her. "Miss Pickens," he said solemnly, "I wouldn't dream of calling you foolish."

They had reached the door to her bed-chamber. Drake pulled it open and, with Miss Pickens's permission, strolled across the small, cold room and checked the window latches. Pooh-poohing her suggestion that they ring for a servant, Drake kindled the fire for her with his own hands, lit the small lamp at the side of her bed, placed her candle on the mantelpiece to give her an additional source of light, and bowed. "All's safe," he promised her.

Miss Pickens was pink with embarrassment and gratification. "Oh, my lord, you are too good," she stammered.

"Nonsense," he said, seeming surprised. "It was my pleasure."

Lilah had watched the scene from the open doorway, leaning against the doorjamb and smiling in spite of herself. Drake seemed utterly unaware that it was unusual for a man of his rank to wait on a governess. There was a task to be done and he did it, soothing Miss Pickens's alarms and seeing to her comfort with no more fuss than if she were a cherished aunt.

She was still puzzling over why she found this quality so endearing when she looked up to see that the moment was over; Miss Pickens was bidding them good night and Drake now stood beside her, closing the door. Lilah straightened hurriedly. She was about to be alone with Drake, and her wits immediately began to scatter. She swallowed hard, then, as the door before her shut tight, she sneaked a peek at his face.

Drake had one hand on the doorknob while the other held the lamp high, its circle of mellow light keeping the darkness of the passage at bay. His eyes glinted down at her. Their expression made her heart race with excitement—and an overpowering sense of danger. "I hope," he said softly, "that you are in no hurry to return to the drawing room."

At his words, Lilah's hand shook and her candle suddenly jumped and wavered. Drake took it from her, blew it out, and set it on the low table beside Miss Pickens's door. Lilah knew what was coming. She knew it in her bones. She made one last, feeble attempt to forestall the inevitable.

"I thought you had decided to avoid being alone with me," she said. Her voice came out suspiciously weak and quavery.

His eyes met hers squarely. "I changed my mind."

And then, as she had hoped—as she had feared—he pulled her roughly to him with his free hand and kissed her, his arm encircling her waist, holding her fast. Holding her up, for surely she would have sunk to the floor otherwise; her knees seemed to melt like so much sealing wax. All of her, all of her was melting.

She moaned and sagged against him, limp and delirious, while he kissed her as if he had all night to do it, all night to kiss her senseless.

But it wouldn't take him all night to kiss her senseless. She had obviously lost her mind already.

Helpless tears spilled down her cheeks. When he tasted salt he groaned and murmured, "Lilah. Lilah, don't cry. Don't cry, sweeting." He kissed the tear tracks with a gentleness she had not glimpsed in him before. Then he pulled her down the passage to a tiny windowed alcove. The rain drummed against the mullioned windows, muffling their conversation from any listening ears. Drake set the lamp on the window bench and took Lilah silently into his arms.

She leaned her cheek against his lapel and gave a loud sniff, hugging him tightly. "Drake," she said dolefully, "we are truly in the suds."

His chuckle rumbled in her ear. "That we are," he agreed.

Frustrated, she beat her fist against his chest. "Why did you kiss me?" she asked indignantly. "I could bear it until you kissed me."

"I had to kiss you," he said tensely. "For one thing, I had to make sure I wasn't imagining this. But I wasn't. It's real." He took her by the shoulders and held her away from him. His expression was grim. "I kissed Eugenia yesterday. It felt like kissing my sister."

285

"Oh, dear," said Lilah faintly. "You mean you had never kissed her before?"

"No. I wish I had thought of that before I proposed marriage to her." Drake looked disgusted. "Then, to make matters worse, she sat me down this afternoon and filled my ears full of the most maudlin pap I ever heard. Mewling about her marital duties and all that, as if she expected me to torture her in the marriage bed. She intends to *submit* to me, for God's sake!" He shuddered. "She intends to do her duty."

Lilah blinked at him. "But isn't that what you want? A submissive wife?"

"Hell, no!" He let go of her and thrust his hands through his hair. It was the first time she'd seen him use both hands. The gesture did twice as much damage as usual. *Adorable,* thought Lilah, besotted. But Drake was talking again, pacing back and forth with an expression of horror that made her want to laugh out loud.

"I wish you could have heard her," he exclaimed. "Fairly made my blood run cold. She means to obey me in all things. Never set up her will in opposition to mine. I'm to be the master, the head of the house, and she's to be the heart, whatever that means. Of all the mealy-mouthed, colorless, boring, timid—"

"Drake," she interrupted, breaking into laughter. "That is *exactly* what you said you wanted. You are describing the very qualities you told me you admired in a woman. The qualities Eugenia has, and I lack."

He halted in midstride, then abruptly pulled her against him again. The fierce, possessive gesture took her breath away. "And what of the qualities you have and Eugenia lacks?" he demanded. He brought his face within inches of hers, his eyes glowing like twin pools of fire. She stared into them and felt that odd lassitude coming over her again, turning her dizzy. "Tell me," he whispered. His lips trailed over her cheek. *Oh, heaven.* "Are you submitting to me, Lilah? Is what you feel now—obedience?"

She shivered. "No," she admitted weakly. "I'd have to say it is . . . something else."

"And what I feel isn't mastery," he growled. "I never felt less in control in my life."

He took her lips again, with an unmistakable hunger that went straight to Lilah's heart. *I cannot have this man,* she thought, aching with loss. *He is not for me.* "Stop," she said at last. Her voice was faint and lacked conviction, but at least she got the words out. "Please stop, Drake."

He did stop kissing her, but rested his forehead against hers, his breathing ragged. "You've ruined my life," he groaned. "I had everything planned."

"So did I," said Lilah mournfully.

"Now I don't want any of it. Not Eugenia,

nor a life of peace and order, nor a perfect, dutiful wife." His hands came up and cradled her cheeks, framing her face, and he pulled his head back to look at her. "I want you, Lilah," he said hoarsely. His eyes studied her features as if memorizing them, lingering on each curve and plane of her face. "I want imperfect, amazing, maddening you. I want a life of chaos and laughter and endless arguments." His voice lowered and roughened. "And I don't want *submission* in my bed. I want passion."

His words made her tremble. *Passion.* How could any woman share Drake's bed and not feel passion? His eyes darkened as he saw her expression change, as he felt the quiver go through her. She could hide nothing from him. His fingertips traced her cheekbones, lightly; then his hands ran back and tangled in her hair. "Lilah," he whispered. The need in his voice made her name sound like prayer. And then his mouth came down on hers, crushing her lips, demanding the response that her eyes had promised him.

She gave it willingly.

Lilah felt her hair come loose and tumble down her back. She registered a moment's fleeting regret that she could not, now, return to the drawing room—and then she didn't care anymore. Her arms snaked around Drake's neck and pulled him closer. She kissed him with a ferocity that matched his, arching her back, reaching up on tiptoe, anything, anything to connect with him.

She could feel the heat of his hands through the thin silk of her gown. They slid down her back, spanned her waist. So warm. So strong. They moved lower, cupping her behind, and she gave a little gasp of mingled shock and desire. Then, with a deep groan of longing, Drake bent and slid one arm beneath her thighs, lifting her. Lilah pulled her face back, startled. "Drake—what—"

"Sit with me," he muttered thickly. He carried her to the window bench. The storm still beat against the windowpanes and the cold seeping through the glass made Lilah shiver. Drake leaned back against the wall and pulled her across his lap, cradling her. "I'll keep you warm," he whispered.

She leaned against him, relishing the feel of him. The strength of him. He was a solid wall of muscle, warm but unyielding. She felt, idiotically, that nothing bad could happen to her in the haven of Drake's arms—although she knew perfectly well that this was the most dangerous place she could possibly be.

The lamp had been set on the other end of the bench. Drake played with her hair, running his fingers through it and watching it shimmer in the lamplight. The infatuated expression on

289

his face as he watched the light play on her hair made her smile, but her smile quickly faded. She was in a terrible fix, she thought, and had little to smile about.

Drake's gaze lifted from her hair to her face. Heat still burned in the amber depths of his eyes. "Tell me. How many men have you kissed?"

"Four," she said demurely. Charlie Brewer hardly counted, since she had been nine years old at the time and had kissed him on a dare, but Drake didn't need to know that.

He looked taken aback. "Four?"

She smiled, tracing the outline of his lips with her finger. "Does that seem too many, or too few?" she asked him teasingly.

He scowled. "Too many."

She looked down her nose at him, one eyebrow raised. "And how many women have you kissed, pray tell?"

His lips twitched. "More than four," he said grudgingly.

"Aha! I thought so."

But then his eyes searched hers, deadly serious. "Was it ever like this?"

Her arch smile faded. "No," she whispered. "Never."

His warm hands framed her face again. "Nor for me," he murmured. His lips brushed against hers with infinite tenderness. "No matter how I kiss you," he whispered against her mouth, "or how many times I kiss you, I cannot get enough."

His words sent a rush of heat through her. Oh, she was undone.

He held her with one arm, tipping her slant-wise as he kissed her, and she lay back across his arm, pliant. Unresisting. The skimpy sleeve of her gown bared her upper arm; his hands now moved to caress the tender flesh, sliding intimately across her slender limb, encircling it. It was a liberty no man had ever dared to take. Lilah almost swooned at the exquisite sensation; his fingers were so warm against her cool skin, his touch so delicious.

He ran his hand up over her shoulder and swept his palm down, following the line of satin piping across the low-cut bodice, warming her delicate skin. And then, as gentle as a whisper, he fanned his fingers out and covered her breast with his hand. The heat of his palm through the silk made her gasp; she arched her back instinctively, trembling and mindless. No man had touched her like this before. Not her body, nor her soul.

She opened her eyes and saw Drake's face, his powerful, fierce, beloved face, hovering over hers. His eyes were fixed on her body, watching his own hand as he caressed her. His expression made her shake with need; seeing his desire fu-

eled her own. She watched his eyes as they traveled up her throat and met her gaze. His voice
was hoarse when he spoke. "I have never
wanted anything as much as I want you." But
he stilled his hand and tore his gaze from hers,
tilting his chin to force his focus at the ceiling,
breathing deeply. He then lifted his hand, carefully, so carefully, and placed it chastely at her
waist. "This is wrong," he said, his voice rasp-
ing with the effort it cost him. "But I swear to
you, I will make it right."

His words seemed to rip at her heart.
"Drake," she said miserably, "I—"

"Ssh. Hush, sweeting," he crooned, his arms
tightening around her. "We'll save our tears for
later." And he kissed her again, compelling her
silence. She surrendered without a fight. It
seemed, to her, the only thing to do. Yes. She
would save her tears for later. For now there
was Drake, and the rain, and the lamplight. And
that was enough.

18

They drifted in time, drugged with kisses and whispers. Heat curled between them, slow and sensuous, linking them in a trancelike haze. Drake, more experienced than Lilah, took great care to keep the fire they shared from blazing out of control. This much, but no more. This far, but no farther. His hands did not wander beyond the boundaries he seemed to have set in his mind, and Lilah willingly followed wherever he led, trusting that he would keep her safe. Trusting him was part of the dream, part of the wonder that she felt.

That it was costing him something became obvious to her, even in her innocence. His body seemed to hum with tension. His breathing grew ever more ragged. Eventually he called a halt, pressing his cheek against the top of her head while he struggled for control. Held tightly against him, Lilah could feel the pounding of his heart.

Still caught in the dream, Lilah lifted her lips

and kissed his throat. "I wish I could kiss more of you," she murmured drunkenly. "I wish I could kiss you all night long."

Drake uttered a strangled sound that fell somewhere between a groan and a laugh. "Lilah, you're killing me. If we don't go back to the drawing room soon, we never shall."

She chuckled. "Oh, it's far too late to return to the party. And look at my hair! I'm ruined."

Drake took a deep breath. "No, you're not," he said steadily. "But you soon will be, if we don't stop now. I'm only flesh and blood."

Reality was knocking. Lilah wished she could bolt the door and hide. She tucked herself more snugly against him, feeling bereft as the shreds of dream slipped away. "I suppose we can't stay here forever," she said sadly. "Much as I would like to."

He kissed the top of her head, then thrust her away from him with both hands. "Off, now," he ordered briskly. "I'm going to do the right thing, for once, and let you go."

She frowned, resisting his attempts to dislodge her. "But I don't want to go."

A glint of humor lit his eyes. "I should have made myself clear. I'm letting you go for now. But not forever." He picked a hairpin off her lap where it had fallen, and tried, unsuccessfully, to return it to her coiffure. "I can't lose you now, Lilah," he said softly. "I couldn't bear it."

His words made her feel better. Which was absurd, really. Nothing had changed. Lilah sighed at her own foolishness, and took the pin from him. "What are we going to do, Drake? I confess, I can't see my way clear. We're in a dreadful tangle."

"Tangle or not, I can't marry Eugenia. That's certain."

Lilah rolled her eyes in mock exasperation. "Then perhaps you shouldn't have asked her. Twice." She wriggled off his lap. "When I think how *determined* you were, just the other day—"

"Yes, well, everything's changed," he said shortly. "I'm going to marry you. Come along." He pulled her to her feet.

"Was that an offer of marriage?" asked Lilah indignantly. "It wasn't very romantic."

His rare grin flashed. "You'll have to make allowances for my natural exhaustion. I've made three offers of marriage in less than three days. Wears a man out."

He reached for the lamp, but Lilah put out her hand and stopped him before he could pick it up. "Drake," she said softly, "in all seriousness. Were I Eugenia, I would not let you go. Why did she accept you? She must want to marry you." She lifted one hand and placed it against his cheek, needing to touch him. Pain tore at her. "Are you hoping to convince her that she should wed my father after all? I don't think you will succeed. I want to believe it, but I can't. Were I in her place, I would never give you up. Not for worlds."

His chin jutted stubbornly. "Your father still means to wed her. Let him. I'll bow out."

"It won't be that easy. Eugenia has already written to my father. We're too late." She closed her eyes to keep tears from welling.

"Balderdash," said Drake bracingly. "Remember, my supposed engagement to Eugenia has been kept secret. Nothing's been announced. I'll simply tell her I made a mistake."

Lilah's eyes flew open. "You would *cry off*? Oh, Drake, you can't!"

He shifted his feet uneasily. "I know it's not the gentlemanly thing to do—"

"It certainly isn't!"

"—but she'll understand. We've known each other forever; she knows how I am. Impulsive. When I offered her marriage, I hadn't thought the matter through."

Lilah shook her head, troubled. "That's not strictly true," she pointed out. "This was not an impulsive decision. You planned for years to marry Eugenia."

"Plague take it!" Drake exploded. "I hadn't met *you*!" He crushed her body against his, as if fearing she would escape him unless he held her tight. "Why the devil did we meddle?" he groaned. "Everything was sewn up nicely until we blundered in."

Lilah's arms went around him gratefully. Just to hold him was a comfort. "If we hadn't meddled," she said wistfully, "we never would have met."

"Is that a good thing or a bad thing?"

She had to think about that for a minute. Would she be happier had she never met Drake? Probably. Would she trade this evening for anything in the world? No.

"I don't know," she admitted. "Since you *would* propose to Eugenia, I suppose it's a bad thing that we met." She frowned. "I do wish you had discussed it with her a little more before committing yourself, or at least tried kissing her. You might have discovered your mistake before it was too late."

She felt the arms around her loosen. "I told you two days ago that I had lost my desire to wed Eugenia," he reminded her. "It was your bright idea that we stay the course."

"It seemed a good idea at the time," said Lilah defensively. She lifted her cheek from his chest. "We knew we weren't thinking straight. All I said was that we should trust the choices we made when we weren't feeling rattled. You agreed with me."

"That'll teach me. I won't agree with you so

readily the next time you make some hare-brained suggestion."

Lilah pulled back against the circle of his arms and glared up at him. "Whose harebrained suggestion was it to attend the masquerade uninvited?" she asked tartly. "Whose harebrained suggestion was it to switch targets? If I had spoken to Papa instead of trying to soften up Eugenia, everything might have come out beautifully."

"If you had just stayed put and minded your own business in the first place," he growled, "everything *would* have come out beautifully. I would have nipped in and stolen Eugenia from your father, and I would have been glad to marry her. I would have been perfectly content with my lot. Now I never shall be."

"Don't try to lay this disaster in my dish," she warned him. "If *you* had stayed put and minded your own business, I would have persuaded Papa to send Eugenia packing, she would have rushed to you for consolation, and everything would still have come out beautifully."

"This is a singularly pointless discussion," said Drake, evidently hanging on to his patience by the slenderest of threads. "We'll never know what might have been. We must deal with the immediate problem."

"And which of our problems do you consider

immediate?" inquired Lilah in a voice of ice. "We have several to choose from."

His jaw tightened. "My most pressing problem is that I have fallen in love with a shrew," he said grimly. "All other difficulties pale before that one. You can't converse with me for ten minutes without ripping up at me."

She tilted her head and regarded him saucily. "It's irresistible," she told him. "You are so badly in need of a good set down, I simply *must* poke you a little."

His eyes gleamed, and Lilah knew, with a little thrill of discovery, that he found their battles as stimulating as she did. "All I ask is a quiet life. And what happens? I meet you." He shook his head, looking gloomy. "You're the worst fate that can befall a man. I think you've bewitched me."

Lilah bit back a ripple of laughter. "Humbug. Besides, we get along together perfectly when you are not arguing with me. Why must you be so quarrelsome? If you would refrain from hurling wild accusations—"

"If you would stop provoking me—"

"If you would show the slightest consideration for my feelings—"

"If you wouldn't interrupt me every two seconds—"

"If you would stop trying to control me—"

"If you would only listen to me with the *pretense* of respect for my authority—"

"Authority, my eye!" The word jarred her out of her laughter for a moment. She pushed indignantly against his chest. "You have no authority over me."

His arms tightened around her waist again. "I will have," he promised her. "I will have." Devils danced in his eyes. "I can hardly wait."

Something in his expression made her feel suddenly hot and breathless. He seemed to be picturing things he might compel her to do, if she ever granted him authority over her. She glanced sideways at him, through her lashes. "You don't frighten me," she told him softly, daring him. "I am no man's chattel."

The lamplight seemed to leap and flare in his eyes. "That you are not," he said. "And never will be, as God is my witness." His head bent, and she lifted her lips to his gladly.

"Marry me, Lilah," he whispered. "I promise you, you won't regret it. I adore you."

She clung to him, hardly knowing whether to laugh or cry. "Oh, Drake! I would marry you tomorrow if I could."

She felt his body go utterly still. Then he took her by the shoulders and held her away from him a bit, staring at her as if seeing her for the first time. "That's it," he said slowly. "That's the answer."

Lilah was confused. "The answer to what?"

"That's what we'll do." He took a breath, excitement kindling in his eyes. "We'll be married tomorrow."

She was too stunned to reply. Drake gave her shoulders a little shake. "Lilah, will you do it? Say yes."

He saw the refusal in her eyes and placed one hand firmly over her mouth. "Do not argue with me," he commanded. "Not this time! This is the surest way out of our difficulties. We'll make a clean break. We'll give them no chance to wring their hands or scold us. We'll be gone and the deed will be done before they know what hit them. And once we're man and wife, by God, they can't touch us."

Lilah tapped her foot against the carpet, waiting grimly for Drake to lift his hand from her mouth. He finally did so. "Drake," she said, in the calm tones one would use to address a lunatic, "you are asking me to elope with you."

"That's right." He waggled his eyebrows at her like a villain in a melodrama. "And if you don't agree, my pretty, I'll abduct you."

She tried not to laugh. "This is *not* amusing."

"I'm not joking."

Lilah looked skeptical. "You would steal me by force?"

"You'd love it."

His words gave her a secret, shameful thrill.

She bit her lip to hide it. "Elopements are for fallen women and fortune hunters and other riffraff," she said loftily. "I've no desire to start a scandal."

"Pshaw," he scoffed. "There's nothing to fear. What's a little gossip? It always dies down eventually. Let people say what they like about us— we won't hang about to hear it." He gave her a sly wink. "I'll take you home to Drakesley. Have you ever seen the Lakes?"

"The Lakes," repeated Lilah, feeling overwhelmed. She had longed all her life to see the lake country. "Oh, my. Is that where Drakesley is?"

"Yes. You will love it there, as I do." His enthusiasm was contagious. "We'll tour the entire district, if you like. We'll dawdle about for weeks. I'll hide you till the next seven-day wonder comes along and the world turns its eyes away from us. By the time we see London again, sweetheart, our wedding will be old news."

Hope and doubt warred in Lilah's heart. "Oh, if it were only possible!" she exclaimed.

"Possible? Why, there's nothing to it." A clock chimed in the distance. Drake held up a finger to warn her to silence, and listened intently. "Two o'clock. Excellent. We can easily be ready in three hours." His eyes returned to hers, bright with reckless determination. "I'll meet you outside your door when the clock chimes five. No sense in leaving earlier; we're not that far from London. We'll borrow Uncle Nat's gig. It won't be as fast as my curricle would have been, but no matter. We'll reach Doctor's Commons before breakfast. Ha! We'll be waiting on the doorstep when the offices open." When she still stared at him, seeming not to comprehend, he squeezed her shoulders with playful impatience. "Doctor's Commons is where I can buy a special license, goose. No need to publish banns. No need to wait for anything. You'll be Lady Drakesley by noon."

The enormity of it struck her, and she gasped, one hand flying to cover her mouth. "Lady Drakesley," she repeated, dazed. "Great heavens above. Oh, Drake, we can't elope! You're not a clerk or a sailor; your marriage is a matter of importance. You must have pomp and splendor and dignity. There ought to be parties and announcements and—"

"I don't care about that," he said impatiently. "The biggest nuisance imposed by rank is the legal folderol. We'll have to have marriage settlements and dowers and portions and all that rot drawn up. But we can tackle it later." Something occurred to him and he sobered briefly, searching her face for clues to her thoughts. "Don't tell me you've nothing to wear," he warned her. "I don't care if you walk down the aisle in a burlap sack."

She gave a little spurt of laughter. "It won't be as bad as that, although I do wish I had something wonderful to honor the occasion." Happiness welled in her, irrepressible and sweet. She felt suddenly giddy with it. "Let's do it," she said, her eyes sparkling. "I know it's rash and ill advised and shocking. I know all the gossips will dine out on our news for a fortnight. I don't care."

Drake seized her in a bear hug and swung her round in a circle. "That's my girl!" he exclaimed.

And that was how Lilah found herself tiptoeing out of Wexbridge Abbey in the gray light of dawn, clutching a valise.

19

The sun was coming up. They had been traveling in silence for a while, with no sound but the beat of the horse's hooves, the jingle of the harness, and the creak and rattle of the gig itself as its wheels spun steadily beneath them, pulling them ever closer to London. The combined rhythm of these sounds seemed to be chanting words in Lilah's brain, repeating an endless refrain: not *clippety clop, clippety clop* but *runaway bride, runaway bride.*

She had a cold feeling in the pit of her stomach. Why did everything look different in the clear light of day? It wasn't fair. Eloping with Drake had seemed such a grand adventure. Now, as the light slowly grew and gathered, bringing the sleepy countryside to life around them, shame was dawning in her.

Just nerves, she told herself staunchly. Every bride feels nervous on her wedding day.

Except that she didn't feel nervous. She felt guilty. She stole a glance at Drake, sitting

305

ramrod-straight beside her. His eyes were, naturally, focused on the road. Was she imagining it, or was there a grim set to his mouth? Were those lines of strain around his eyes? Was he feeling what she was feeling?

She hoped not. A lump rose in her throat. One of them had better be wholehearted about this venture, or it was likely to fail. And although she was feeling far from easy in her mind, she desperately wanted to marry Drake. She just wished he had abducted her, as he had threatened to do. It would be lovely to wake up married to Drake . . . if it were all his doing, and none of her responsibility.

Well, it *was* all his doing, she told herself. This wasn't her idea. He had talked her into it. Lilah hugged herself against the cold morning air, trying to remember the arguments that had seemed so persuasive a few hours ago. They eluded her.

She must be tired. She didn't feel tired, but after all, she hadn't slept all night. Her brain must not be working properly. She wanted to marry Drake, didn't she? Yes, indeed she did. She didn't want him stolen away by Eugenia Mayhew, did she? No, she certainly didn't. Very well, then. She was doing the only possible thing. Since it was the only possible thing, it must be the right thing.

But it didn't feel right. It didn't feel right at all.

She sneaked another peek at her companion. This time, he was looking at her. His expression was grave, and when his eyes met hers and he read the unhappiness on her face he slowed the horse, muttering rueful curses under his breath. "Out with it, brat," he said shortly. "You're having second thoughts."

"No, no," said Lilah quickly. "Not that, precisely. And kindly stop calling me *brat*."

"I'll try." He gave her a twisted smile. "But that's not what's troubling you. Is it?"

She tucked one cold hand into the pocket of his greatcoat and snuggled against him a little, sighing. "No. I'm sorry, Drake. I suppose I'm just greedy. I want to marry you, but I also want an untroubled conscience." She gave a shaky little laugh. "So far, I have been unable to reconcile the two. If I must choose between you and my conscience, I choose you."

His arm went around her, warm and comforting, but he said nothing. They drove slowly on. "I own, I'm not feeling as brash as I felt earlier," he admitted glumly. "Plague take it! A conscience is more a hindrance than a help."

"Yes," she said listlessly. "Often it is."

The arm around her tightened. "I won't give you up," he said fiercely.

"Good," she said in a small voice.

"But here's the thing, Lilah. We've been sniping at Sir Horace and Eugenia for days, despis-

ing their cowardice, and now we are acting like
the biggest cowards of the lot." He reined in the
horse, drawing the carriage to the side of the
road so he could turn to her. "Lilah, my love,"
he said, with unaccustomed gentleness, "we
can't do this. We must go back and face them."

She clung to his hands. "Must we?" she asked
miserably. "I am so afraid it will end badly."

"It may end badly. It won't be easy and it
won't be fun. But we must see it through, that's
all. We must stand firm. I will be reviled for
breaking my word to Eugenia, and you will be
scolded for luring me away from her, and everyone will rip up at the both of us for meddling
in the first place. Well, why not? They have a
right to be angry. We've behaved abominably.
But running off with each other to avoid a scene
is . . . well, it's unworthy of us."

She gave a rather watery chuckle. "Oh, yes.
Unworthy of two such brave and noble persons
as we are."

He grinned. "That's the dandy. We'll keep re-
minding ourselves how brave and noble we are,
and that will shame us into right conduct."

"I'm not feeling particularly brave. Or noble,"
said Lilah forlornly. She snuggled against his
shoulder, wishing she could burrow like a rabbit
into his solid warmth. "Aunt Polly and Uncle
Ned are fond of Eugenia, you know. They are
her family as much as yours. I'm afraid they

will convince you to give me up and wed her. And even if it *is* the right thing to do—which, I have the most lowering suspicion, it probably is—I don't want you to do it."

He held her, patting her comfortingly. "Hush, now. There's no chance of anyone convincing me to marry Eugenia. You may have noticed, I'm a rather stubborn chap."

She had to smile. "Yes. I'm so glad." Her best hat was being crushed against his greatcoat, but she didn't care. It was worth anything to feel Drake's arms around her.

She felt his laughter rumbling against her ear, and heard it change to a deep growl. "I wish I could pull this blasted gig into that copse over there and ravish you," he muttered.

She pulled back so she could look at him. "If you are trying to shock me, you will have to try harder than that," she told him primly. "It sounds a lovely idea, and I hope you will bear it in mind. I rely upon it, in fact—to make you hold your ground while your family rings a peal over you."

"I'll hold my ground, all right and tight." He gave her a crooked grin. "So—are we agreed? We turn round, go back to the house, and confess all. We then listen with patience to whatever my family has to say, beg their pardons most humbly, and stick to our guns."

"Right," said Lilah, trying to sound more confident than she felt.

He tapped her nose with his index finger. "Trust me. I'm not as changeable as the past few days have made me seem."

She forced herself to smile. "I'm delighted to hear *that,* at any rate."

His expression softened as he looked down into her face. "One kiss. To seal the bargain." He tilted her chin up with one finger and bent his head to hers. His lips moved gently across her mouth in a kiss that was cherishing and tender. Lilah clung to the lapels of his coat and kissed him back, aching. It was terrible to fear, in spite of his assurances, that this might be their last kiss.

The light was full, now, and she was dimly aware that their scandalous behavior had drawn the interest of a group of farm laborers in a nearby field. She felt their eyes on her, but didn't care. There was a carriage approaching from the opposite direction, too, despite the earliness of the hour. She didn't care about that, either. She didn't care who saw Drake's kiss; she defied anyone to make her feel ashamed of kissing the man she would marry. For she *would* marry him somehow, she vowed to herself. She would make it happen, come hell or high water.

Or Sir Horace. For it was neither hell nor high water approaching in that oncoming coach; it was Sir Horace Chadwick. He stared at the couple wantonly embracing at the side of the road—first with amusement and then, as he recognized the parties, with disbelief. He shouted to his driver to stop, stop!

Sir Horace's outraged bellow, combined with the sound of his traveling coach being hastily drawn to a halt beside them, caused the couple to stop kissing. Lilah's eyes flew open and she saw, past Drake's shoulder, her father's face—nearly unrecognizable with astonishment and fury, but definitely her father's face, leaning halfway out the coach window. His face was larger and redder than she had ever seen it, and his eyes appeared to be starting from their sockets. Lilah squeaked. It was an inelegant sound, but it was the only utterance she was capable of at the moment.

Sir Horace spluttered incoherently for a second or two, then managed to shout in a terrible voice, "Delilah Chadwick! Get down from that carriage this instant!"

"Papa!" she cried. "Drake, look—it is my father!" She squirmed out of Drake's grasp, nearly climbing over him in her haste to reach Sir Horace. "Papa, what are you doing here?"

He goggled at her. "What am *I* doing? How, in heaven's name, can you ask what *I* am doing? I have driven half the night to reach this place with whatever haste I could muster, only to find—" Words seemed to fail him for a moment. "What are *you* doing here, missy?" he shouted

311

at last. His wrathful gaze lit on Drake. "And you, sirrah—earl or no earl, I'll have the law on you if you dare to molest my daughter!"

"So I should hope," remarked Drake. "Lilah, pray remove yourself from my lap. I wish to get down from here and speak with your father."

"Oh, good. I wish to speak with him, too." She straightened eagerly and held out her hand. Drake jumped lightly down from the gig and turned to help Lilah navigate the step.

Sir Horace watched these maneuvers with angry amazement. "You are very nonchalant, the two of you—upon my word! Have you no shame?"

"Not much," Drake admitted. He kept Lilah's hand firmly in his once she stood beside him on the ground. "I hope you will join us, sir, in a brief walk," he said politely. "I trust your driver can look after our horses while we converse for a moment or two."

Sir Horace did not wait for the steps to be let down. The door to the coach flew open with a bang and he fairly tumbled out in his haste. "I'll speak with you," he promised, wrath still burning in his eyes. "And you'll hear what I have to say, begad, or there'll be the devil to pay!"

"Oh, Papa, of course we will listen to you," said Lilah soothingly. "But you must listen to Lord Drakesley, too."

Sir Horace shot her an angry glance. "I suggest you say nothing at present, kitten. I'm far too displeased with you to give you a hearing."

Lilah clamped her mouth shut, deciding that the most prudent course—for the present—was to obey. Drake stepped neatly between Lilah and her father, and she clung to Drake's other arm, doing her best to duck behind his large body and stay out of Papa's sight. They had barely walked out of the driver's earshot before Sir Horace exploded in wrath.

"I am glad for the chance to speak with you, i'faith! I have a bone to pick with you, my lord. I received a message last night from Miss Mayhew—such a message as I have never received in my life! I could scarce make heads or tails of it, but the gist of it seemed to be that you, sir—you!—were pressing attentions on both Miss Mayhew *and* my daughter, with what object I cannot conceive! Good God, sir, what are you about? If I understood her correctly— which is by no means certain—you renewed your offer of marriage to her. An offer I would not have believed it possible you could make, had I not witnessed with my own eyes and ears your utter disregard for propriety and decency!"

Drake winced. "Now, then, sir, it's not as bad as that—"

"It is every bit as bad as that!" shouted Sir Horace, waving his fist in the air. "I have never seen anything like it! You will give me leave

313

to tell you, my lord, that I find your behavior incredible! Incredible! I cannot express myself strongly enough. I'm a patient man, my lord, but you have driven me beyond the bounds of what any man can tolerate! Proposing marriage to my fiancée—*my* fiancée, sir!—not once, but twice! Without so much as a by-your-leave! With the *banns* already read—why, she's as good as mine! Your transgression is hardly less severe than if you had attempted to woo my *wife*. For she is my affianced wife, my lord, and you would do well to bear that in mind!"

Lilah was really alarmed. She had never known her father to fly into such a passion. He was normally a placid soul. She leaned forward and peeked past Drake's shoulder, trying to see Papa's face, but Drake smoothly interposed his arm, pushing her back out of sight. "Well, as to that point—" Drake began, but Sir Horace interrupted him again.

"Is it your object to insult and humiliate *me*?" he demanded. "It must be, for I cannot credit that you, or, indeed, any man of sense, would deliberately embarrass Miss Mayhew. What have I done, my lord, to offend you? I have no recollection of ever meeting you before! What have I done to earn your enmity?"

"Nothing, nothing in the world," said Drake hastily. "In fact—"

"For it is not only my fiancée whom you have

targeted, but my daughter as well! What do you mean by it, my lord? What can you possibly mean by such marked disrespect, such shocking contempt for my daughter's fair name? The first time I laid eyes on you, you were touching my Lilah in a way that struck me as suggestive—*suggestive,* my lord, and I promise you I understate the matter! And now I come upon you—having been informed that you plan to snap your fingers in the face of the world and marry Miss Mayhew, despite her lawful betrothal to me—*kissing* my daughter in the public road! With no more respect for her than if she were a milkmaid!" Overcome with fury, Sir Horace halted at this point in his peroration and moved to seize Lilah's hand, yanking it away from Drake's clasp. "And as for *you,* Lilah, I am deeply ashamed of your conduct. More than ashamed, I am incredulous! I am astonished! I am mortified."

To Lilah's dismay, Papa's beloved face suddenly crumpled and tears started in his eyes. He shook his head, struggling to command his emotions, and Lilah cried out in distress. "Oh, Papa, do not look so!" She flew into his arms with a sob. "I cannot bear it. Pray, pray do not be angry with me."

He patted her awkwardly. "I am angry with you, Lilah, I cannot deny it. I thought you knew better, kitten. I never would have believed that any man could turn your head so easily, or make you behave in a manner you know full well to be wrong."

"Oh, Papa," said Lilah miserably. "If you would only let me explain—"

"I do not blame you totally, child." She could feel the anger in his tense arms as he pushed her resolutely away, the better to face Drake. "I know where the blame lies. If I were a younger man, Lord Drakesley, I would be strongly tempted to call you out."

Drake looked harassed. "I can't say I blame you, for I don't. My actions may seem strange on the surface—"

"Strange? Is that how you would characterize your behavior? *Inexplicable* comes nearer the mark! Bizarre! Outlandish! Incomprehensible!"

"Yes, yes, yes, whatever you like," snapped Drake, his patience with being scolded obviously wearing thin. "But if you would listen to me for three minutes—"

"By Jove! The more I think on it, the angrier I become! Kissing my Lilah, and at the same time trying to fix your interest with Miss Mayhew—by heaven, sir, I hope my Eugenia read you a lecture you won't soon forget!"

"Well, she didn't," said Drake, nettled. "She accepted my offer. Which, if you read her letter, you should already know."

"Drake!" exclaimed Lilah. "The fact that she accepted you is entirely beside the point!"

Drake looked sulky. He jerked his chin to indicate Sir Horace. "Well, he's beginning to annoy me," said Drake truculently. "Carrying on as if he expects every woman to show me the door when I propose. Confound it, I'm an earl! Why shouldn't Eugenia accept me if she wishes to? Why shouldn't you?" he added, seeing that Lilah's eyes were growing round with outrage.

"Tut! Tut!" said Sir Horace testily. "Eugenia has not accepted you, my lord, and well you know it. She is engaged to me. Kindly stop annoying her, which is what you do when you persist in your suit. It cannot prosper, my lord. It cannot prosper, and you are making a figure of yourself."

Drake and Lilah looked blankly at each other. Drake rubbed his chin. "He said her letter was unclear. Apparently it left out the most important part."

"Perhaps that's just as well," said Lilah anxiously. "Lucky, in fact. For if she hasn't broken off her engagement to Papa, why, that lets us all off the hook. Doesn't it?"

"Hook?" Sir Horace looked suspiciously from Drake to Lilah and back again. "What hook? You're talking nonsense, the pair of you. I didn't say Miss Mayhew's letter was unclear. It was perfectly *clear*. The reading of it gave me no trouble; understanding what it all meant was the difficulty! At the end she begged me, in plain English, to come to her without delay, and I have done so. I would be with her now, had I not been waylaid by the two of you."

Drake frowned. "She wants to see you so that she can explain the breaking of her promise to you."

"God grant me patience!" shouted Sir Horace. "She has *not* broken her promise to me." He shook both fists in the air, as if appealing to heaven. "Are you dense, man? Are you deaf? Eugenia and I will be married within a fortnight!"

Drake and Lilah exchanged bewildered looks. "She told you I renewed my proposal," Drake said impatiently. "Didn't she tell you she accepted it?"

"No!" barked Sir Horace. "She told me she *pretended* to accept it. And that, my lord, is what I cannot comprehend! She warned me at the outset that you seldom take no for an answer. But—"

"Wait a moment!" In his eagerness, Drake seized Sir Horace's shoulders. "She told you she was *pretending*? She never meant to have me?"

"That's right, that's right. Unhand me, if you please!" Drake let go, with a very queer expression on his face, and Sir Horace dusted his shoulders crossly. "She did not explain how one can *pretend* to accept a gentleman's proposal. That portion of her message made no sense. It seemed to me she was playing a very dangerous game, and despite all her assurances that nothing had changed between us—that I was to entertain no fears on that head—I could not help feeling some degree of alarm that Miss Mayhew had plunged into deep water. And she went on, if you please, to inform me that my daughter was on the point of contracting a most eligible betrothal, and that if I wished to seal the bargain I should return to Wexbridge Abbey without delay." He rounded angrily on Lilah. "What have you to say to that, kitten? Is there any truth in it? For I promise you, no respectable suitor will stand for your jauntering about the countryside with *this* lunatic"—he jerked a thumb at Lord Drakesley—"And if you have frightened off a decent man with these foolish indiscretions—"

Sir Horace broke off in bewildered incredulity as Drake and Lilah suddenly burst out laughing. Drake seized Lilah round the waist and swung her into an exuberant two-step. "She saw it all!" exclaimed Lord Drakesley. "Clever, clever Jenny! I should have known she'd never let me down."

Lilah pulled a face. "And in marrying you,

she certainly *would* have let you down! You always told me she was a woman of sense. I am relieved to find that you were right."

Sir Horace, spluttering with frustration, tried unsuccessfully to dislodge Drake's hands from his daughter's waist. Lilah caught at his coat sleeve, her eyes bright with happiness. "Papa, pray—! Do you not see? You are to marry Miss Mayhew, and Drake will marry me. Everything has turned out perfectly."

Sir Horace suddenly went very still. His eyes searched Lilah's face, perturbation in his expression. "My dear Lilah, what can you mean? What are you saying? You don't wish to marry Lord Drakesley."

Lilah blushed. "On the contrary, Papa. I wish very much to marry Lord Drakesley."

"And I would like to marry Lilah, sir," Drake added. "I suppose I should mention that, in case you were wondering."

Sir Horace's eyes, round with doubt, traveled to Drake's face. "You just told me, half a minute ago, that you wanted to marry Miss Mayhew."

"Oh, no, sir," Drake assured him. "I said I had *proposed* to her. I never said I wanted to marry her."

Sir Horace flushed angrily. "Now, look here—" he began, but Lilah pulled herself out of Drake's grip and clutched her father's arm affectionately.

"Papa, don't mind Drake. He's not joking

you. It's just that the situation is rather difficult to explain."

"I can see that," said Sir Horace sharply. "Lilah, I think Lord Drakesley must excuse us for a moment. I wish to speak privately with you."

He marched her back to the berline and ushered her inside, then climbed in after her and closed the door. He then sat facing her and took her hands in his, studying her features intently. "Lilah, what are you doing?" he asked her softly. Trouble was in every line of his face. "It isn't like you, child, to behave so wildly. Why have you encouraged Lord Drakesley to think you might accept his suit? It is incomprehensible. I cannot believe that a promise of rank and great wealth would move you."

"Oh, Papa, no," said Lilah miserably. "How could you think that? I love him." She saw the astonishment and perplexity on her father's features and leaned earnestly forward. "I do," she insisted. "Is that so difficult to believe?"

"Yes," said Sir Horace bluntly. "His affections seem to list with the wind. He bestows them first on one lady and then on another. And he has no more regard for propriety than a baboon! You'd be happier wed to a Hottentot."

Lilah had to chuckle, although it pained her to see her father so distressed at her choice. "Well, I haven't met any Hottentots, so I cannot say whether your statement is true or false. But, Papa, if Lord Drakesley is a Hottentot there must be a little of the Hottentot in me, as well. We are as like as two peas in a pod, and understand each other perfectly."

"Understand each other? I thought you quarreled day and night."

"Oh, we do! I didn't say we *agreed* with each other. We understand each other. Agreement is something else." Lilah bit her lip. "It's very difficult to explain, and I know it must sound strange to you," she admitted. "To you, mutual agreement is the very essence of harmony. With Drake and me . . . Oh, how can I express it? Our souls are in harmony even when our opinions differ, so disagreement is no bar to understanding. We respect each other, Papa. We find our arguments entertaining, not alienating."

Sir Horace did not seem reassured by her answer. He stared very hard at her, shaking his head. "Good heavens, child. I begin to think you are as mad as he is."

Lilah gave him a rather misty smile. "Oh! I am."

He still looked worried. "And yet you believe you love him?"

"I know I do," said Lilah fervently. "Although I don't suppose I can ever make you understand it. It seems a little strange to me, as well. You must know I had thought to marry a . . . a less forceful man. Drake was not what I had in mind at all. But now that I have met him"—she shrugged helplessly—"I can't imagine life with any other man. Compared to him, everyone else is boring."

Sir Horace, frowning, was sunk in thought for a few moments. When he looked up at Lilah again, his expression was both pensive and humorous. "There is much in what you say, daughter. Opposites may attract, but a marriage of like minds is more apt to bring happiness. Or so I have come to believe." An apologetic twinkle lit his eyes. "I adored your mother, but our union was far from tranquil. She thrived on a level of drama and excitement that I found exhausting. Now that I am older, I have even less interest in a *thrilling* sort of life. I daresay my choice of Eugenia Mayhew may have baffled you, for she is nothing like your dear Mama—"

Lilah shook her head quickly. "Papa, do not apologize. I own, I was taken aback at first, but all that is forgotten. I see now that Eugenia is the perfect match for you. She is clever, but in a quiet way, and I think you will both enjoy your life of peace and tranquillity." She wrinkled her nose, her eyes sparkling with amusement. "It is, of course, a life that would drive Drake and me quite mad."

Sir Horace chuckled and patted her hand. "One man's peace and quiet is another man's tedium, eh?"

Lilah smiled with relief. "Yes. Just as one couple's stimulating discussion is another couple's ghastly quarrel."

A knock sounded on the berline's door. Lilah pulled it open. Drake leaned in, glancing politely from Lilah to her father. "I hesitate to interrupt while you two are deciding my fate, but perhaps you should consider that the horses are still standing—and that there might be some anxiety back at the Abbey regarding our whereabouts."

"Oh, yes!" exclaimed Lilah. "Papa, we must go back without delay. We didn't leave a note, you know, and everyone will suppose that Drake and I have run off."

"We did run off," Drake reminded her.

"Yes, but we have changed our minds. There's no need for us to elope now. Do let's go back before we start a scandal."

Sir Horace took a deep breath. It was plain that this horror had not occurred to him, in all the excitement of the past half hour. "You were *eloping*?"

"Well, yes," Lilah admitted. "But never mind that! We can do the thing properly now—if you are quite, quite sure that Miss Mayhew did not break faith with you."

Sir Horace covered his eyes with one hand. "Lilah, how could you?" he moaned. "Are you so lost to all proper feeling?"

She opened her eyes in surprise. "Of course not! Which is why I am very glad that we need not elope after all. Papa, what did you think Drake and I were doing, so far from the Abbey at this hour of the morning?"

"Later," ordered Drake. "Can you not see, my love, that your father requires time to digest this surfeit of information? Give over, or you'll send him into a fever! I'm taking the gig back to Wexbridge Abbey. We can tell everyone we drove out to meet Sir Horace, if you like. Lilah, stay with your father—and comfort him if you can." He disappeared, closing the door behind him.

Sir Horace stared. "I cannot say I like his manners," he muttered.

"No, they are atrocious," agreed Lilah serenely. "He orders everyone about, Papa. Do not mind it. It's just his way."

Sir Horace looked very hard at his daughter. "Bless my soul! I never thought I'd see the day when you, of all women, would accept that tone from a man!"

Lilah looked mischievous. "You haven't yet heard the tone he accepts from me."

20

Drake arrived at the Abbey well before the Chadwicks and was waiting impatiently on the steps, pacing to and fro, as they drove up. Higgins appeared in the doorway behind him at the sound of approaching carriage wheels, but Drake strode down to the berline ahead of the staff and jerked the door open. Lilah tumbled happily out, letting Drake catch her rather than wait for the steps to be let down.

"Oh, Drake, it is the most famous thing! Papa has decided that we may be married—if you can convince him that you are *not* deranged, which I feel certain you will be able to do if you set your mind to it."

A glimmer of a smile lightened Drake's features. "I will try," he promised. Keeping one hand on Lilah, he turned to let the steps down for Sir Horace. Sir Horace watched him carefully, his expression still a trifle strained.

"Lilah has a flair for flippant remarks," he said gruffly. "I don't mean any disrespect to you, my lord, as I hope you know. But my daughter's future happiness is at stake. I am disinclined to rush to judgment in such an important matter. Prudence is called for, my lord. I must give her betrothal the careful attention it deserves. I do not intend to make a hasty decision."

"Unlike Lilah and me," Drake supplied, reaching to help Sir Horace alight. "I don't blame you in the least, sir. You hardly know me. Lilah hardly knows me, for that matter."

"I know you," Lilah murmured, glowing. She was clinging to his arm in a most besotted manner. "I know you through and through."

Drake grinned down at her. "Be that as it may, sweetheart, your father may need a little convincing. At any rate, let's go in and face the music. Higgins tells me the family is at breakfast, so we can confess our perfidy to everyone at once."

Lilah took his arm to climb the steps to the front door, but frowned in puzzlement at this news. "Breakfast. That's odd," she remarked. "Who could want breakfast at a time like this? Our absence must have been noticed by now."

Drake chuckled. "I daresay it has, but no mere elopement would throw off Nat Peabody's appetite. The ladies may be in high fidgets, or they may not—but Uncle Nat must have his breakfast."

They entered the Abbey arm in arm, with Sir Horace bringing up the rear. In spite of Drake's sanguine assessment that breakfast would be going forward as usual, Lilah braced for an out-cry when she and Drake walked in. She was confident that Miss Pickens, at least, would be too excited and anxious to do anything as mun-dane as eating breakfast—so she was both amused and annoyed to find that Drake was right, and the entire party was placidly consum-ing coddled eggs. An outcry did occur, but it was filled with glad welcome rather than relief and anger, and it was directed at her father rather than herself. Apparently Lilah and Drake's sensational elopement was less interest-ing than Sir Horace's return from Uxbridge.

There was a general exclamation when Sir Horace was glimpsed, and Nat fairly jumped from his place, wiping his mouth hastily and extending his hand. "Horace, dear chap! Wel-come, welcome. Have you broken your fast yet, old man?" He wrung Sir Horace's hand and waved at the table. "Sit you down, sit you down—no, I won't hear of it; no trouble at all. Eh, Higgins, is that you? Tell Gaston we've three more for breakfast; there's a good fellow. I say, Horace, why'd you run off like that, all in a quack? Gave us quite a turn."

Polly nodded at Sir Horace, but her gaze then slid to Drake and Lilah. The corners of her eyes crinkled. "Here you are, you naughty children," she observed, with mock severity. "For pity's sake, come in and close the door. I dare not ask where you have been."

Nat glanced at his wife in surprise. "Thought they ran off to be married. Wasn't that what you said?" His expression brightened and he turned to Drake. "I say—am I to wish you happy, my boy? Have you done the thing already? Bless me, what fast work!"

"Nat, dear, do sit down," said Polly. "They can't have been married yet." She smiled approvingly at Eugenia. "You were right, my love, as usual. They came back to us safe and sound, and no harm done."

Drake looked down at Lilah. "We might have known," he muttered. "So much for preening ourselves on our cleverness—or our noble resolve to come back here with the deed undone, for that matter. The whole time, we were dancing to Eugenia's tune."

But Lilah was watching, with strangely mixed emotions, her father greeting Miss Mayhew. He had responded genially to Nat Peabody's enthusiastic welcome, but his eyes had continually strayed to Eugenia, and the instant he had been released he had walked to her side, a light in his eyes that Lilah could not mistake. Under Sir Horace's gaze Eugenia turned a most becoming shade of pink, and the smile she gave him glowed with quiet happiness. She extended her hand, and Sir Horace took it.

All Sir Horace said was, "How do you do, my dear? I missed you." He patted her hand and dropped the lightest of kisses on her upturned cheek, then let her go. Eugenia replied composedly, and Sir Horace took his place at the table. That was all that passed between them, but Lilah felt she had glimpsed something tender and private. It was unsettling to see one's father in the throes of strong affection for a woman other than one's mother . . . but under the circumstances, Lilah's predominant emotion was relief. Since Papa *would* marry, she could only thank God that he was going to the altar with love in his heart—and that, miracle of miracles, his chosen bride plainly returned his regard.

The Peabodys' staff entered and flew unobtrusively about, setting additional places and carrying full serving dishes in and empty ones out, while Drake and Lilah meekly seated themselves. Aunt Polly was still fixing them with what was, for her, a gimlet glare. When the last footman had departed, she pointed her spoon at Drake.

"Adam Arthur Beresford Harleston," she said sternly, "*what* were you thinking?"

Drake looked sheepish. "To tell the truth, Aunt, I don't believe I *was* thinking. In fact, I cannot recall having a genuine, unrattled, reasoned thought since I met Miss Chadwick." He glanced uneasily at Eugenia. "I daresay I owe you an apology, Jenny."

Eugenia choked back a laugh. "What, for jilting me? Or for bullying me into that absurd betrothal in the first place?"

His eyes gleamed with sardonic appreciation. "For underestimating you."

She smiled. "Ah. For *that*, my friend, you may apologize."

Miss Pickens set down her fork and looked around the table in bewilderment. "Forgive me, but I do not perfectly understand. Is Miss Mayhew correct that Lilah and Lord Drakesley have formed an attachment?"

"Miss Mayhew is indeed correct," said Drake, managing to bow while still seated.

"Then—is Miss Mayhew betrothed to Sir Horace rather than to you, my lord?"

"Yes, she is," said Sir Horace firmly.

Miss Pickens brightened. "Why, this is delightful. For I have been meaning to tell you, Lilah my love, that I have formed a very high opinion of Miss Mayhew. She seems to be a very clever young woman, and is excessively poised for a girl of her age. I would have been sorry to lose her to Lord Drakesley, for I believe she will make Chadwick Hall an excellent mistress after all."

"Of course she will," said Sir Horace firmly.

"And is our Lilah to marry Lord Drakesley, then?" Miss Pickens clasped her hands before her in an attitude of rapture. "So romantic! I think it's perfectly lovely."

"Well, well, that remains to be seen," said Sir Horace hastily. "Lilah is of age now, and I'm sure I don't wish to stand in her way, but—"

"What!" exclaimed Nat. "Is there any question, my dear Horace? Great heavens! I should think it an excellent match. Excellent."

Sir Horace was turning a dull red. "Oh, well, no offense, Nat. No offense meant. It's just—my own little girl, you know! Can't marry her off in a great, tearing hurry."

"Pooh!" Lilah sat very straight in her chair. "And what of your own marriage, pray? If I had not rushed down here, you would have wed Eugenia without so much as introducing her to me. Or showing her her future home, for that matter! I call that a great, tearing hurry."

Drake nudged her. "Address your father with a little more respect, sweeting, or we'll be forced to elope after all."

Lilah would doubtless have ignored this excellent advice, but Eugenia's soft voice intervened. "I own, I am a little surprised to learn that you object to the match, Horace. Pray, what are your reasons?"

Sir Horace's complexion reddened further. "Tut! I do not like to appear unreasonable, my

332

love. But you must understand that I know little of the man. Whatever his rank, you cannot expect me to view with enthusiasm my daughter's alliance with—" He broke off abruptly.

Drake assisted him to finish his awkward sentence. "With a chap who tried to steal your bride from you. Perfectly understandable. Sir Horace does not like to say it in so many words, but he has no wish to encourage me to hang about—in the bosom of his family, no less! Who knows whether I may make another attempt to steal Eugenia? Or to make off with some other lady? To him, I seem dangerously unhinged."

"Yes, but you are *not*," said Lilah staunchly.

Eugenia smiled. "Lilah is not an impartial observer. But I have known Drake all my life, Horace, and do not hesitate to assure you—if assurance you require—that he is a man of intelligence and principle. His ways may be eccentric, but his heart is sound."

Sir Horace looked doubtful. "I am inclined to rely upon your judgment, Eugenia, but—"

"And," she continued smoothly, "from what I have seen, he loves Lilah ardently, as she loves him. Often these violent attachments burn themselves out, but I believe that Drake and Lilah may prove to have formed a lasting passion. They seem exceptionally well suited."

"She's quite right, Horace," stated Polly, peering kindly at him through her spectacles. "I understand your hesitation, naturally. Drake has behaved like a perfect ass, and you have every reason to think he would make Lilah a dreadful husband. But you must bow to his family's superior knowledge of him—and Eugenia's ability to judge character, which I believe is quite remarkable. Only look at how unerringly she ascertained that *you* were the man to make *her* happy."

Nat winked. "And just wait till you see Drakesley! It's in all the guidebooks, but pictures don't do it justice. Overlooks Lake Windermere, you know. Scenic beauty and all that. Quite a place, quite a place. Your Lilah will live like a queen."

Sir Horace chuckled. "She'd like that," he admitted. "Wouldn't you, kitten?"

But Drake was staring very hard at Eugenia. "Hold on. If you knew all along that I had formed a *lasting passion* for Lilah, why the deuce did you let me make such a cake of myself? You could have saved us all a lot of grief, Jenny, had you simply turned me down flat."

Her eyes twinkled. "You have conveniently forgotten that I *did* turn you down flat. My initial refusal had no effect on you whatsoever," she pointed out. "I was forced to accept you, for if I had not, I would never have heard the end of it. I know you, Drake. You are tenacious as a bulldog. The only way I could induce you to let go of the bone was to let you have it. As soon as I gave you what you *thought* you wanted . . ." She shrugged delicately.

Respect dawned in Drake's eyes. "Egad. You're right. I had a sinking feeling the instant you said yes."

Lilah covered her mouth with her hand to hide her laughter. "What a fellow I am marrying! I thank you, Eugenia, for this valuable example of how to handle Drake."

Eugenia chuckled. "I warn you, it only works when Drake is chasing after something from pure stubbornness—which won't happen as often as your experience of him might lead you to believe."

Drake bowed ironically. "I thank you," he said dryly. "I hope Miss Pickens and Sir Horace can provide me with a few tips on handling Lilah, to level the playing field."

"I am being outmaneuvered," complained Sir Horace. "Everyone speaks of Lord Drakesley's marriage to my daughter as a sure thing."

"So it is," said Nat happily. "Give over, Horace! I don't mind saying, now that things seem to be ending happily, that I was worried, there, for a bit—thinking Eugenia was turning short about, jilting you and all. Polly told me I should have faith in Eugenia's good sense and, by Jove, she was right. Come along, old chap—let Lilah marry Drake. Can't have them running off again, you know. It would cause the very devil of a scandal."

Sir Horace's lips twitched. "Oh, very well," he said grudgingly. "I suppose Nat has the right of it."

Pandemonium ensued. Lilah gave a little shriek of joy and flew to embrace her father, then Drake, then everyone at the table in turn. Drake shook hands all around, grinning, the coddled eggs were forgotten, and a cacophony of chatter broke out. Eventually it was decided that Sir Horace would draft the notice for the papers, and the task of writing the announcement letters that must be sent to various dignitaries and family members was parceled out among the remaining parties.

At last the group scattered, and Drake pulled Lilah into the music room for a few moments alone. Quiet settled around them as the door closed, and she sighed blissfully as he took her into his arms.

"Tired, sweeting?" he murmured.

"Very! But I'm too excited to feel sleepy." She pulled back against the circle of his arms and looked up at him, the better to watch his expression. "Did it feel strange to you," she asked him softly, "to see Eugenia so happy with my father?"

"Not as strange as it doubtless felt to you, to see your father so happy with Eugenia." He pulled a strand of her hair away from her face and tucked it behind her ear, studying her gravely. "You don't really mind it, do you?"

"Oh! No," she said quickly. "It was wrong of us to meddle. Now that I feel certain Papa has made a good choice—an excellent choice—it would be even more wrong to begrudge them their joy." She paused, looking a little doubtful. "They did look happy, didn't they, Drake?"

"That's as happy as Eugenia gets," he explained. "She is not an effusive person."

"Papa isn't, either." She bit her lip. "Drake?"

"Yes, my heart?"

"If you and I are ever separated for any considerable length of time, don't you *dare* greet me with a kiss on the cheek."

Drake emitted a low, growling laugh and tightened his arms around her. "I don't think I could. So if I ever do, don't you dare look happy about it."

She chuckled, but a tiny, niggling doubt gnawed at the edges of her delight. Her smile faded, and she lifted her hands to gently frame his face. His eyes darkened at her touch. Her heart raced at this evidence of his desire for her, but she forced herself to keep her distance. This was important. "Drake," she whispered, troubled. "We will be happy together, too. Won't we?"

Something gleamed in his eyes. He turned his

head and planted a kiss on her palm. The touch of his mouth to her skin was electric. She snatched her hand away. "I don't mean *that*," she said breathlessly.

He reached up and caught her wrists. "I know you don't." He brought her hands down and cradled them at his chest, looking soberly into her face. "If you're asking me whether we'll share the kind of happiness your father will enjoy with Eugenia . . . I doubt that we will." Sly heat flicked at the back of his eyes. "Doubtless you'll always be a brat."

As always, his provoking remarks sparked answering heat in her. She tilted her chin at him. "And you'll always be a brute," she said tartly.

His teeth flashed in a swift grin. "The thing is, you wouldn't want me any other way."

A smile tugged at her unwilling mouth. "No," she admitted at last. "You must be exactly who you are. Even if it drives me mad."

There was no sense in fighting it. This was simply the way it was with them. Annoyance spiced with desire. Admiration and exasperation mixed in a strange, irresistible potion. Fascination and friction. Their relationship wouldn't be everyone's cup of tea . . . but now that they had tasted it, neither Drake nor Lilah wanted a milder brew.

His fingers played softly in her hair. "Our life together may be one row after another," he said softly. "We may never know a moment's peace. But I tell you honestly, Lilah, I don't care. You are the most exciting woman I have ever met, and I will pay any price to keep you at my side."

"We'll never be bored," she offered in a tiny voice. "That's something."

"Hell, yes." His hands stilled. "Do you think we're shallow, that that is so important to us?"

"No. I've known a number of unhappy marriages where the partners were simply . . . bored. It's a sad state of affairs because it's almost impossible to mend."

"So I think. That fate, at least, will never befall us." His expression softened, and his hands dropped to her shoulders. "Lilah. Sweetheart. Whatever the future holds for us, we'll be stronger for having each other. I love everything about you from your head to your toes. Even your willful, crazy, stubborn little brain." He saw the warning in her face and grinned. "*Especially* your brain."

Her lips twitched. "Our servants will quake with fear whenever we disagree, you know."

"Yes. The butler will probably hide all the weapons in the house. Even the crossed swords over the mantel in the great hall."

She looked a bit gloomy. "And no one will understand us. They'll bless themselves and shake their heads and marvel that two people can be so much in love and yet quarrel so constantly."

"A fig for that," scoffed Drake. "I don't care a rap what anyone says or thinks. Do you? They can hang themselves for all I care. We understand each other, and that's what matters."

"Yes." Her arms snaked up around his neck. "It won't be a conventional marriage. But it will be perfect for us."

"That's right." His voice was husky with emotion. "If I'd wanted a conventional marriage, I would have married one of those pretty ninnyhammers you meet at Almack's. I've trotted any number of them around the dance floor, Lilah, and I must tell you—they all left me cold. Until you."

Lilah blushed. "And I must admit," she said shyly, "that of all the men I have kissed—"

"All four of them?"

"—yours is the only kiss that ever . . . preyed on my mind. Afterward."

"Heaven help me," groaned Drake, crushing her against his body. "Marry me soon, Lilah. A man can only take so much."

She smiled against his waistcoat. "It's not easy for me to wait, either," she murmured provocatively. "So I hope you will be very, very pleasant to Papa—and not argue overmuch about settlements and things."

"I'll give him whatever he wants," Drake said fervently. "If he will give me what I want. You. And the sooner, the better."

She laughed. "I'll tell him to ask for a great deal. Properties for each of our children, however many we have. A house in London, one in Bath, and an enormous income for me—"

"In the event I predecease you."

"Oh, no! Pin money. I shall require several thousand per annum."

"Done, madam. Done." He bent, seeking her mouth, but she pushed him laughingly away.

"You can't be as rich as all that."

"I certainly can." He paused and looked at her, his eyes gleaming. "Seems to me I warned you, once upon a time."

She blinked at him. "That you were as rich as Croesus?"

"That's right, love. Kiss me."

Lilah felt a little faint. She held him off a moment, searching his face for clues, but in spite of the teasing light in his eyes he appeared to be speaking the truth. "Good heavens. I was only joking you."

"I know you were. But I wasn't. Kiss me."

"Drake! I am *not* interested in your money."

"Good. Since we're on the subject, I may as well tell you I'm not interested in your money, either."

She squirmed in his arms. "I haven't any. Or, at least, not enough to tempt a—Drake! This is important!"

He held her firmly at arm's length. "I'm afraid I must correct you on that point, my love. You may take it from one who knows: money is utterly *un*important." Heat simmered in his eyes. "I'll show you what's important."

He pulled her back into his arms and covered her mouth with his. Every thought she had immediately flew out of her head and she relaxed against him, mindlessly returning his kiss. Oh, he was right. This was all that mattered. This connection between them, strong and joyous.

Eventually he lifted his head, and she snuggled against him, sighing. He held her, placing his cheek against the top of her head. "You truly don't care about my blasted money, do you, Lilah?" he asked. His tone was more tender than she had ever heard it. "And my rank means nothing to you, either."

"No. For I do love you, Drake," she whispered, lifting her lips for his kiss. "I just love you. And always will."